The Editors

Isaac Asimov is a biochemist who has taught at the Boston University School of Medicine. Not only is he one of the foremost contemporary science writers, but he exercises an imaginative power that enables him to write vivid science fiction as well. His story, "The Fun They Had," is included in this collection. Among Dr. Asimov's factual works published by Collier Books are *The Clock We Live On, The Kingdom of the Sun, The World of Carbon, The World of Nitrogen,* and *The Bloodstream: River of Life.*

Groff Conklin, a pioneer in recognizing and evaluating the merits of science fiction, is also a distinguished science and technical writer. The diversity of his talents has expressed itself in such works as *The Best of Science Fiction,* one of the first science fiction anthologies, and *The Weather Conditioned House,* a standard work for architects.

Other Asinov and Conklin anthologies of science fiction published by Collier Books include:

Great Science Fiction by Scientists, edited by Groff Conklin

Soviet Science Fiction, with an introduction by Isaac Asimov

More Soviet Science Fiction, with an introduction by Isaac Asimov

The Supernatural Reader, edited by Groff Conklin

Great Science Fiction About Doctors, edited by Groff Conklin and Noah D. Fabricant

Fifty Short Science Fiction Tales

EDITED, AND WITH INTRODUCTIONS, BY

ISAAC ASIMOV AND GROFF CONKLIN

COLLIER BOOKS

A Division of Macmillan Publishing Co., Inc.

NEW YORK

COLLIER MACMILLAN PUBLISHERS

LONDON

Library of Congress Catalog Card Number: 62-21646

First Collier Books Edition 1963

Twentieth Printing 1979

Macmillan Publishing Co., Inc.
866 Third Avenue, New York, N.Y. 10022
Collier Macmillan Canada, Ltd.

PRINTED IN THE UNITED STATES OF AMERICA

ACKNOWLEDGMENTS

Karen Anderson, *Six Haiku*. Copyright 1962 by Mercury Press. Reprinted by permission of the author.

Poul Anderson, *Ballade of an Artificial Satellite*. Copyright 1958 by Mercury Press. Reprinted by permission of the author.

Isaac Asimov, *The Fun They Had*. Copyright 1951 by NEA Service, Inc. Reprinted by permission of the author.

Alan Bloch, *Men are Different*. Copyright 1954 by Groff Conklin. Reprinted by permission of the author.

Anthony Boucher, *The Ambassadors*. Reprinted by permission of Willis Kingsley Wing Copyright © 1952 by Anthony Boucher.

Fredric Brown, *The Weapon*. Copyright 1951 by Street &

Smith Publications, Inc. Reprinted by permission of the author and Scott Meredith Literary Agency, Inc.

T. P. Caravan, *Random Sample*. Copyright 1953 by Fantasy House, Inc. Reprinted by permission of Charles C. Munoz.

Cleve Cartmill, *Oscar*. Copyright 1941 by Street and Smith Publications, Inc. Reprinted by permission of the author.

Peter Cartur, *The Mist*. Copyright 1952 by Fantasy House, Inc. Reprinted by permission of Forrest J. Ackerman.

James Causey, *Teething Ring*. Copyright 1953 by Galaxy Publishing Corp. Reprinted by permission of Forrest J. Ackerman.

Arthur C. Clarke, *The Haunted Space Suit*. Copyright 1958 by United Newspapers Magazine Corp. Reprinted by permission of the author and Scott Meredith Literary Agency, Inc.

Mildred Clingerman, *Stair Trick*. Copyright 1952 by Fantasy House, Inc. Reprinted by permission of Barthold Fles.

Roger Dee, *Unwelcome Tenant*. Copyright 1950 by Love Romances Publishing Co. Reprinted by permission of Harry Altshuler.

Arthur Feldman, *The Mathematicians*. Copyright 1953 by Ziff-Davis Publishing Co.

Jack Finney, *The Third Level*. Copyright 1952 by Fantasy House, Inc. Reprinted by permission of the author.

Stuart Friedman, *Beautiful, Beautiful, Beautiful!* Copyright 1952 by Columbia Publications, Inc. Reprinted by permission of the author and Scott Meredith Literary Agency, Inc.

Edward Grendon, *The Figure*. Copyright 1947 by Street and Smith Publications, Inc. Reprinted by permission of Lawrence LeShan.

David Grinnell, *The Rag Thing*. Copyright 1951 by Fantasy House, Inc. Reprinted by permission of Forrest J. Ackerman.

Marion Gross, *The Good Provider*. Copyright 1952 by Marion Gross. Reprinted by permission of Barthold Fles.

Robert A. Heinlein, *Columbus Was a Dope*. Copyright 1949 by Standard Magazines, Inc. Reprinted by permission of Lurton Blassingame.

Albert Hernhuter, *Texas Week*. Copyright 1954 by King Size Publications. Reprinted by permission of Forrest J. Ackerman.

H. B. Hickey, *Hilda*. Copyright 1952 by Fantasy House, Inc. Reprinted by permission of Forrest J. Ackerman.

W. Hilton-Young, *The Choice*. Copyright by *Punch*, London. Reprinted by permission of The Ben Roth Agency, Inc.

Damon Knight, *Not with a Bang*. Copyright 1950 by Fantasy House, Inc. Reprinted by permission of the author and General Artists Corp.

C. M. Kornbluth, *The Altar at Midnight*. Copyright 1952 by Galaxy Publishing Corp. Reprinted by permission of Mary Kornbluth.

Fritz Leiber, *A Bad Day For Sales*. Copyright 1953 by Galaxy Publishing Corp. Reprinted by permission of the author and General Artists Corp.

Jack Lewis, *Who's Cribbing?* Copyright 1953 by Better Publications, Inc. Reprinted by permission of Forrest J. Ackerman.

John D. MacDonald, *Spectator Sport*. Copyright 1950 by Standard Magazines, Inc. Reprinted by permission of Littauer and Wilkinson.

Avro Manhattan, *The Cricket Ball*. Copyright by Avro Manhattan; published in 1955 by Fantasy House, Inc. Reprinted by permission of the author.

Winston K. Marks, *Double-Take*. Copyright 1953 by Future Publications, Inc. Reprinted by permission of the author and Scott Meredith Literary Agency, Inc.

John P. McKnight, *Prolog*. Copyright 1951 by Fantasy House, Inc. Reprinted by permission of the author.

Lion Miller, *The Available Data on the Worp Reaction*. Copyright 1953 by Fantasy House, Inc. Reprinted by permission of the author.

Alan Nelson, *Narapoia*. Copyright 1951 by Fantasy House, Inc. Reprinted by permission of the author.

Alan E. Nourse, *Tiger by the Tail*. Copyright 1951 by Galaxy Publishing Corp. Reprinted by permission of Harry Altshuler.

Peter Phillips, *Counter Charm*. Originally published in *Slant*,

North Ireland. Reprinted by permission of the author and Scott Meredith Literary Agency, Inc.

Arthur Porges, *The Fly*. Copyright 1952 by Fantasy House, Inc. Reprinted by permission of the author and Scott Meredith Literary Agency, Inc.

Mack Reynolds, *The Business, As Usual*. Copyright 1952 by Fantasy House, Inc. Reprinted by permission of the author and Scott Meredith Literary Agency, Inc.

Frank M. Robinson, *Two Weeks in August*. Copyright 1951 by Galaxy Publishing Corp. Reprinted by permission of the author and Curtis Brown, Ltd.

Edward G. Robles, Jr., *See?* Copyright 1954 by Galaxy Publishing Corp. Reprinted by permission of the author.

Eric Frank Russell, *Appointment at Noon*. Copyright 1954 by Ziff-Davis Publishing Co. Reprinted by permission of the author and Scott Meredith Literary Agency, Inc.

James H. Schmitz, *We Don't Want Any Trouble*. Copyright 1953 by Galaxy Publishing Corp. Reprinted by permission of the author and Scott Meredith Literary Agency, Inc.

Howard Schoenfeld, *Built Down Logically*. Copyright 1951 by Fantasy House, Inc. Reprinted by permission of the author.

Idris Seabright, *An Egg a Month from All Over*. Copyright 1952 by Fantasy House, Inc. Reprinted by permission of Margaret St. Clair.

Robert Sheckley, *The Perfect Woman*. Copyright 1954 by Ziff-Davis Publishing Co. Reprinted by permission of the author.

Walt Sheldon, *The Hunters*. Copyright 1952 by Better Publications, Inc. Reprinted by permission of Harry Altshuler.

Evelyn E. Smith, *The Martian and the Magician*. Copyright 1952 by Fantasy House, Inc. Reprinted by permission of the author.

Will Stanton, *Barney*. Copyright 1951 by Fantasy House, Inc. Reprinted by permission of the author and Rogers Terrill.

Theodore Sturgeon, *Talent*. Copyright 1953 by Galaxy Publishing Corp. Reprinted by permission of the author.

William Tenn, *Project Hush*. Copyright 1954 by Galaxy Publishing Corp. Reprinted by permission of Philip Klass.

A. E. Van Vogt, *The Great Judge*. Copyright 1948 by Fantasy

Publishing Co., Inc. Reprinted by permission of Forrest J. Ackerman.

Ralph Williams, *Emergency Landing*. Copyright 1940 by Street and Smith Publications, Inc. Reprinted by permission of the author and Scott Meredith Literary Agency, Inc.

S. Fowler Wright, *Obviously Suicide*. Copyright 1951 by *Suspense* Magazine.

Introductions

Introduction No. 1

I love to read reviews of science fiction books. For this, I have many ignoble motives. For instance, if a book of my own is involved, I read the review on the off-chance that the reviewer, struck by an unaccustomed bolt of benevolence, will proceed to lavish praise on me. If someone else's book is involved, I read the review with at least the spark of a hope that if unkind words *must* be said, the entire supply be lavished at this point, with none left for me next time around.

Needless to say, my ignobility is not always pampered, and I have been, on occasion, irritated to find that praise and blame are assigned without the kind of partiality I would like to see.

Nevertheless, the irritation I feel on such occasions is minor, if the reviewer is a member of the science fiction fraternity. If he is, he at least knows the rules of the game; he knows the proper manner in which to judge science fiction. An outsider, on the other hand, often does not.

It is supremely irritating (frustrating, even) to watch an outside reviewer discuss a science fiction book and miss the point completely. As, for instance, when he complains (as he sometimes does) of the inadequate depth and richness of characterization and never says a word about the completely adequate depth and richness of background. For in science fiction, more than in any other branch of literature, background's the thing.

Consider: In a murder mystery, there is no need to describe

11

a gun or explain what is meant by footprints. In a western, horses, sheriffs, gamblers, and steers are all familiar objects that require no detailed word-pictures. In love stories, the mores and customs of our society are well known, and, if you are the least bit sophisticated, you even know what a line of asterisks means.

In short, almost all books have known backgrounds, and the reader is an ally of the author, filling in details and elaborating on mere hints. Even when the background is exotic, a tropic jungle, the inside world of Washington politics, seventeenth-century France, most of the basic facts of life remain the same, and a few paragraphs of explanation will do the rest.

The author of such a book, relieved of the necessity to do more than nail two sticks together to supply the background, has ample time to devote to the minutiae of characterization. How fortunate he is!

But consider the one exception to the rule—the writer of the science fiction story.

A science fiction story is usually set on another world or in a future time. In either case, the background usually is a society that differs from our own, sometimes radically. The gadgetry is different; the customs are different; sometimes the most accepted things are different.

Thus a story that has its setting on the Moon must at all times keep the reader aware that the gravity is only one-sixth that of the Earth and that the very walk of a human being is changed. Since there is no air, there is, in the open, no sound in the usual manner of sounds. In a proper story, these differences may make up the nub and kernel of the complications of the plot.

I remember a story, for instance, in which two men found that Moondust caked their suits and covered their faceplates thanks to the effect of static electricity. They were then faced with the problem of removing that dust under the conditions that prevailed on the Moon. (They succeeded.)

Or, more subtly, suppose the setting is on Earth, an Earth reasonably similar, physically speaking, to our world of today but with a radically different culture. Suppose it is so overcrowded that no one can possibly own a private bathroom and that a whole set of accepted rules of behavior in using a public bathroom has been developed.——And suppose a facet of the plot hinges on those rules.

Suppose tobacco is outlawed and adultery accepted. Suppose robots do the world's work and humanity lives in enforced and resented leisure. Suppose some men can live for centuries while other men cannot. Suppose an intelligent form of life visits our planet and suppose they (or we) happen to be good to eat?

In such cases, how does the author go about explaining a completely strange background?

He can't just stop the story and write a little sociological tract and then say, "Now go on with the story. . . ." The reader won't sit still for it.

He can't refuse to explain and simply have his hero put in jail for scratching his chin in public without having the reader understand why this is an enormity.

Sometimes there is a strong temptation to have it all explained via conversation. One character tells another character how the "frammistant" works as he turns it on. This, alas, is too artificial a device to impress anyone over twelve. After all, in our own culture, a man doesn't casually explain to his friend how an electric light works. He just flicks the switch and both accept the light as a fact even when one knows how it works and the other doesn't.

What is the answer, then?

Well, I can do it, but I can't explain it. All I can say is that there are ways of inserting sentences, statements, remarks, asides here and there in a story which help explain the background little by little, without perceptibly slowing the progress of the story.

There is a disadvantage to this—and an advantage.

The disadvantage is that the background, however cleverly introduced, takes up time. I should judge about half the space in a good science fiction story must be devoted to detailing the background. This leaves only half the space for such things as characterization, and in a novel of the usual length it is no wonder that the science fiction author sometimes misses a bit in these areas.

Also, the background is introduced little by little and the

first portion of the book may therefore be unclear. To the science fiction reader, this actually supplies an added dimension of enjoyment for it is pleasant to watch apparent paradoxes smooth out and obscurities clear up as the story progresses. An outsider without the necessary patience may simply feel confused and give up.

The chief advantage, though, is that the background itself, if properly done, can be completely fascinating not only to the reader but to the author as well. (I speak from experience on both sides of the fence.) There is a creative delight in constructing a different world or a different society from scratch, putting it together, and making it three-dimensional in every detail. This delight cannot help but communicate itself to the reader.

The advertising-society background of Frederik Pohl's novel, *The Space Merchants*, for instance, or the telepathic-society background of Alfred Bester's novel, *The Demolished Man*, are far more fascinating and rewarding than the plots that work out their details in the foreground. And I say this despite the fact that the plots, in both cases, are most competently constructed.

Now then, it is only in science fiction that this special creative joy in background is possible. If science fiction had no other justification, this would be enough, for surely to supply a new and unique pleasure is enough to ask of a particular branch of literature.

But does this mean that only the science fiction *novel* is possible? Does it take at least fifty to a hundred thousand words to paint an appropriate background picture, or can it be done in less? And if it can be done in less, then in how much less?

Human ingenuity is remarkable. It can be done within the limits of the short-short story.

The short-short is, in itself, a popular, if difficult, form of literature. Because it is so short, it can be read quickly, and in our hectic times a "bite-size" piece of writing, designed to be nibbled at between meals, is always welcome. Because it is so short, it must pack a final punch to be effective; and there is then the added delight of trying to outguess the author and (we hope) failing, and therefore being at once surprised, shocked, and delighted at the final sentence.

But consider the extra dimension of the science fiction short-short. There must be the concise writing and the final punch of the ordinary short-short, and on top of that there must *also* be the evocation of a background differing from our own.

As an example, consider my story "The Fun They Had," which is included in this anthology. (By talking about it, I may spoil its effect, and if I must spoil a story in this book, let it be my own.) In a little over a thousand words, I must not only describe the feelings and frustrations in the mind of a little girl, but I must get across, somehow, the entire educational system of a future society, compare it with our own, and do it all without being obvious. It was sheer fun for me to work out a way of doing so.

And so it is that Groff Conklin and I have selected fifty short-short stories for you to enjoy, I hope, in twofold fashion. You can read them casually for the events they contain and the kicker with which they usually conclude. Or you can read them analytically for the joy of noting how so much can be crammed into so little space.

Or you can read them both ways.

Isaac Asimov

August 1962

Introduction No. 2

(Short-Short Version)

There really is little left for this appreciative nonpractitioner of the art of fiction to add to Isaac Asimov's definitive analysis of the short-short, or brief, story—except a few practical notes, historical, technical, and legal-economic.

First, here is a loose-jointed definition of what actually constitutes a "short-short" in terms of length. When it was first used, the term was limited to tales that ran to no more than an average of 1,000 words, give or take a hundred or so. This was back in the days of the fierce fiction competition (golden days!) between those magazine behemoths of the 1930's, Bernarr MacFadden's *Liberty* and the late, great, lamented *Collier's*. This is not to suggest that short-shorts did not exist before that—only that those were the publications that made a fad out of them, elevating them to the status of a popular art form. Technically, of course, the short-short was always exactly long enough to fill a page in the magazine, plus an illustration—no more and no less.

Many precisians (a word I like to use for grammarians, Aristotelians, and mathematical physicists) will claim, and with justification, that this collection really does not play fair with the definition. Sure enough, it doesn't—because we hold that such finicky word-counting is ridiculous, and rules based on it are made to be broken. Consequently, you will find stories within these covers that range from as few as 300 to as many as 3,000 words.

Another point may need a bit of explanation: Why do we open and close with verses—and both of them in the Anderson family? We have the best of all possible reasons: we wanted to. Asimov suggested Poul's the year it came out, 1958; and I brought it up again this year, along with Karen's *Haiku*. Thus we now have a first-rate poetic bracket between which the prose of the book fits beautifully, for our pleasure and (we hope) yours.

Finally, it will be noted that two of the acknowledgments do *not* contain the phrase "Reprinted by permission of. . . ." The reason in both instances is that we could not locate the author from whom we could obtain permission. Every reasonable effort was made to do so, and we hope that if these authors do learn of the use of their stories in this book, they will write to us so that we can regularize our relations with them.

Groff Conklin

August 1962

Contents

Fifty Short Science Fiction Tales

Prelude

Ballade of an Artificial Satellite

Poul Anderson

Thence they sailed far to the southward along the land, and came to a ness; the land lay upon the right; there were long and sandy strands. They rowed to land, and found there upon the ness the keel of a ship, and called the place Keelness, and the strands they called Wonderstrands for it took long to sail by them.

Thorfinn Karlsefni's *Voyage to Vinland*

> *One inland summer I walked through rye,*
> *a wind at my heels that smelled of rain*
> *and harried white clouds through a whistling sky*
> *where the great sun stalked and shook his mane*
> *and roared so brightly across the grain*
> *it burned and shimmered like alien sands.—*
> *Ten years old, I saw down a lane*
> *the thunderous light on Wonderstrands.*

> *In ages before the world ran dry,*
> *what might the mapless not contain?*
> *Atlantis gleamed like a dream to die,*
> *Avalon lay under faerie reign,*
> *Cíbola guarded a golden plain,*
> *Tir-nan-Og was fair-locked Fand's,*
> *sober men saw from a gull's-road wain*
> *the thunderous light on Wonderstrands.*

23

Such clanging countries in cloudland lie;
but men grew weary and they grew sane
and they grew grown—and so did I—
and knew Tartessus was only Spain.
No galleons call at Taprobane
(Ceylon, with English); no queenly hands
wear gold from Punt; nor sees the Dane
the thunderous light on Wonderstrands.

Ahoy, Prince Andros Horizon's-bane!
They always wait, the elven lands.
An evening planet gives again
the thunderous light on Wonderstrands.

The Fun They Had

Isaac Asimov

Margie even wrote about it that night in her diary. On the page headed May 17, 2155, she wrote, "Today Tommy found a real book!"

It was a very old book. Margie's grandfather once said that when he was a little boy *his* grandfather told him that there was a time when all stories were printed on paper.

They turned the pages, which were yellow and crinkly, and it was awfully funny to read words that stood still instead of moving the way they were supposed to—on a screen, you know. And then, when they turned back to the page before, it had the same words on it that it had had when they read it the first time.

"Gee," said Tommy, "what a waste. When you're through with the book, you just throw it away, I guess. Our television screen must have had a million books on it and it's good for plenty more. I wouldn't throw *it* away."

"Same with mine," said Margie. She was eleven and hadn't seen as many telebooks as Tommy had. He was thirteen.

She said, "Where did you find it?"

"In my house." He pointed without looking, because he was busy reading. "In the attic."

"What's it about?"

"School."

Margie was scornful. "School? What's there to write about

school? I hate school." Margie always hated school, but now she hated it more than ever. The mechanical teacher had been giving her test after test in geography and she had been doing worse and worse until her mother had shaken her head sorrowfully and sent for the County Inspector.

He was a round little man with a red face and a whole box of tools with dials and wires. He smiled at her and gave her an apple, then took the teacher apart. Margie had hoped he wouldn't know how to put it together again, but he knew how all right and, after an hour or so, there it was again, large and black and ugly with a big screen on which all the lessons were shown and the questions were asked. That wasn't so bad. The part she hated most was the slot where she had to put homework and test papers. She always had to write them out in a punch code they made her learn when she was six years old, and the mechanical teacher calculated the mark in no time.

The inspector had smiled after he was finished and patted her head. He said to her mother, "It's not the little girl's fault, Mrs. Jones. I think the geography sector was geared a little too quick. Those things happen sometimes. I've slowed it up to an average ten-year level. Actually, the over-all pattern of her progress is quite satisfactory." And he patted Margie's head again.

Margie was disappointed. She had been hoping they would take the teacher away altogether. They had once taken Tommy's teacher away for nearly a month because the history sector had blanked out completely.

So she said to Tommy, "Why would anyone write about school?"

Tommy looked at her with very superior eyes. "Because it's not our kind of school, stupid. This is the old kind of school that they had hundreds and hundreds of years ago." He added loftily, pronouncing the word carefully, "*Centuries* ago."

Margie was hurt. "Well, I don't know what kind of school they had all that time ago." She read the book over his shoulder for a while, then said, "Anyway, they had a teacher."

"Sure they had a teacher, but it wasn't a *regular* teacher. It was a man."

"A man? How could a man be a teacher?"

Well, he just told the boys and girls things and gave them homework and asked them questions."

"A man isn't smart enough."

"Sure he is. My father knows as much as my teacher."

"He can't. A man can't know as much as a teacher."

"He knows almost as much I betcha."

Margie wasn't prepared to dispute that. She said, "I wouldn't want a strange man in my house to teach me."

Tommy screamed with laughter, "You don't know much, Margie. The teachers didn't live in the house. They had a special building and all the kids went there."

"And all the kids learned the same thing?"

"Sure, if they were the same age."

"But my mother says a teacher has to be adjusted to fit the mind of each boy and girl it teaches and that each kid has to be taught differently."

"Just the same, they didn't do it that way then. If you don't like it, you don't have to read the book."

"I didn't say I didn't like it," Margie said quickly. She wanted to read about those funny schools.

They weren't even half finished when Margie's mother called, "Margie! School!"

Margie looked up. "Not yet, mamma."

"Now," said Mrs. Jones. "And it's probably time for Tommy, too."

Margie said to Tommy, "Can I read the book some more with you after school?"

"Maybe," he said, nonchalantly. He walked away whistling, the dusty old book tucked beneath his arm.

Margie went into the schoolroom. It was right next to her bedroom, and the mechanical teacher was on and waiting for her. It was always on at the same time every day except Saturday and Sunday, because her mother said little girls learned better if they learned at regular hours.

The screen was lit up, and it said: "Today's arithmetic lesson is on the addition of proper fractions. Please insert yesterday's homework in the proper slot."

Margie did so with a sigh. She was thinking about the old

schools they had when her grandfather's grandfather was a little boy. All the kids from the whole neighborhood came, laughing and shouting in the schoolyard, sitting together in the schoolroom, going home together at the end of the day. They learned the same things so they could help one another on the homework and talk about it.

And the teachers were people. . . .

The mechanical teacher was flashing on the screen: "When we add the fractions 1/2 and 1/4 . . ."

Margie was thinking about how the kids must have loved it in the old days. She was thinking about the fun they had.

Men Are Different

Alan Bloch

I'm an archaeologist, and Men are my business. Just the same,
I wonder if we'll ever find out about Men—I mean *really*
find out what made Men different from us Robots—by digging around on the dead planets. You see, I lived with a Man
once, and I know it isn't as simple as they told us back in
school.

We have a few records, of course, and Robots like me are
filling in some of the gaps, but I think now that we aren't
really getting anywhere. We know, or at least the historians
say we know, that Men came from a planet called Earth. We
know, too, that they rode out bravely from star to star; and
wherever they stopped, they left colonies—Men, Robots, and
sometimes both—against their return. But they never came
back.

Those were the shining days of the world. But are we so old
now? Men had a bright flame—the old word is "divine," I
think—that flung them far across the night skies, and we have
lost the strands of the web they wove.

Our scientists tell us that Men were very much like us—
and the skeleton of a Man is, to be sure, almost the same as
the skeleton of a Robot, except that it's made of some cal-
cium compound instead of titanium. Just the same, there are
other differences.

It was on my last field trip, to one of the inner planets, that I met the Man. He must have been the last Man in this system, and he'd forgotten how to talk—he'd been alone so long. Once he learned our language we got along fine together, and I planned to bring him back with me. Something happened to him, though.

One day, for no reason at all, he complained of the heat. I checked his temperature and decided that his thermostat circuits were shot. I had a kit of field spares with me, and he was obviously out of order, so I went to work. I turned him off without any trouble. I pushed the needle into his neck to operate the cut-off switch, and he stopped moving, just like a Robot. But when I opened him up he wasn't the same inside. And when I put him back together I couldn't get him running again. Then he sort of weathered away—and by the time I was ready to come home, about a year later, there was nothing left of him but bones. Yes, Men are indeed different.

The Ambassadors

Anthony Boucher

Nothing so much amazed the first Martian expedition—no, not even the answer, which should have been so obvious from the first, to the riddle of the canals—as the biological nature of the Martians themselves.

Popular fiction and scientific thought alike had conditioned the members of the expedition to expect either of two possibilities: a race more or less like ourselves, if possibly high-domed and bulge-chested; or a swarm of tentacled and pulpy horrors.

With either the familiar or the monstrously unfamiliar we were prepared to make contact; we had given no thought to the likeness-with-a-difference which we encountered.

It was on the night of the expedition's official welcome to Mars, after that exchange of geometrical and astronomical diagrams which had established for each race the intelligence of the other, that the zoologist Professor Hunyadi classified his observations.

That the Martians were mammals was self-evident. Certain points concerning their teeth, their toes, and the characteristic tufts of hair on their cheekbones led Professor Hunyadi to place them, somewhat to the bewilderment of his nonzoological colleagues, as fissipede arctoids. Further technicalities involving such matters as the shape of the nozzle and the number and distribution of the nipples led him from the family

31

Canidae through the genus *Canis* to the species *lupus*.

"My ultimate classification, gentlemen," he asserted, "must be *Canis lupus sapiens*. In other words, as man may be said to be an intelligent ape, we are here confronted with a race of intelligent wolves."

Some Martian zoologist was undoubtedly reaching and expounding analogous conclusions at that same moment; and the results were evident when the First Interplanetary Conference resumed its wordless and symbolic deliberations on the following day.

For if it was difficult for our representatives to take seriously the actions of what seemed a pack of amazingly clever and well-trained dogs, it was all but impossible for the Martians to find anything save amusement in the antics of a troupe of space-touring monkeys.

An Earthman, in those days, would use "You cur!" as an indication of contempt; to a Martian, anyone addressed as "You primate!" was not only contemptible but utterly ridiculous.

By the time the First Conference was over, and the more brilliant linguists of each group had managed to master something of the verbal language of the other, traces of a reluctant mutual respect had begun to dawn. This was particularly true of the Earthmen, who had at heart a genuine, if somewhat patronizing fondness for dogs (and even wolves), whereas the Martians had never possessed any warmth of feeling for monkeys (and certainly not for great apes).

Possibly because he had first put his finger on the cause, it was Professor Hunyadi who was especially preoccupied, on the return voyage, with the nagging thought that some fresh device must be found if the two races were to establish their interplanetary intercourse on a solid footing. It is fortunate indeed that the professor had, as he tells us in his *Memoirs*, spent so many happy hours at the feet of his Transylvanian grandmother; for thus he alone, of that crew of superb specialists, was capable of conceiving the solution that was to revolutionize the history of two planets.

The world press alternated between roars of laughter and screams of rage when the returned zoologist issued his eloquent plea, on a world-wide video hookup, for volunteer werewolves as ambassadors to the wolves of Mars.

Barbarous though it may seem to us now, mankind was at that time divided into three groups: those who disbelieved in werewolves; those who hated and feared werewolves; and, of course, those who were werewolves.

The fortunate position of three hitherto unsuspected individuals of this last category served to still both the laughter and the rage of the press.

Professor Garou of Duke University received from Hunyadi's impassioned plea the courage at last to publish his monumental thesis (based on the earlier researches of Williamson) proving once and for all that the lycanthropic metamorphosis involves nothing supernatural, but a strictly scientific exercise of psychokinetic powers in the rearrangement of molecular structure—an exercise at which, Garou admitted, he was himself adept.

This revelation in turn emboldened Cardinal Mezzoluppo, a direct descendant of the much misinterpreted Wolf of Gubbio, to confess the sting of the flesh which had long buffeted him and, taking his text from II Cor. 11:30, *pro me autem nihil gloriabor nisi in infirmitatibus meis* ("If I must needs glory, I will glory of the things which concern mine infirmities"), magnificently to proclaim the infinite wisdom of God in establishing on earth a long misunderstood and persecuted race which could now at last serve man in his first great need beyond earth.

But it was neither the scientific demonstration that one need not disbelieve nor the religious exhortation that one need not hate and fear that converted the great masses of mankind. That conversion came when Streak, the Kanine King of the Kinescope, the most beloved quadruped in the history of show business, announced that he had chosen an acting career as a wolf-dog only because the competition was less intense than among human video-actors ("and besides," he is rumored to have added privately, "you meet fewer bitches . . . and their sons").

The documentary which Streak commissioned for his special use, *A Day in the Life of the Average Werewolf*, removed the last traces of disbelief and fear and finally brought forth the needed volunteers, no longer hesitant to declare themselves lest they be shot down with silver bullets or even forced to submit to psychoanalysis.

As a matter of fact, this new possibility of public frankness cured immediately many of the analysts' most stubborn cases, hitherto driven to complex escapes by the necessity of either frustrating their very nature by never changing or practicing metamorphosis as a solitary vice.

The problem now became one, not of finding volunteers, but of winnowing them. Fortunately, a retired agent of the Federal Bureau of Investigation (whose exploits as a werewolf of good will have been recounted elsewhere) undertook the task of cleaning out the criminal element, which statistical psychology has since established as running no higher (allowing for the inevitable historical effects of repression and discrimination) than in other groups. Professor Garou devised the requisite aptitude tests.

One minor misfortune of the winnowing process may be mentioned: A beautiful Australian actress, whose clarity of diction (in either form) and linguistic talent strongly recommended her, proved to metamorphose not into the European wolf (*Canis lupus*) but into the Tasmanian (*Thylacynus cynocephalus*); and Professor Garou, no doubt rightly, questioned the effect upon the Martians of her marsupial pouch, highly esteemed though it was by connoisseurs of such matters.

The rest is history. There is no need to detail here the communicative triumphs of that embassy and its successors; the very age of interplanetary amity in which we live is their monument.

Nor should we neglect to pay tribute to the brilliant and charming wereapes who so ably represent their mother planet in the Martian embassies here on earth.

For once the Martians had recognized the perfection of the Hunyadi solution, their folklorists realized that they too had long suffered a minority problem whose existence the majority had never suspected; and Cardinal Mezzoluppo's tribute to divine wisdom was echoed by the High *Vrakh* himself, that monster of legend, the were-primate who took his rightful place among the valued citizens of Mars.

It would be only fitting if this brief sketch could end with a touching picture of the contented old age of Professor Hunyadi, to whom two worlds owe so infinitely much. But that restless and unfulfilled genius has once more departed on an interplanetary expedition, trusting ever that the God of the Cardinal and the *Vrakh* has somewhere designed a planet peopled by a batlike race *(Vampyrus sapiens)* to which he will be the ideal first ambassador.

The Weapon

Fredric Brown

The room was quiet in the dimness of early evening. Dr. James Graham, key scientist of a very important project, sat in his favorite chair, thinking. It was so still that he could hear the turning of pages in the next room as his son leafed through a picture book.

Often Graham did his best work, his most creative thinking, under these circumstances, sitting alone in an unlighted room in his own apartment after the day's regular work. But tonight his mind would not work constructively. Mostly he thought about his mentally arrested son—his only son—in the next room. The thoughts were loving thoughts, not the bitter anguish he had felt years ago when he had first learned of the boy's condition. The boy was happy; wasn't that the main thing? And to how many men is given a child who will always be a child, who will not grow up to leave him? Certainly that was rationalization, but what is wrong with rationalization when— The doorbell rang.

Graham rose and turned on lights in the almost-dark room before he went through the hallway to the door. He was not annoyed; tonight, at this moment, almost any interruption to his thoughts was welcome.

He opened the door. A stranger stood there; he said, "Dr. Graham? My name is Niemand; I'd like to talk to you. May I come in a moment?"

Graham looked at him. He was a small man, nondescript, obviously harmless—possibly a reporter or an insurance agent.

But it didn't matter what he was. Graham found himself saying, "Of course. Come in, Mr. Niemand." A few minutes of conversation, he justified himself by thinking, might divert his thoughts and clear his mind.

"Sit down," he said, in the living room. "Care for a drink?"

Niemand said, "No, thank you." He sat in the chair; Graham sat on the sofa.

The small man interlocked his fingers; he leaned forward. He said, "Dr. Graham, you are the man whose scientific work is more likely than that of any other man to end the human race's chance for survival."

A crackpot, Graham thought. Too late now he realized that he should have asked the man's business before admitting him. It would be an embarrassing interview—he disliked being rude, yet only rudeness was effective.

"Dr. Graham, the weapon on which you are working—"

The visitor stopped and turned his head as the door that led to a bedroom opened and a boy of fifteen came in. The boy didn't notice Niemand; he ran to Graham.

"Daddy, will you read to me now?" The boy of fifteen laughed the sweet laughter of a child of four.

Graham put an arm around the boy. He looked at his visitor, wondering whether he had known about the boy. From the lack of surprise on Niemand's face, Graham felt sure he had known.

"Harry"—Graham's voice was warm with affection—"Daddy's busy. Just for a little while. Go back to your room; I'll come and read to you soon."

"*Chicken Little?* You'll read me *Chicken Little?*"

"If you wish. Now run along. Wait. Harry, this is Mr. Niemand."

The boy smiled bashfully at the visitor. Niemand said, "Hi, Harry," and smiled back at him, holding out his hand. Graham, watching, was sure now that Niemand had known: the smile and the gesture were for the boy's mental age, not his physical one.

The boy took Niemand's hand. For a moment it seemed that he was going to climb into Niemand's lap, and Graham pulled him back gently. He said, "Go to your room now, Harry."

The boy skipped back into his bedroom, not closing the door.

Niemand's eyes met Graham's and he said, "I like him," with obvious sincerity. He added, "I hope that what you're going to read to him will always be true."

Graham didn't understand. Niemand said, "*Chicken Little*, I mean. It's a fine story—but may *Chicken Little* always be wrong about the sky falling down."

Graham suddenly had liked Niemand when Niemand had shown liking for the boy. Now he remembered that he must close the interview quickly. He rose, in dismissal.

He said, "I fear you're wasting your time and mine, Mr. Niemand. I know all the arguments, everything you can say I've heard a thousand times. Possibly there is truth in what you believe, but it does not concern me. I'm a scientist, and only a scientist. Yes, it is public knowledge that I am working on a weapon, a rather ultimate one. But, for me personally, that is only a by-product of the fact that I am advancing science. I have thought it through, and I have found that that is my only concern."

"But, Dr. Graham, is humanity *ready* for an ultimate weapon?"

Graham frowned. "I have told you my point of view, Mr. Niemand."

Niemand rose slowly from the chair. He said, "Very well, if you do not choose to discuss it, I'll say no more." He passed a hand across his forehead. "I'll leave, Dr. Graham. I wonder, though . . . may I change my mind about the drink you offered me?"

Graham's irritation faded. He said, "Certainly. Will whisky and water do?"

"Admirably."

Graham excused himself and went into the kitchen. He got the decanter of whisky, another of water, ice cubes, glasses. When he returned to the living room, Niemand was just leaving the boy's bedroom. He heard Niemand's "Good night, Harry," and Harry's happy " 'Night, Mr. Niemand."

Graham made drinks. A little later, Niemand declined a second one and started to leave.

Niemand said, "I took the liberty of bringing a small gift to your son, doctor. I gave it to him while you were getting the drinks for us. I hope you'll forgive me."

"Of course. Thank you. Good night."

Graham closed the door; he walked through the living room into Harry's room. He said, "All right, Harry. Now I'll read to—"

There was sudden sweat on his forehead, but he forced his face and his voice to be calm as he stepped to the side of the bed. "May I see that, Harry?" When he had it safely, his hands shook as he examined it.

He thought, *only a madman would give a loaded revolver to an idiot.*

Random Sample

T. P. Caravan

If you don't give me another piece of candy I'll cry. You'd be surprised how loud I can cry. Mother wouldn't like that.

Thank you. I just love candy.

I'm very polite for my age; everybody says so. I can get more candy that way. Old ladies are best. I'm also a very intelligent little girl, but I suppose you found that out from your tests. They gave me the same kind of tests, but they didn't give me any candy, so I was bad and didn't answer anything right.

Thank you. I'll take two this time. Do you have any hard candies? The heat's melted these chocolates a little.

My father says to get all I can out of you, because all you Viennese head-thumpers are quacks. He says you cost an awful lot of money. He says only an old fraud would have a beard like a billy goat. He says . . .

Are you getting angry?

All right, then, if you give me just one more piece of candy I'll tell you all about it.

Merci. That's French, you know.

My brother Johnny and I were out in the back yard, stomping ants, when the space ship came down. It's fun sometimes to watch ants, they run around so hopefully going about their business, carrying little bits of twigs and things in their mouths; and they don't even seem to know you're there until your foot just about touches them. Then they run away, waving their feelers before they squish. But the big red ants are the really good ones. You can jump right spang on them and they don't even seem to notice it. I guess they sink into the ground a little ways, because if you pound one between two rocks he squishes without any trouble. They taste funny. Once Johnny saw a red one fighting a black one and they kept on fighting until he burned them both up with his magnifying glass.

Will you buy me a magnifying glass if I tell you about it? I'd just love to have a magnifying glass. I bet the ant thinks the sun is spread out over the whole sky. I bet he thinks the whole world is burning up. I bet it hurts. I bet I could burn up more ants than Johnny can, even though I'm a whole year younger. He's ten.

Please, can I have a magnifying glass? Please? Please? Can I? Can I? I'll cry.

When can I have it?

Thank you.

It was his birthday so I let him take the ones near the ant hill. I'm really very generous at times. You let them get almost down the hole before you jump on them. That's the most fun. I was watching one I'd pulled the legs off, waiting to see if the others would eat it, when Johnny yelled for me to come quick and I went running over. He showed me one ant carrying another on its back, trying to get it down into the ant hill before we squished it. We were just about to stomp on its little head when we heard the noise in the sky. It was the kind of skreeky sound I make when I pull my fingernail along the blackboard in school and make old Miss Cooper get the shivers. I hate Miss Cooper. She doesn't give me any candy—thank you—and I never answer any questions for her.

We looked up and saw the rocket ship coming down for a landing in the woods. It didn't look like a ship to me, but that's what Johnny says it was. It looked like a big washing machine to me. Father says it was a hallucination—I like big words—but he didn't even see it, so how could he know?

Sometimes I hate Father. Are you writing that down? Was that the right thing to say? Can I have some more candy?

Thank you.

This is very good, even if it is melted. I should think you could afford to have your office air conditioned, then the candy wouldn't melt at all. If you were smart you'd think of these things.

What happened? I've told it over and over but nobody believes me. Isn't that sad? I don't think I'll tell anybody else about it.

The whole box? For me? Thank you. I just love chocolates.

Your beard isn't really much like a billy goat's.

We saw it come down in the woods and we ran over to the place. Nobody else was there. The grass and underbrush was burning a little but they were putting it out, and when they saw us they stopped still and made little noises to each other. I held up my hand and I said, "I'm queen here. You must all bow down." And Johnny held up his hand and said, "I'm king." He never thinks of anything for himself.

I hate them. They didn't bow down to me. One of them picked up a squirrel that had been burned a little when they landed, and he was petting it and putting something on the burned place, and he didn't pay any attention to me. I hated him most of all, so I went over and kicked him. He was smaller than Johnny, so Johnny kicked him too. I kicked him first, though, and he was just my size.

What did they look like? They didn't look like little old billy goats.

They took us inside their space ship, and they started to give us some tests like the one you gave me. They were very simple tests, but I didn't like them so I got them all wrong. Johnny got them all wrong too, because I told him I'd scratch his eyes out if he didn't. I remember some of them. They drew little triangles with boxes on two of the sides and then they gave me the pen and waited to see what I'd do. I fooled them. I took the pen and threw ink all over them. It wasn't a pen, exactly, but it was like one. Then they held up one little block, then two, then three, then four. They did this a few times, and then they held up one block, then two. Then they waited for me to pick up three. I picked up all the blocks and hit them over the head with them. I had a lot of fun. I was very bad.

They got Johnny off in a corner, and before you could say "boo!" he was telling them about all the people he'd killed in the war. He wasn't really in the war, of course, but he likes to pretend he was. He likes television best when they kill lots of people. I don't think they really knew what he was talking about, but they looked as if they did. He's a very good actor.

I suppose they thought we were grownups; they were pretty much the same size we are. Anyway, they paid a lot of attention to him, so I went over and punched him a couple of times. I'm afraid we broke up the insides of their space ship a little.

They looked pretty mad. I guess they were disgusted with Johnny; a lot of people are. I always try to make a good impression on strangers, even when they don't give me any candy, so I took some of them outside and showed them how to stomp ants. It was very funny. One of them got sick. Johnny and I were still jumping up and down, stomping ants, when they took off. I hated them. They were nasty; they didn't bow down to me.

That's all. Nothing else happened.

Father says not to take up too much of your expensive old time. He says no honest man could afford a penthouse for his office. You have a very nice view, don't you? You can see all over the city from here.

My, isn't it hot? I wish I had a refrigerator to keep my candy in.

Look there. Look at the fires springing up across the river. Aren't they pretty? Look. Look. And some on this side.

Take me away from here. It's too hot.

Look at the sun. Look at it. It's spreading out over the whole sky. It's burning up the city. Billy goat, help me! Save me. I'm sorry I was bad.

Oscar

Cleve Cartmill

Paul Rockey parked his roadster in front of the beer joint.

"She lives in that corner apartment house," he said. "We'll meet here, after."

"I'd like to raise an objection," Michael Corbyn said.

Terence Finnegan and Paul Rockey regarded Corbyn with patient annoyance. Corbyn's lean face flushed.

"My objection is valid," he protested. "Suppose this girl goes nuts. We'd be in a hell of a jam."

Terence Finnegan laid a large fatherly hand on Corbyn's shoulder.

"Mike, my son, we rehearsed for two hours with Elsie. Did she turn a hair? No. Nor will this friend of Paul's."

"Elsie is a tailor's dummy."

"Aren't all women?"

"Don't be so glib, Terry. I contend it's dangerous. According to Paul, this girl has occult leanings. She wants to believe in such phenomena as our imaginary Oscar. If we play our parts well enough, I tell you we're running a risk."

"I'm not as concerned for Linda's sanity," Paul Rockey interposed, "as I am about your acting."

"O.K. Let's go."

In the third-floor corridor of the apartment building, Paul Rockey rapped on a door. It was presently opened by a pretty brunette in blue slacks.

"Oh, good," she said. "Company."

The three young men trooped inside. Paul Rockey made a vague motion toward his companions.

"Linda, may I present Terry Finnegan, and—"

He broke off. Michael Corbyn was following an Unseen Something around the walls with cold, blue eyes.

Rockey cleared his throat. "Ah, er, Mike."

Corbyn started. "Sorry," he murmured to the girl. "How do you do?"

"—and Michael Corbyn. Linda Houseman."

Finnegan closed the door. He and Rockey exchanged a significant glance, turned compassionate eyes on Corbyn, shook their heads in brief pity. Linda, observing the byplay, frowned fleetingly and motioned them to chairs.

"Would you like a whisky and soda?"

Three contented sighs were born.

As ice tinkled in the kitchen, Corbyn asked a question with his eyebrows. Two nods of affirmation answered him.

Linda brought a tray of drinks, tucked a leg under her on a divan, and raised her glass.

"Do we drink to something, or do we just drink?"

"To our beautiful barmaid," Corbyn responded. "My father told me only last week—"

"Last night you said he was killed in the Big Wind of 1906," Rockey interrupted.

"That wasn't the blow that killed father. He told me only last week that brunettes, as compared to blondes—"

He halted. Again his eyes followed an Unseen Something across the walls.

Rockey and Finnegan dropped embarrassed glances to their drinks.

Rockey made a hollow effort to break the tension. "What have you been doing lately, Linda?"

She, intent upon Corbyn, did not heed the question. Finnegan nodded at Rockey.

"He's got it again," Rockey said in disgust.

"Mike!" Finnegan snapped.

Corbyn jumped. Like a man awakening from heavy sleep, he blinked and gradually oriented himself.

"As I was saying," he mumbled, ". . . where was I?"

"I think we'd better explain," Rockey said to the wide-eyed Linda. "Mike thinks he's a psychic phenomenon. He has a familiar spirit, who, in a spirit of familiarity, he calls Oscar."

"Nuts!" Finnegan snorted. "There's nothing the matter with him, except he's crazy."

"He sees a Thing," Rockey continued smoothly. "It follows him. He can't or won't, describe it. It is not always visible. He sees it, or claims he does, only on some nights in an enclosure—a room, auditorium, or a similar place. It never manifests itself in daylight. Don't feel ill at ease. It never bothers anybody. Terry and I don't pay attention to it any more."

"All we can do," Finnegan added, "is apologize for him. Of course, this peculiarity of his distracts attention from some of his more obvious defects, and people get the impression that he's a pretty nice guy except for his fixation."

Michael Corbyn watched Linda narrowly during the conversation. When she looked at him, he spoke confidentially.

"I feel that we are kindred spirits, Miss Houseman. We know that forces, beings, exist that cannot be explained in terms familiar to such clods as my friends. But you and I, and others like us . . . we know."

Linda's lips were parted, her forgotten drink clutched in both hands.

"Yes," she whispered. "Yes."

"Don't let him sell *you* on it, Miss Houseman," Finnegan said. "And drink your drink before it gets warm."

"Let's talk of something else," Rockey proposed. "If Mike gets started, he'll talk all night on other-plane beings. I remember one drunk and stormy night—"

His voice died. His jaw dropped. His eyes, as Corbyn's had, followed an Unseen Something along the base of a wall. He became rigid.

"What is this, a gag?" Finnegan snarled.

Corbyn flung him a smug and sardonic look. Linda's wide, dark eyes moved slowly from one to the other. With a slight shudder, she set aside her drink.

Rockey, in the manner of a sleepwalker, set down his drink

and walked stiffly from the apartment without a glance at Linda or a word of farewell.

"What the hell's the matter with you?" Finnegan snapped. "Where you going?"

After the door had closed behind Rockey, the three sat quietly. Corbyn's lips formed a faint smile. Finnegan gulped the last of his drink and set the glass on the floor. Linda's glance moved fearfully about the room, questing, searching each corner.

"This is a lot of nonsense!" Finnegan growled.

"Be a good boy, Oscar," Corbyn tossed over his shoulder at an empty corner.

"It's gone far enough," Finnegan continued. "I never told you before, Mike, but I think this is just a pose on your part to get attention you wouldn't receive otherwise because of a colorless and stupid nature. I'll grant that the accumulated effect of these painful incidents might persuade a weak-minded visionary like Paul that he saw something for a moment. Your low cunning broke through for an instant. Well, I resent this pose of yours, and you either drop it or I don't want your friendship." He paused. "May I have another drink, Miss Houseman?"

Linda took his glass solemnly and went into the kitchen. Corbyn and Finnegan grinned at each other.

When Linda came into the room again Finnegan smiled his thanks for the fresh drink and continued, directing his remarks at the girl.

"Hope you'll excuse my vehemence, but I'm fed up with this gag. I don't like to be made feel a fool, and when Paul walked out of here like a corpse, it was embarrassing. If he had brains enough to come in out of an air raid, he'd have known he didn't see anything; he only thought he did. Mike doesn't see anything, either. He—"

Finnegan gasped. His eyes froze on Something in the kitchen doorway.

Corbyn turned lazily, looked toward the kitchen, and shrugged. Linda put a taut hand to her throat.

Finnegan got stiffly to his feet. With the glass still in his hand, he backed to the door. He reached behind him, opened it, and backed into the hallway, his eyes still riveted on the kitchen entrance.

When the door closed and the sound of footsteps receded, Corbyn looked at his watch.

"Now we are alone with it," he said in sepulchral tones. "In five minutes it will be midnight, the end of an old day. This is the first time anyone else has ever seen Oscar. Perhaps that is an omen." He mused silently for a second. "Perhaps . . . this time . . . it won't follow me out."

"No . . . no!" Linda whimpered as he rose.

A strangling scream gurgled in her throat as she fastened her eyes on the kitchen doorway. Corbyn followed her glance. The short hairs on his neck stiffened, and a chill fluttered down his spine.

In the kitchen doorway squatted a dark Thing. It had two living snakes for arms, and a large green eye.

"Well?" it snarled in a hoarse voice. "Well?"

The Mist

Peter Cartur

The big man grunted, then spoke slowly. "Can't do that, mister. I go into town Saturday nights. This is Saturday night."

The little man on the porch was trembling as he leaned forward, trying to catch the words above the noise of the hounds baying in the side yard. His small, alert face was pale, drawn, his eyes too eager. He gave the appearance of being smaller, somehow, than he should be—as though he were shrunken. His clothes hung on him, too large. His eyes were tired, lostlooking.

"Mr.—Mr. Brown, please listen. If this is real, this time— not a rumor—please!"

Brown shook his head slowly, his eyes careful.

"But it's what I've searched for, Mr. Brown. You've seen it. Others have. You've sworn to the truth of it."

"Sure." Brown spat, nodded his head. "Sure. And them as says we ain't are liars for sure."

"I know. . . . Mr. Brown, I'm an investigator of psychic phenomena—of ghosts and things. I *must* see that apparition tonight." The shrunken man closed his eyes for an instant, leaned against the porch post.

"Saturday night."

"But, Mr. Brown—this will be the last night."

"Might be here right along, now. I dunno."

"*I* know, Mr. Brown." The little man rubbed at his finger

with the big golden ring on it. "I know. Another ten minutes at the most. And I've got to—" He stopped, let his eyes beg for him.

"Well, I reckon it's worth lookin' at, right enough."

"You're—sure of what it looks like?"

"I know what I seen. Golden and glowing, it is. You gotta have dark to see it. Real dark. It don't move, exactly. Just stays still but sorta shimmies like."

"That's it, Mr. Brown. I've got to see it!"

"Reckon that's out, mister. I'm goin' to town."

Brown watched the little man's eyes, saw the pain in them. "Course, if it's worth somethin'—reckon it'd have to be for me to stay home Saturday night."

"It would take a minute—a moment."

"I gotta be getting along."

"It's worth everything to me, Mr. Brown. Everything."

"How much?"

"I—I don't have money."

"Hunh!"

"I begged rides for seven hundred miles to get here."

Brown shook his head. "Nice ring you got. . . . Well, I gotta be gettin' to town."

The little man dropped his hand to his side. Then he raised it again. His eyes, too, moved to the curiously shaped ring on his finger.

"I—can't let you have that."

Brown shrugged his big shoulders, stepped back, and fingered the inside doorknob.

"I gotta lock up now an' let out the hounds. . . . Don't be hangin' around the yard when I let out the hounds."

"No. . . . Wait—you can have the ring."

Brown closed his eyes. "I don't know—"

"You can have it."

The big man opened the screen door, took the ring. He stepped back so the little man could come through the doorway. Brown struck a match, lit the lamp on the table. He turned the ring over and over, very slowly, in his thick fingers. His eyes squinted shrewdly. Golden, but not gold. Too heavy for gold—or any other metal. Much too large for the little man's fingers. Brown pushed it on his last finger, felt it grip the flesh.

The little man, moving nervously, found the bedroom door.

Brown gave him a rough shove. "Go ahead. You paid, and it ain't nothin' to hurt a man."

But the little man stood aside, let Brown lead the way.

It was a golden blot in the air, shimmering in the center of the bedroom. Eight feet high, perhaps, and about four wide.

Brown laughed coarsely. "Not a spook, is it, mister? I knew it wasn't. Reckon you was paying for a spook. Course I didn't say it was a spook."

The little man's face hardened. He looked at Brown appraisingly, sadly. Then he shrugged.

"I can't quite believe you really walked through that, Brown."

"Sure." The big man laughed. "Sure I did. Watch."

"Wait. I'll walk with you. Wait!" The little man stepped forward, then, as though still uncertain, put his fingers on Brown's arm. "All right."

Together they moved forward into the golden mist.

It was different for the big man—this time. As they entered the mist he felt sharp tingles dance over his skin. Before, there had been nothing but the feel of air. He started to step back, was stopped by surprising strength from the little man. Brown was forced forward.

The tingling was almost unbearable. It seemed to come in hot flashes, now, from the finger that wore the ring. Brown hurried, trying to get back to the familiar bedroom.

They stepped out of the mist.

There was no familiar bedroom. The house was gone, and with it the night.

Daylight. Daytime on a countryside where the grass was blue as Brown had never seen it, and where trees were slender, unbranched needles reaching for an orange sky. A sky in which Brown could see three gigantic suns.

The big man ripped free, swore, spun back to face the mist. The little man shook his head.

"We just made it, Brown. The mist is gone."

The little man was changing. He seemed to grow, fill out his clothes. "I'm sorry, Brown. I couldn't get through except with the ring—or with someone wearing the ring. . . . That meant it had to be you."

"This is crazy. Where—" The big man stopped, looked again at the suns. He rubbed his forehead.

"Home. *My* home. . . . Find another mist while you wear the ring. Then go home . . . to your home."

"But—a mist?"

"You'll hear rumors. Wild tales. We have stories of ghosts here, too. Be an investigator. Track down those rumors."

"But—"

"Good luck, Brown."

The little man turned quickly, began walking across the strange blue grass. Once he looked back, saw Brown staring helplessly after him. He hesitated for an instant, then hurried on. In a moment he was among the needle trees, then out of Brown's sight.

Teething Ring

James Causey

Half an hour before, while she had been engrossed in the current soap opera and Harry Junior was screaming in his crib, Melinda would naturally have slammed the front door in the little man's face. However, when the bell rang, she was wearing her new Chinese-red housecoat, had just lustered her nails to a blinding scarlet, and Harry Junior was sleeping like an angel.

Yawning, Melinda answered the door and the little man said, beaming, "Excellent day. I have geegaws for information."

Melinda did not quite recoil. He was perhaps five feet tall, with a gleaming hairless scalp and a young-old face. He wore a plain gray tunic, and a peddler's tray hung from his thin shoulders.

"Don't want any," Melinda stated flatly.

"*Please.*" He had great, beseeching amber eyes. "They all say that. I haven't much time. I must be back at the university by noon."

"You working your way through college?"

He brightened. "Yes. I suppose you could call it that. Alien anthropology major."

Melinda softened. The initiations those frats pulled nowadays—shaving the poor guy's head, eating goldfish—it was criminal.

"Well?" she asked grudgingly. "What's in the tray?"

"Flangers," said the little man eagerly. "Oscilloscopes. Portable force field generators. A neural distorter." Melinda's face was blank. The little man frowned. "You use them, of course? This *is* a Class IV culture?" Melinda essayed a weak shrug, and the little man sighed with relief. His eyes fled past her to the blank screen of the TV set. "Ah, a monitor." He smiled. "For a moment I was afraid—may I come in?"

Melinda shrugged, opened the door. This might be interesting, like a vacuum-cleaner salesman who had cleaned her drapes last week for free. And *Kitty Kyle Battles Life* wouldn't be on for almost an hour.

"My name is Porteous," said the little man with an eager smile. "I'm doing a thematic on Class IV cultures." He whipped out a stylus, began jotting down notes. The TV set fascinated him.

"It's turned off right now," Melinda said.

Porteous's eyes widened impossibly. "You mean," he whispered in horror, "that you're exercising Class V privileges? This is terribly confusing. I get doors slammed in my face, when Class IV's are supposed to have a splendid gregarian quotient—you *do* have atomic power, don't you?"

"Oh, sure," said Melinda uncomfortably. This wasn't going to be much fun.

"Space travel?" The little face was intent, sharp.

"Well," Melinda yawned, looking at the blank screen, "they've got *Space Patrol, Space Cadet, Tales of Tomorrow. . . .*"

"Excellent. Rocket ships or force fields?" Melinda blinked. "Does your husband own one?" Melinda shook her blonde head helplessly. "What are your economic circumstances?"

Melinda took a deep rasping breath, said, "Listen, mister, is this a demonstration or a quiz program?"

"Oh, my excuse. Demonstration, certainly. You will not mind the questions?"

"Questions?" There was an ominous glint in Melinda's blue eyes.

"Your delightful primitive customs, art forms, personal habits—"

"Look," Melinda said, crimsoning. "This is a respectable neighborhood, and I'm not answering any Kinsey report, understand?"

The little man nodded, scribbling. "Personal habits are taboo? I so regret. The demonstration." He waved grandly at the tray. "Anti-grav sandals? A portable solar converter? Apologizing for this miserable selection, but on Capella they told me—" He followed Melinda's entranced gaze, selected a tiny green vial. "This is merely a regenerative solution. You appear to have no cuts or bruises."

"Oh," said Melinda nastily. "Cures warts, cancer, grows hair, I suppose."

Porteous brightened. "Of course. I see you can scan. Amazing." He scribbled further with his stylus, glanced up, blinked at the obvious scorn on Melinda's face. "Here. Try it."

"You try it." Now watch him squirm!

Porteous hesitated. "Would you like me to grow an extra finger, hair—"

"Grow some hair." Melinda tried not to smile.

The little man unstopped the vial, poured a shimmering green drop on his wrist, frowning.

"Must concentrate," he said. "Thorium base, suspended solution. Really jolts the endocrines, complete control . . . see?"

Melinda's jaw dropped. She stared at the tiny tuft of hair which had sprouted on that bare wrist. She was thinking abruptly, unhappily, about that chignon she had bought yesterday. They had let her buy that for eight dollars when with this stuff she could have a natural one.

"How much?" she inquired cautiously.

"A half-hour of your time only," said Porteous.

Melinda grasped the vial firmly, settled down on the sofa with one leg tucked carefully under her.

"Okay, shoot. But nothing personal."

Porteous was delighted. He asked a multitude of questions, most of them pointless, some naive, and Melinda dug into her infinitesimal fund of knowledge and gave. The little man scribbled furiously, clucking like a gravid hen.

"You mean," he asked in amazement, "that you live in these primitive huts of your own volition?"

"It's a GI housing project," Melinda said, ashamed.

"Astonishing." He wrote: *Feudal anachronisms and atomic power, side by side. Class IV's periodically "rough it" in back-to-nature movements.*

Harry Junior chose that moment to begin screaming for his lunch. Porteous sat, trembling. "Is that a security alarm?"

"My son," said Melinda despondently, and she went into the nursery.

Porteous followed, and watched the ululating child with some trepidation. "Newborn?"

"Eighteen months," said Melinda stiffly, changing diapers. "He's cutting teeth."

Porteous shuddered. "What a pity. Obviously atavistic. Wouldn't the crèche accept him? You shouldn't have to keep him here."

"I keep after Harry to get a maid, but he says we can't afford one."

"Manifestly insecure," muttered the little man, studying Harry Junior. "Definite paranoid tendencies."

"He was two weeks premature," volunteered Melinda. "He's real sensitive."

"I know just the thing," Porteous said happily. "Here." He dipped into the glittering litter on the tray and handed Harry Junior a translucent prism. "A neural distorter. We use it to train regressives on Rigel Two. It might be of assistance."

Melinda eyed the thing doubtfully. Harry Junior was peering into the shifting crystal depths with a somewhat strained expression.

"Speeds up the neural flow," explained the little man proudly. "Helps tap the unused eighty per cent. The presymptomatic memory is unaffected because of automatic cerebral lapse in case of overload. I'm afraid it won't do much more than cube his present IQ, and an intelligent idiot is still an idiot, but—"

"How dare you?" Melinda's eyes flashed. "My son is *not* an idiot! You get out of here this minute and take your . . . things with you." As she reached for the prism, Harry Junior squalled. Melinda relented. "Here," she said angrily, fumbling with her purse. "How much are they?"

"Medium of exchange?" Porteous rubbed his bald skull.

"Oh, I really shouldn't—but it'll make such a wonderful addendum to the chapter on malignant primitives. What is your smallest denomination?"

"Is a dollar okay?" Melinda was hopeful.

Porteous was pleased with the picture of George Washington. He turned the bill over and over in his fingers, at last bowed low and formally, apologized for any taboo violations, and left via the front door.

"Crazy fraternities," muttered Melinda, turning on the TV set.

Kitty Kyle was dull that morning. At length Melinda used some of the liquid in the green vial on her eyelashes, was quite pleased at the results, and hid the rest in the medicine cabinet.

Harry Junior was a model of docility the rest of that day. While Melinda watched TV and munched chocolates, did and re-did her hair, Harry Junior played quietly with the crystal prism.

Toward late afternoon, he crawled over to the bookcase, wrestled down the encyclopedia and pawed through it, gurgling with delight. He definitely, Melinda decided, would make a fine lawyer someday, not a useless putterer like Big Harry, who worked all hours overtime in that damned lab. She scowled as Harry Junior, bored with the encyclopedia, began reaching for one of Big Harry's tomes on nuclear physics. One putterer in the family was enough! But when she tried to take the book away from him, Harry Junior howled so violently that she let well enough alone.

At six-thirty, Big Harry called from the lab, with the usual despondent message that he would not be home for supper. Melinda said a few resigned things about cheerless dinners eaten alone, hinted darkly what lonesome wives sometimes did for company, and Harry said he was very sorry but this might be *it*, and Melinda hung up on him in a temper.

Precisely fifteen minutes later, the doorbell rang. Melinda opened the front door and gaped. This little man could have been Porteous's double, except for the black metallic tunic, the glacial gray eyes.

"Mrs. Melinda Adams?" Even the voice was frigid.
"Y-Yes. Why—"

"Major Nord, Galactic Security." The little man bowed. "You were visited early this morning by one Porteous." He spoke the name with a certain disgust. "He left a neural distorter here. Correct?"

Melinda's nod was tremulous. Major Nord came quietly into the living room, shut the door behind him. "My apologies, madam, for the intrusion. Porteous mistook your world for a Class IV culture, instead of a Class VII. Here—" He handed her the crumpled dollar bill. "You may check the serial number. The distorter, please."

Melinda shrunk limply onto the sofa. "I don't understand," she said painfully. "Was he a thief?"

"He was . . . careless about his spatial coordinates." Major Nord's teeth showed in the faintest of smiles. "He has been corrected. Where is it?"

"Now look," said Melinda with some asperity. "That thing's kept Harry Junior quiet all day. I bought it in good faith, and it's not my fault—say, have you got a warrant?"

"Madam," said the Major with dignity, "I dislike violating local taboos, but must I explain the impact of a neural distorter on a backwater culture? What if your Neanderthal had been given atomic blasters? Where would *you* have been today? Swinging through trees, no doubt. What if your Hitler had force fields?" He exhaled. "Where is your son?"

In the nursery, Harry Junior was contentedly playing with his blocks. The prism lay glinting in the corner.

Major Nord picked it up carefully, scrutinized Harry Junior. His voice was very soft.

"You said he was . . . playing with it?"

Some vestigial maternal instinct prompted Melinda to shake her head vigorously. The little man stared hard at Harry Junior, who began whimpering. Trembling, Melinda scooped up Harry Junior.

"Is *that* all you have to do—run around frightening women and children? Take your old distorter and get out. Leave decent people alone!"

Major Nord frowned. If only he could be sure. He peered stonily at Harry Junior, murmured, "Definite egomania. It doesn't seem to have affected him. Strange."

"Do you want me to scream?" Melinda demanded.

Major Nord sighed. He bowed to Melinda, went out, closed the door, touched a tiny stud on his tunic, and vanished.

"The manners of some people," Melinda said to Harry Junior. She was relieved that the Major had not asked for the green vial.

Harry Junior also looked relieved, although for quite a different reason.

Big Harry arrived home a little after eleven. There were small worry creases about his mouth and forehead, and the leaden cast of defeat in his eyes. He went into the bedroom, and Melinda sleepily told him about the little man working his way through college by peddling silly goods and about that rude cop named Nord. Harry said that was simply astonishing, and Melinda said, "Harry, you had a drink!"

"I had two drinks," Harry told her owlishly. "You married a failure, dear. Part of the experimental model vaporized, *wooosh*, just like that. On paper it looked so good—"

Melinda had heard it all before. She asked him to see if Harry Junior was covered, and Big Harry went unsteadily into the nursery, sat down by his son's crib.

"Poor little guy," he mused. "Your old man's a bum, a useless tinker. He thought he could send Man to the stars on a string of helium nucleii. Oh, he was smart. Thought of everything. Auxiliary jets to kick off the negative charge, bigger mercury vapor banks—a fine straight thrust of positive alpha particles." He hiccuped, put his face in his hands.

"Didn't you ever stop to think that a few air molecules could defocus the stream? Try a vacuum, stupid."

Big Harry stood up.

"Did you say something son?"

"Gurfle," said Harry Junior.

Big Harry reeled into the living room like a somnambulist. He got pencil and paper, began jotting frantic formulae. Presently he called a cab and raced back to the laboratory.

Melinda was dreaming about little bald men with diamond-studded trays. They were chasing her, they kept pelting her with rubies and emeralds, all they wanted was to ask questions, but she kept running, Harry Junior clasped tightly in her arms. Now they were ringing alarm bells. The bells kept ringing and she groaned, sat up in bed, and seized the telephone.

"Darling." Big Harry's voice shook. "I've got it! More auxiliary shielding plus a vacuum. We'll be rich!"

"That's just fine," said Melinda crossly. "You woke the baby."

Harry Junior was sobbing bitterly into his pillow. He was sick with disappointment. Even the most favorable extrapolation showed it would take him nineteen years to become master of the world.

An eternity. Nineteen years!

The Haunted Space Suit

Arthur C. Clarke

When Satellite Control called me, I was writing up the day's progress report in the observation bubble—the glass-domed office that juts out from the axis of the space station like the hubcap of a wheel.

It was not really a good place to work, for the view was too overwhelming. Only a few yards away I could see the construction teams performing their slow-motion ballet as they put the station together like a giant jigsaw puzzle. And beyond them, twenty thousand miles below, was the blue-green glory of the full Earth, floating against the raveled star-clouds.

"Station supervisor here," I answered. "What's the trouble?"

"Our radar's showing a small echo two miles away, almost stationary, about five degrees west of Sirius. Can you give us a visual report on it?"

Anything matching our orbit so precisely could hardly be a meteor; it would have to be something we'd dropped—perhaps an inadequately secured piece of equipment that had drifted away from the station. So I assumed; but when I pulled out my binoculars and searched the sky around Orion, I soon found my mistake. Though this space traveler was man-made, it had nothing to do with us.

"I've found it," I told Control. "It's someone's test satellite—cone-shaped, four antennas. Probably U.S. Air Force, early 1960's, judging by the design. I know they lost track of several when their transmitters failed. There were quite a few attempts to hit this orbit before they finally made it."

After a brief search through the files, Control was able to confirm my guess. It took a little longer to find that now, in 1988, Washington wasn't in the least bit interested in our discovery and would be just as happy if we lost it again.

"Well, we can't do *that*," said Control. "Even if nobody wants it, the thing's a menace to navigation. Someone had better go out and haul it aboard; get it out of orbit."

That someone, I realized, would have to be me. I dared not detach a man from the closely knit construction teams; we were already behind schedule, and a single day's delay on this job cost a million dollars. All the radio and TV networks on Earth were waiting impatiently for the moment when they could route their programs through us, and thus provide the first truly global service, spanning the world from pole to pole.

"I'll go out and get it," I answered, and though I tried to sound as if I were doing everyone a great favor, I was secretly not at all displeased. It had been at least two weeks since I'd been outside.

The only member of the staff I passed on my way to the air lock was Tommy, our recently acquired cat. Pets mean a great deal to men thousands of miles from Earth, but there are not many animals that can adapt themselves to a weightless environment. Tommy mewed plaintively at me as I clambered into my spacesuit, but I was in too much of a hurry to play with him.

At this point, perhaps I should remind you that the suits we use on the station are completely different from the flexible affairs men wear when they want to walk around on the Moon. Ours are really baby space ships, just big enough to hold one man. They are stubby cylinders, about seven feet long, fitted with low-powered propulsion jets, and have a pair of accordion-like sleeves at the upper end for the operator's arms.

As soon as I'd settled down inside my very exclusive space craft, I switched on power and checked the gauges on the tiny instrument panel. All my needles were well in the safety zone, so I gave Tommy a wink for luck, lowered the transparent hemisphere over my head and sealed myself in. For a short trip like this, I did not bother to check the suit's internal lockers, which were used to carry food and special equipment for extended missions.

As the conveyor belt decanted me into the air lock, I felt like an Indian papoose being carried along on its mother's back. Then the pumps brought the pressure down to zero, the outer door opened, and the last traces of air swept me out into the stars, turning very slowly head over heels.

The station was only a dozen feet away, yet I was now an independent planet—a little world of my own. I was sealed up in a tiny, mobile cylinder, with a superb view of the entire universe, but I had practically no freedom of movement inside the suit. The padded seat and safety belts prevented me from turning around, though I could reach all the controls and lockers with my hands or feet.

In space, the great enemy is the Sun, which can blast you to blindness in seconds. Very cautiously, I opened up the dark filters on the "night" side of my suit, and turned my head to look out at the stars. At the same time I switched the helmet's external sunshade to automatic, so that whichever way the suit gyrated my eyes would be shielded.

Presently, I found my target—a bright fleck of silver whose metallic glint distinguished it clearly from the surrounding stars. I stamped on the jet control pedal and felt the mild surge of acceleration as the low-powered rockets set me moving away from the station. After ten seconds of steady thrust, I cut off the drive. It would take me five minutes to coast the rest of the way, and not much longer to return with my salvage.

And it was at that moment, as I launched myself out into the abyss, that I knew that something was horribly wrong.

It is never completely silent inside a space suit; you can always hear the gentle hiss of oxygen, the faint whir of fans and motors, the susurration of your own breathing—even, if you listen carefully enough, the rhythmic thump that is the pounding of your heart. These sounds reverberate through the suit, unable to escape into the surrounding void; they are the unnoticed background of life in space, for you are aware of them only when they change.

They had changed now; to them had been added a sound which I could not identify. It was an intermittent, muffled thudding, sometimes accompanied by a scraping noise.

I froze instantly, holding my breath and trying to locate the alien sound with my ears. The meters on the control board gave no clues; all the needles were rock-steady on their scales, and there were none of the flickering red lights that would warn of impending disaster. That was some comfort, but not much. I had long ago learned to trust my instincts in such matters; it was their alarm signals that were flashing now, telling me to return to the station before it was too late. . . .

Even now, I do not like to recall those next few minutes, as panic slowly flooded into my mind like a rising tide, overwhelming the dikes of reason and logic which every man must erect against the mystery of the universe. I knew then what it was like to face insanity; no other explanation fitted the facts.

For it was no longer possible to pretend that the noise disturbing me was that of some faulty mechanism. Though I was in utter isolation, far from any other human being or indeed any material object, I was not alone. The soundless void was bringing to my ears the faint, but unmistakable, stirrings of life.

In that first, heart-freezing moment it seemed that something was trying to get into my suit—something invisible, seeking shelter from the cruel and pitiless vacuum of space. I whirled madly in my harness, scanning the entire sphere of vision around me except for the blazing, forbidden cone towards the Sun. There was nothing there, of course. There could not be—yet that purposeful scrabbling was clearer than ever.

Despite the nonsense that has been written about us, it is not true that spacemen are superstitious. But can you blame me if, as I came to the end of logic's resources, I suddenly remembered how Bernie Summers had died, no further from the station than I was at this very moment?

It was one of those "impossible" accidents; it always is. Three things had gone wrong at once. Bernie's oxygen regulator had run wild and sent the pressure soaring, the safety valve had failed to blow—and a faulty joint had given way. In a fraction of a second, his suit was open to space.

I had never known Bernie, but suddenly his fate became of overwhelming importance to me, for a horrible idea had come into my mind. One does not talk about these things, but a damaged space suit is too valuable to be thrown away, even if it has killed its wearer. It is repaired, renumbered—and issued to someone else. . . .

What happens to the soul of a man who dies between the stars, far from his native world? Were you still here, Bernie, clinging to the last object that linked you to your lost and distant home?

As I fought the nightmares that were swirling around me—for now it seemed that the scratchings and soft fumblings were coming from all directions—there was one last hope to which I clung. For the sake of sanity, I had to prove that this wasn't Bernie's suit—that the metal walls so closely wrapped around me had never been another man's coffin.

It took me several tries before I could press the right button and switch my transmitter to the emergency wave length. "Station!" I gasped, "I'm in trouble! Get records to check my suit—"

I never finished; they say my yell wrecked the microphone. But what man, alone in the absolute isolation of space, would *not* have yelled when something patted him softly on the back of the neck?

I must have lunged forward, despite the safety harness, and smashed against the upper edge of the control panel. When the rescue squad reached me a few minutes later, I was still unconscious, with an angry bruise across my forehead.

And so I was the last person in the whole satellite relay system to know what had happened. When I came to my senses an hour later, all our medical staff was gathered around my bed, but it was quite a while before the doctors—

and certainly that cute little space nurse—bothered to look at me. They were much too busy playing with the three little kittens our badly misnamed Tommy had been rearing in my space suit's Number Three storage locker.

Stair Trick

Mildred Clingerman

Day after day the bartender did his fool's routine of a man going down stairs. The regular customers loved it. Of course there weren't any stairs, but sooner or later somebody would call down the long length of bar, "Dick, old boy, I'd like a bottle of that Chateau Margaux '29 to take home to the wife. How about it?"

After twenty years of it, Dick could recognize his cue. "Certainly, sir," he'd say gravely. "It won't take me a minute. You'll excuse me while I step down to the cellar?"

The regulars would grin and nudge the newcomers, the un-initiated. "Watch it," they'd say. "Just watch this." And the newcomers would set their faces in accommodating lines, tinged with the resentment of those who aren't in on the joke, and watch Dick carefully. Dick, his bald head gleaming in the overhead light, would start his stately descent into the cellar, until, step by step, the bald head had disappeared from view.

"What's so hot about that?" Nine times out of ten some disgruntled stranger would challenge the regulars. "Hell, I can still walk down a few stairs."

"Just wait. Just wait and *listen*." Gleefully the regulars would shush the unimpressed stranger until reluctantly he sub-sided and listened.

Nobody knew, or cared to inquire too closely, just what it

67

was Dick had rigged under the bar for his sound effects, but they were good. One heard the rattle of a chain lock, the squeak of the heavy door at the foot of the steps, a clicking light switch, and then the stone-muffled tramp, tramp of Dick's feet to the wine racks. Some hesitation then followed while the customers imagined Dick selecting the wine asked for, then they heard him crossing the stone floor. They heard again the click of the light switch and the door closing behind him with a hollow booming sound, the rattle of the lock, and Dick (a heavy man) was climbing the stairs, puffing a little. As he gradually came into view, one often saw a wisp of cobweb trailing across the bald head, and in his arms he cradled a dusty bottle. The bottle was always the same, but the puzzled stranger didn't know that.

"Now!" the regulars would shout. "Look! Look!" Everybody would raise himself from his bar stool to peer over the bar, pointing at Dick's feet and the floor he stood on, the stranger along with the rest. It was always a pleasure to watch the stranger's face as he took in the solid cement floor that showed through the slatted walkway running unbroken behind the bar. The grin breaking on the newcomer's face always started out a little sickly, but as light dawned and the illusion faded, the usual verdict was, "I'll be damned." And everybody was happy.

"Let's see what you got in the bottle" . . . but the regulars were quick to explain, low-voiced, that Dick was funny about the bottle. It was just an old empty bottle, but Dick didn't go handing it around. If you wanted to get snubbed, try making a grab for it.

Dick, as always after he'd finished the stair trick, just stood there for a while, holding the empty bottle, and anybody looking at him would have been surprised at the expression on his face. Nobody really looks at a bartender. The man behind the bar is either a smile or a mild grouch, and in any case, a pair of willing hands—reaching, setting down, polishing, ringing the cash register. Even the bar philosophers (the dreariest customers of all) prefer to study their own faces in the back-bar mirror. And however they accept their reflected images, whether shudderingly or with secret love, it is to this aloof image that they impart their whisky-wisdom, not to the bartender. Dick knew that. For twenty years he had watched his customers with growing bewilderment. His small, kind eyes assessed his world and found it very lonely.

Occasionally Dick, too, took note of his own face in the back-bar mirror, but most of all he used the mirror for watching The Game. The Game went on and on, year in and year out, but Dick never tired of watching it. Just as the customers smiled and narrowed their eyes at his stair trick, wanting to believe, so too did he take in all the nuances of The Game, and even after twenty years of it he kept on wanting to believe. Nightly he assured himself that people do fall in love in bars . . . well, anyway, that one couple . . . maybe. He hoped so.

Dick was almost used to the loneliness of his room in the musty old hotel. Every night when he unlocked his door he found the steaming foot bath waiting. How many bellboys had he trained to that attention? Too many, perhaps. . . . Oh, well, there was the evening paper on the arm of the shabby easy chair, and the slippers waiting for his feet to emerge from the good hot water. A wife now . . . might remember he liked hot tea waiting, too, but then again she might not relish such tasks around 1:00 a.m. And, anyway, what was the use of wondering about that? It certainly wasn't very likely at this point that Dick would ever marry. Marriage happened to other men. Well, didn't it? He would gladly have married if the chance had ever . . . happened. How else did you get married? Nobody sets forth with the thought: I'm going to find somebody, *today*, for instance, and get myself married. No, it wasn't that way at all.

First, somebody catches your eye. You look at each other, past the mask, beyond all the things life does to cover people up, hide them, and your eyes meet in a far place that's familiar to each of you. And that's a frightening thing. That's the beginning of The Game, and the fear is part of the fascination. The Game is really just hide and seek, until neither can bear to hide any longer. But you can't play The Game until you meet the right pair of eyes. Now, can you?

Dick had looked into a lot of eyes, but none had been

right. He had watched hundreds of people experience that shock of recognition, though. That's how he knew so much about it. Well, admit it. . . . He'd also seen it assumed, counterfeited. He'd watched the Hunters of both sexes mark their prey. Usually they avoided their own kind, but sometimes, like jungle beasts meeting on a narrow path, they challenged each other. Then it was a battle to the death. Whenever this happened in Dick's bar, he could almost feel the charged atmosphere. You could see that it affected the customers, too. The laughter grew louder, the drinks went down quicker, and quarrels sprang up in the room like little fires. A good time for the stair trick—it helped to clear the air.

This night Dick had gone through the routine and was still puffing from his exertions, just standing there, holding the empty bottle with that strange look on his face, when somebody down at the end of the bar called to him in a high, clear voice:

"Tell me, bartender, what's it like in the cellar?"

Dick turned slowly towards the voice and his hands shook so much he was afraid he'd drop the bottle. Nobody else had ever asked that question. Laughter and head-shaking admiration were supposed to be the end of it. This woman, now . . . she only came around once or twice a month. How did she know the cellar was . . . very real to Dick? He hurried to set the empty bottle before her so that she could examine it—the emptiness of it, the carefully preserved dust and cobwebs.

"The cellar. . . " Dick said. "It's nice."

She lifted her look to his. "I know," she said.

Their eyes met in the far place, and yet Dick trembled with unbelief. She was a Hunter, and Hunters were clever enough to find your far place, or to pretend they had.

"You're a liar," Dick whispered. "You don't really know."

The woman tucked a dark lock of hair behind her ear and smiled at him. "Don't believe me," she said. "Forget it. I'm just tight. But . . . tell me, in your cellar . . . have you found the door to the other side?"

"I don't know what you mean." Dick moistened his dry lips and glanced up and down the bar and out to the crowded tables. The customers were engrossed in their own talk, their glasses almost full.

The woman sighed and shook her head at him gently. "You're afraid," she said. "You know what I am, and now— this minute—I'm drunk enough to admit it. Also drunk enough and crazy enough to try to find the way out. . . . You know you can't go through the door alone? Even if you find it?"

Dick looked long at her before he nodded his head. Yes, he knew. And here, at last, was the woman, if only he could believe in her.

"Aren't you lonely, too?" the woman asked softly. "Don't you want me? I'd be different beyond the door. . . . What do you think I've been hunting for, all these years?"

"Why didn't you speak sooner?" Dick whispered. "Years ago . . ."

"You wouldn't look at me," she said. "You'd never really look at me."

That was true. He was afraid of the Hunters, and most afraid of the few quiet, lovely women who did not look the part. Like this one.

"I can't believe it," he said. "You don't want me." He shook his head dazedly.

The woman tried to smile. "All right," she said. "I was crazy to think you'd listen, that you'd believe. . . . I don't blame you. And now the hell with it, I don't believe in anything at all." She slid down from the high bar stool and turned to walk away.

"Wait."

For a moment she hesitated, then turned again to face him. He looked at her soft red mouth and the cloud of dark hair, and at the slender, sweet body before he allowed himself to look again into her eyes. She faced him as if he were Judgment and she standing up pleading for mankind. Her eyes admitted everything. The meanness, the drab cheating, all the niggling subterfuges, the hurt, the fear, and yes . . . the love, to balance them all—to write them all off.

"Come with me now," he said.

Quickly then she ducked under the hinged serving board and was beside him on the slatted walkway behind the bar. He took her hand and smiled at her, and together they went down the stairs.

There was the old bottle standing on the bar—that was the first thing noticed. Then somebody heard the creaking of the door. Somebody else heard it chained and locked again from the other side, and as sounds died in the room, almost everybody in the bar heard the muffled steps of the two of them crossing the stone floor. But they didn't stop at the wine racks. The regulars will tell you that. They went beyond—far beyond—any point Dick had ever reached alone. Until at last the footsteps ceased—brought up short it seemed before the last barrier. And then there was time enough and silence enough for every man in the bar to remember blank closed doors and the sour taste of failure.

The sighing had already begun—the thin, stingy *ahhh* for this latest defeat—when they heard the sound that was new and triumphant. Not one of the customers will swear it was music he heard, but every last one of them swears he heard Dick open the door to the Other Side . . . and close it again behind him.

Unwelcome Tenant

Roger Dee

It happened just before he reached the zero point, the no-man's land in space where the attenuated gravity fields of two planets meet and cancel out.

Maynard was dividing his attention equally between the transparent bubble that housed the Meinz pendulum and the two ports, forward and aft, that broke the steel paneling of the control cubicle. He listened critically to the measured clicking of the Geiger counters and the quiet sibilance of the air purifiers, and in spite of his weightlessness and his total loss of equilibrium he was quite calm.

But deep inside him, under his trained calmness, Maynard felt a steadily growing triumph, a swelling exultation that was a thing quite apart from scientific pride. The feeling that he was a pioneer, an advance guard for a conquering people, elated him and multiplied the eagerness in him when he turned his eyes to the forward port where Mars hung, full and ruddy, a spotted enigmatic disc of promise.

Earth hung in the after port behind and below him, a soft emerald crescent in its first thin quarter. A warm green sickle that was home, a hustling verdant young world impatient to push its way across black empty space and satisfy its lusty curiosity about its cosmic neighbors.

He was at the end of his second day out, and he had covered roughly half of the distance he must travel. The

atomic jets had cut off long ago, at escape velocity, and
would not come on again until they were needed to slow his
approach. The mid point lay just ahead; in a matter of
minutes now he would leave Earth's waning field and fall free
into the grasp of the red planet.

He was watching the cobalt ball of the Meinz pendulum
quiver on its thin quartz thread with the first fluttering release
of Earth's gravity when the fear came.

Terror struck him suddenly, galvanically, blanking out all
reason and all sensation. The control cubicle whirled giddily
before his eyes, and the abysmal panic that gripped his mind
was a monstrous thing boiling up out of unguessed subconscious depths. It froze him, breathing, like a man paralyzed
under an overwhelming electric shock.

It was not fear of death. It was not even his own fear.

It was the blind panic of Something inside him whose
existence he had never remotely suspected, Something that
shrieked soundlessly in senseless maniac terror and fought
to tear Itself free of him.

He was torn by the struggle for an interminable instant,
and then it was over. He felt It writhe loose from the encum-
brance of his mind, like a madman writhing out of a strait-
jacket, and then It was falling back toward Earth, away from
him. He could sense It plainly, once It was outside him—a
malevolent, intangible Thing that fell back swiftly toward the
emerald crescent of Earth.

He sat for a moment dazed while breath came back into
his lungs and the steel-paneled cubicle grew steady again before his staring eyes. And, when It had gone in the distance
and he could no longer feel the frenzy of Its terror, he felt
the swift unbounded freedom that a spirited horse feels when
it has, unexpectedly, lost its rider.

He was still Robert Maynard, but with a difference.
He was free.

The feeling of utter freedom staggered him. For the first
time in his life he possessed himself entirely, without doubt
or reservation, a complete and serene entity. He could feel
his consciousness still expanding, reaching into every hidden

corner of his mind and taking control of functions he had not dreamed of before.

An analogy occurred to him in perfect exactness of detail: he was like a man waking from a vague world of sleep to find that what he had thought a single small room was in reality a spacious house. There were other rooms than the cramped chamber he had lived in all his life—rooms that had been tenanted a moment before by Something else, but which lay open and ready for his own use now that their Tenant was gone. A moment before his ego had occupied a meager one-twelfth of his brain; with Its departure the whole of his mind was his.

As suddenly as that he knew what had happened to him and why, and his incredibly multiplied intelligence arranged the details of it precisely for his consideration.

He had been host to a parasitic intelligence, without knowing it, all his life. He had moved at Its dictates, following his own will only when It slept or tired or was distracted, never succeeding fully in any endeavor of his own because It was in control and must be obeyed. He knew when he had explored the vacated premises of his newly freed mind that It was only one of many, that all Earthmen had Tenants like It, intangible parasitic entities subsisting upon and controlling the human life force.

He thought: *No wonder we have wars on Earth! We have no common ground for agreement because we are under Their compulsion. They know our inherent abilities and keep us at each others' throats lest we learn of and destroy Them. Everything that Man has accomplished has been done in spite of Them.*

He looked with new eyes at the instrument panel under the forward port and was astonished at the crudity of the engines it controlled. He was primarily an astrophysicist, and his understanding of atomic propulsion had been negligible; now its every function was clear to him at a glance. Experimentally he drew a graph of the arc he described through space and knew to a minute how long it would be before the braking jets slowed his speed for landing.

He raised his eyes to the forward port where the ruddy

disc of Mars hung framed against the black velvet backdrop of space like a red jewel burning dully among a random display of lesser brilliants, beckoning him on with the future's illimitable promise.

He sat quite still for a time on the padded control couch, thinking intently, testing the new powers of his mind as he might have flexed a newly discovered limb.

His first conclusion was inescapable: his Tenant had left him because It could not exist outside Earth's gravity. It had been forced to quit him or perish, and Its departure had made him the first really free man.

They were not invincible. They were not even particularly intelligent, in spite of Their gift of parasitic control, or his own Tenant would have known Its danger. The fact that They were gravity-bound entities gave him the first vulnerable chink in Their armor, an Achilles heel that offered eventual salvation for men. There would be other ways to be rid of Them, and it was his responsibility as the first free man to see that others of his kind were freed as he had been.

He pictured the harmonious integration of an Earth peopled by free men and saw clearly the heights men might reach unhampered by their Tenants. His own possibilities, when he had summed them up, awed him in their extent. There were no limits to what he could do, no bounds to the knowledge he could accumulate and use.

This is what being a man is really like. I can liberate a world. Like Moses, I can set my people free.

The thought set his face shining, suffused him with a glow of anticipated triumph. It was all so simple, now that he was free. . . .

In a few hours he would land on Mars, and in a matter of minutes he could set up a beam transmitter to report back to the scientific foundation that had sent him out. He could not tell his fellows the truth because they were still captive, and their Tenants must not be warned; but he could invent a plausible story of easily acquired wealth on Mars that would bring other and larger commercial expeditions swarming after him. With the help of other freed men he could found a new civilization on the red planet, develop means to carry the fight back to Earth and exterminate the Tenants utterly. It would take time, but in the end men would be free.

The Meinz centrifuge spun slowly, and with the swing of its cobalt ball Maynard felt the shift from terrestrial to Martian gravity. He felt the first tiny tug of weight and the slow returning of equilibrium as his body oriented itself to the growing pull of the new attraction.

With the return of equilibrium he suddenly realized that he was upside down and turned to the control board for correction. The cubicle righted itself, rotating gently until the ruddy expanding disc of Mars hung below and ahead of the forward port. The Meinz pendulum ceased to oscillate, the little cobalt ball hanging stiffly at the end of its taut quartz filament.

He was well into the Martian attraction field by now. He made a quick calculation (which once would have taken painstaking hours) and knew that he would release the first braking blast from his forward jets in precisely ten hours. The little ship would nose into a slowly tightening spiral, avoiding the odd-planed orbits of the two tiny moons and, within minutes of establishing his declaration track, he would be ready to land.

He watched eagerly as the red disc of Mars swelled to a mottled globe, blurred already at the edges by atmospheric refraction. Down there on the dead ground of that ancient world he would set up his equipment and flash back his triumphant message to Earth, a fabulous exultant lie that would bring other men like him swarming to the red planet.

Free men! Supermen, really, in a new free world. Nothing impossible, then!

Later, he shut off the braking blast of the forward jets and felt the soft rubber-foam padding of the couch rise gently under him as deceleration ceased. He was well into his landing spiral, eating up the paltry thousands of miles that lay between him and the shining future.

He lay back on the couch, smiling, his mind busy with the message he would beam back to Earth, planning already the campaign he would carry out. Years must pass before men were freed completely of their Tenants, perhaps decades, but time did not matter. It was essentially a simple task because he and those to come after him would be free of Their compulsion—serene, unhampered supermen to whom time was nothing.

In the end they could not fail. . . .

Something impinged sharply upon his new perception, a chill-groping tentacle of questioning intelligence. The smile froze on his face; he sat up stiffly, numbed with the unforeseen horror of what was happening to him. The groping ceased, and the hungry Intelligence from outside poured into his mind like smoke into an empty room, smothering his feeble attempt at resistance.

He rose and went to the forward port, staring dully down at the uprushing sandy wastes and trying to recall what glorious thing it was that he had been thinking. Or had it been only a dream? Somewhere in the farthest recess of his blunted consciousness a thought formed and floated like a bubble up into his awareness; but like a bubble it burst, and its meaning was lost on him.

There were Tenants on Earth, it said. *Why not on Mars, too?*

The Mathematicians

Arthur Feldman

They were in the garden. "Now, Zoe," said Zenia Hawkins to her nine-year-old daughter, "quit fluttering around, and papa will tell you a story."

Zoe settled down in the hammock. "A true story, papa?"

"It all happened exactly as I'm going to tell you," said Drake Hawkins, pinching Zoe's rosy cheek. "Now: two thousand and eleven years ago in 1985—figuring by the earthly calendar of that time—a tribe of beings from the Dog Star, Sirius, invaded the earth."

"And what did these beings look like, father?"

"Like humans in many, many respects. They each had two arms, two legs, and all the other organs that humans are endowed with."

"Wasn't there any difference at all between the Star beings and the humans, papa?"

"There was. The newcomers, each and all, had a pair of wings covered with green feathers growing from their shoulders, and long, purple tails."

"How many of these beings were there, father?"

"Exactly three million and forty-one male adults and three female adults. These creatures first appeared on Earth on the island of Sardinia. In five weeks' time they were the masters of the entire globe."

"Didn't the Earthlings fight back, papa?"

"The humans warred against the invaders, using bullets, ordinary bombs, super-atom bombs, and gases."

"What were those things like, father?"

"Oh, they passed out of existence long ago. 'Ammunition' they were called. The humans fought each other with such things."

"And not with ideas, like we do now, father?"

"No, with guns, just as I told you. But the invaders were immune to the ammunition."

"What does 'immune' mean?"

"Proof against harm. Then the humans tried germs and bacteria against the Star beings."

"What were those things?"

"Tiny, tiny bugs that the humans tried to inject into the bodies of the invaders to make them sicken and die. But the bugs had no effect at all on the Star beings."

"Go on, papa. These beings overran all Earth. Go on from there."

"You must know, these newcomers were vastly more intelligent than the Earthlings. In fact, the invaders were the greatest mathematicians in the System."

"What's the System? And what does mathematician mean?"

"The Milky Way. A mathematician is one who is good at figuring, weighing, measuring, clever with numbers."

"Then, father, the invaders killed off all the Earthlings?"

"Not all. They killed many, but many others were enslaved. Just as the humans had used horses and cattle, the newcomers so used the humans. They made workers out of some, others they slaughtered for food."

"Papa, what sort of language did these Star beings talk?"

"A very simple language, but the humans were never able to master it. So, the invaders, being so much smarter, mastered all the languages of the globe."

"What did the Earthlings call the invaders, father?"

" 'An-vils.' Half angels, half devils."

"Then papa, everything was peaceful on Earth after the An-vils enslaved the humans?"

"For a little while. Then, some of the most daring of the humans, led by a man named Knowall, escaped into the interior of Greenland. This Knowall was a psychiatrist, the foremost on Earth."

"What's a psychiatrist?"

"A dealer in ideas."

"Then, he was very rich?"

"He'd been the richest human on Earth. After some profound thought, Knowall figured a way to rid the earth of the An-vils."

"How, papa?"

"He perfected a method, called the Knowall-Hughes, Ilinski technique, of imbuing these An-vils with human emotions."

"What does 'imbuing' mean?"

"He filled them full of and made them aware of."

Zenia interrupted, "Aren't you talking a bit above the child's understanding, Drake?"

"No, Mama," said Zoe. "I understand what papa explained. Now, don't interrupt."

"So, Knowall," continued Drake, "filled the An-vils with human feelings such as love, hate, ambition, jealousy, malice, envy, despair, hope, fear, shame, and so on. Very soon the An-vils were acting like humans, and in ten days terrible civil wars wiped out two-thirds of the An-vil population."

"Then papa, the An-vils finally killed off each other?"

"Almost, until among them a being named Zalibar, full of saintliness and persuasion, preached the brotherhood of all An-vils. The invaders, quickly converted, quit their quarrels, and the Earthlings were even more enslaved."

"Oh, papa, weren't Knowall and his followers in Greenland awfully sad the way things had turned out?"

"For a while. Then Knowall came up with the final payoff."

"Is that slang, papa? Payoff?"

"Yes. The *coup de grâce*. The ace in the hole that he'd saved, if all else failed."

"I understand, papa. The idea that would out-trump anything the other side had to offer. What was it, father? What did they have?"

"Knowall imbued the An-vils with nostalgia."

"What is nostalgia?"

"Homesickness."

"Oh, papa, wasn't Knowall smart? That meant, the An-vils were all filled with the desire to fly back to the Star from where they had started."

"Exactly. So, one day, all the An-vils, an immense army, flapping their great green wings, assembled in the Black Hills of North America, and, at a given signal, they all rose up from Earth and all the humans chanted, 'Glory, glory, the day of our deliverance!' "

"So then, father, all the An-vils flew away from Earth?"

"Not all. There were two child An-vils, one male and one female, aged two years, who had been born on Earth, and they started off with all the other An-vils and flew up into the sky. But when they reached the upper limits of the stratosphere, they hesitated, turned tail, and fluttered back to Earth. Their names were Zizzo and Zizza."

"And what happened to Zizzo and Zizza, papa?"

"Well, like all the An-vils, they were great mathematicians. So, they multiplied."

"Oh, papa," laughed Zoe, flapping her wings excitedly, "that was a very nice story!"

The Third Level

Jack Finney

The presidents of the New York Central and the New York, New Haven and Hartford railroads will swear on a stack of timetables that there are only two. But I say there are three, because I've *been* on the third level at Grand Central Station. Yes, I've taken the obvious step: I talked to a psychiatrist friend of mine, among others. I told him about the third level at Grand Central Station, and he said it was a waking-dream wish fulfillment. He said I was unhappy. That made my wife kind of mad, but he explained that he meant the modern world is full of insecurity, fear, war, worry, and all the rest of it, and that I just want to escape. Well, hell, who doesn't? Everybody I know wants to escape, but they don't wander down into any third level at Grand Central Station.

But that's the reason, he said, and my friends all agreed. Everything points to it, they claimed. My stamp-collecting, for example—that's a "temporary refuge from reality." Well, maybe, but my grandfather didn't need any refuge from reality; things were pretty nice and peaceful in his day, from all I hear, and he started my collection. It's a nice collection, too, blocks of four of practically every U.S. issue, first-day covers, and so on. President Roosevelt collected stamps, too, you know.

Anyway, here's what happened at Grand Central. One

night last summer I worked late at the office. I was in a hurry
to get uptown to my apartment, so I decided to subway from
Grand Central because it's faster than the bus.

Now, I don't know why this should have happened to me.
I'm just an ordinary guy named Charley, thirty-one years old,
and I was wearing a tan gabardine suit and a straw hat with
a fancy band—I passed a dozen men who looked just like me.
And I wasn't trying to escape from anything; I just wanted to
get home to Louisa, my wife.

I turned into Grand Central from Vanderbilt Avenue and
went down the steps to the first level, where you take trains
like the Twentieth Century. Then I walked down another
flight to the second level, where the suburban trains leave
from, ducked into an arched doorway heading for the subway—and got lost. That's easy to do. I've been in and out of
Grand Central hundreds of times, but I'm always bumping
into new doorways and stairs and corridors. Once I got into
a tunnel about a mile long and came out in the lobby of the
Roosevelt Hotel. Another time I came up in an office building
on Forty-sixth Street, three blocks away.

Sometimes I think Grand Central is growing like a tree,
pushing out new corridors and staircases like roots. There's
probably a long tunnel that nobody knows about feeling its
way under the city right now, on its way to Times Square,
and maybe another to Central Park. And maybe—because
for so many people through the years Grand Central *has* been
an exit, a way of escape—maybe that's how the tunnel I got
into . . . but I never told my psychiatrist friend about that
idea.

The corridor I was in began angling left and slanting
downward and I thought that was wrong, but I kept on walking. All I could hear was the empty sound of my own footsteps and I didn't pass a soul. Then I heard that sort of hollow
roar ahead that means open space, and people talking. The
tunnel turned sharp left; I went down a short flight of stairs
and came out on the third level at Grand Central Station.
For just a moment I thought I was back on the second level,
but I saw the room was smaller, there were fewer ticket
windows and train gates, and the information booth in the
center was wood and old-looking. And the man in the booth

wore a green eyeshade and long, black sleeve-protectors. The lights were dim and sort of flickering. Then I saw why; they were open-flame gaslights.

There were brass spittoons on the floor, and across the station a glint of light caught my eye; a man was pulling a gold watch from his vest pocket. He snapped open the cover, glanced at his watch, and frowned. He wore a dirty hat, a black four-button suit with tiny lapels, and he had a big, black, handle-bar mustache. Then I looked around and saw that everyone in the station was dressed like 1890 something; I never saw so many beards, sideburns and fancy mustaches in my life. A woman walked in through the train gate; she wore a dress with leg-of-mutton sleeves and skirts to the top of her high-buttoned shoes. Back of her, out on the tracks, I caught a glimpse of a locomotive, a very small Currier & Ives locomotive with a funnel-shaped stack. And then I knew.

To make sure, I walked over to a newsboy and glanced at the stack of papers at his feet. It was the *World;* and the *World* hasn't been published for years. The lead story said something about President Cleveland. I've found that front page since, in the Public Library files, and it was printed June 11, 1894.

I turned toward the ticket windows knowing that here—on the third level at Grand Central—I could buy tickets that would take Louisa and me anywhere in the United States we wanted to go. In the year 1894. And I wanted two tickets to Galesburg, Illinois.

Have you ever been there? It's a wonderful town still, with big old frame houses, huge lawns, and tremendous trees whose branches meet overhead and roof the streets. And in 1894, summer evenings were twice as long, and people sat out on their lawns, the men smoking cigars and talking quietly, the women waving palm-leaf fans, with the fireflies all around, in a peaceful world. To be back there with the first World War still twenty years off, and World War II over forty years in the future . . . I wanted two tickets for that.

The clerk figured the fare—he glanced at my fancy hat-band, but he figured the fare—and I had enough for two coach tickets, one way. But when I counted out the money and looked up, the clerk was staring at me. He nodded at the bills. "That ain't money, mister," he said, "and if you're trying to skin me you won't get very far," and he glanced at the cash drawer beside him. Of course the money was old-style bills, half again as big as the money we use nowadays, and different-looking. I turned away and got out fast. There's nothing nice about jail, even in 1894.

And that was that. I left the same way I came, I suppose. Next day, during lunch hour, I drew $300 out of the bank, nearly all we had, and bought old-style currency (that *really* worried my psychiatrist friend). You can buy old money at almost any coin dealer's, but you have to pay a premium. My $300 bought less than $200 in old-style bills, but I didn't care; eggs were thirteen cents a dozen in 1894.

But I've never again found the corridor that leads to the third level at Grand Central Station, although I've tried often enough.

Louisa was pretty worried when I told her all this and didn't want me to look for the third level any more, and after a while I stopped; I went back to my stamps. But now we're *both* looking, every week end, because now we have proof that the third level is still there. My friend Sam Weiner disappeared! Nobody knew where, but I sort of suspected because Sam's a city boy, and I used to tell him about Galesburg—I went to school there—and he always said he liked the sound of the place. And that's where he is, all right. In 1894.

Because one night, fussing with my stamp collection, I found—Well, do you know what a first-day cover is? When a new stamp is issued, stamp collectors buy some and use them to mail envelopes to themselves on the very first day of sale; and the postmark proves the date. The envelope is called a first-day cover. They're never opened; you just put blank paper in the envelope.

That night, among my oldest first-day covers, I found one that shouldn't have been there. But there it was. It was there because someone had mailed it to my grandfather at his home in Galesburg; that's what the address on the envelope said. And it had been there since July 18, 1894—the postmark showed that—yet I didn't remember it at all. The stamp was a six-cent, dull brown, with a picture of President Garfield.

Naturally, when the envelope came to Granddad in the mail, it went right into his collection and stayed there—till I took it out and opened it.

The paper inside wasn't blank. It read:

> 941 Willard Street
> Galesburg, Illinois
> July 18, 1894

Charley:

I got to wishing that you were right. Then I got to *believing* you were right. And, Charley, it's true; I found the third level! I've been here two weeks, and right now, down the street at the Dalys', someone is playing a piano, and they're all out on the front porch singing *Seeing Nellie Home*. And I'm invited over for lemonade. Come on back, Charley and Louisa. Keep looking till you find the third level! It's worth it, believe me!

The note is signed Sam.

At the stamp and coin store I go to, I found out that Sam bought $800 worth of old-style currency. That ought to set him up in a nice little hay, feed, and grain business; he always said that's what he really wished he could do, and he certainly can't go back to his old business. Not in Galesburg, Illinois, in 1894. His old business? Why, Sam was my psychiatrist.

Beautiful, Beautiful, Beautiful!

Stuart Friedman

It was the eve of Progress-Stage Six, and the daily message had prescribed Stage Five Ecstasy Formula. Everyone, from 000 to 999, in Community Home 8051, for Premating Males in Progress-Stage Five, was experiencing the formula's balanced emotional heightening. Everyone, that is, except G17-AZ(q):444,801,735, category male, known familiarly as 735. 735 stood in a small, mirrored, harshly lighted meditation chamber, cut off from the goodness of the Community Mind. Under the plastiskin contours of his perfect features he felt a flush of shame on his own imperfect face; he couldn't master the formula.

All of the formula's ingredients, from basic joy in beauty through proportionally blended mastered emotions of lower progress-stages, were easy. Except the new one: anticipation of love adventure. 735 knew that, without this ingredient to propel him, he would not wish to leave Stage Five. And not to wish to move beautifully onward would be—735 shuddered—ugly!

Yesterday, he had voiced the courtship chant, saying, *Oh, daughter and mother of the gods, the beat of thy heart is the pulse in my veins. Wilt thou, O Chosen One, G17AZ(q):444,-801,735, category female, co-create the beauty of human life?* She, instead of chanting in turn, *Oh, son and father of the gods,* had said, "I'm 733, not 735."

A member of the Sublime Committee had remedied the error, and 735 had understood again the beauty of everything. The very fact that he couldn't tell one odd-numbered female from another, because of their equal perfection, was guarantee against the blemishes of desire and envy and possessiveness.

Tomorrow he must enter Stage Six if he did not want 735, category female, to suffer delay in fulfillment. Of course, he didn't want any such thing to happen to one whom he loved beautifully. He frowned sternly at himself. Of course not! He shut his eyes and concentrated on feeling anticipation of love adventure. He tried it with his eyes open, thought of the selflessly dedicated career ahead of him in helping construct another wing on the temple of ageless, imperishable beauty. He had a vision of an earthquake, but brief and hazy as it was it gave that balanced emotional heightening which was surely ecstasy formula.

He re-entered the great hall. Here was aesthetic perfection, where tones of light merged with lines of architecture and waves of sound and pleasing odors. Each of his fellows was as flawless of feature as he, differing only in that odd numbers were blond, even brunette. The spiritual symphony of a thousand minds under the baton of Stage Five Ecstasy Formula exalted 735, augmenting his small mind a thousand fold, transforming his ugly aloneness until he was One-All and beautiful again.

He stood, gazing out from a breadth of curving glass upon the vista. As distant as a dream, and with all a dream's wispy texture, stood Community Home 8051, for Premating Females in Progress-Stage Five, upon an eminence of the land similar to the Males' Home. He knew they were also experiencing ecstasy formula.

In the distance between were the many buildings of the city, each a proud curve or angle or mass within the patterned whole. There were vast open greens and areas of intricate floral lacework; some streets thrust, while others meandered, and there were pools and fountains. The dusk sky blending exquisite patterns of sun and cloud, thanks to the committee of artist-meteorologists for the zone, was, as always, superb. 735 regarded a stand of dark evergreens forming an irregular counterbalancing mass, and the outlaw thought raced through his mind that he would like to have a portable sawmill.

He shifted his attention hastily to the contemplation of another aspect. Beyond the weather cone, he noted, it was storming. He kept staring, with an intensity which threatened the balance of his emotional heightening. He sensed that his mind was once more out of harmony and feared that he would taint the whole. He stared fixedly at the dreamlike eminence upon which stood the female home and concentrated on anticipation of love adventure with 733 . . . no! 735, category female.

Suddenly he was running. The violence of his motion left several of his fellows in a state of near collapse. He got out of the great hall, ran through the city. He reached the edge of the weather cone, paused, then rushed through. He stood in the raging downpour of the storm and shivered. He looked back at the indescribable magnificence of the world he had left, feeling like a pauper peering into a castle of yore. He burst out laughing.

He plunged on through the storm. The land was rough and ugly, and he tired quickly. The remedial hue had begun to fade from areas of his imperfectly colored hair. His plastiskin mask had begun to crinkle; he sank down and peeled the mask off.

Now he could never go back; he would have to be the abomination that was himself. He groaned, got up, and trudged on, tired, dirty, hungry, and spiritually loathesome because he was mad as hell. He made the coarsest sort of brutish sounds in his throat. He was ashamed, and then he repeated the sounds and grinned.

735 stopped in his tracks. There was a small, smoke fire ahead. He moved stealthily toward it and saw a female kneeling beside it, hurling raucous, squalling imprecations at the fire. She twisted around and saw him. She had streaked hair, a dirty, off-balance face and a distinctly unpleasant expression. His heart began to slam, and he thought: *This is anticipation of love adventure.*

The female's scowl had vanished, and she got to her feet and came to him

"Who are you?" she said unpleasantly. She snuffed her nose and sneezed.

"I was once known to my fellows as 735, but—"

"Son and father of the gods!" She screeched offensively with laughter. "I'm 735, category female."

"My mate!" He shut his eyes and groaned. Then he peered narrowly at her. "She was beautiful; you're not her."

She was regarding him thoughtfully. "You're not him, either; you look more like an ogre."

"Long ago," he said dreamily, "I saw in a picture book the face of a woman called The Horror. I thought all dreams had already come true, and that I could never hope to find such a one. But here you are!"

"Do you really mean it?" she said, her eyes adoring. Then her voice broke excitedly. "Why, there's not a perfect feature to you!"

"We were made for each other! Look at us; we haven't sense enough to get in out of the rain!"

"I just know we'll make a mess of everything together."

"First we'll build a shelter—"

"No. A fire."

"You see?" he cried triumphantly. "Already we're out of harmony."

And, so saying, they built a house that fell down, a fire that flooded out, and discovered they had both been wrong in not first seeking food. Half-starved, coughing, sneezing, foul-tempered, sour-faced, they set out through the rain.

The Figure

Edward Grendon

It's a funny sort of deal and I don't mind admitting that we're scared. Maybe not so much scared as puzzled or shocked. I don't know, but it's a funny deal—. Especially in these days.

The work we have been doing is more secret than anything was during the war. You would never guess that the firm we work for does this kind of research. It's a very respectable outfit, and as I said, no one would ever guess that they maintained this lab, so I guess it's safe to tell you what happened. It looks like too big a thing to keep to ourselves anyhow, although of course it may mean nothing at all. You judge for yourself.

There are three of us who work here. We are all pretty highly trained in our field and get paid pretty well. We have a sign on our door that has nothing whatsoever to do with our work, but keeps most people away. In any case we leave by a private exit and never answer a knock. There's a private wire to the desk of the guy who hired us and he calls once in awhile, but ever since we told him that we were making progress he has more or less left us alone. I promised him— I'm chief here insofar as we have one—that I'd let him know as soon as we had something to report.

It's been a pretty swell setup. Dettner, Lasker, and myself have got along fine. Dettner is young and is an electrical physicist—as good as they make them. Studied at M.I.T., taught at Cal. Tech., did research for the Army, and then came here. My own background is mostly bioelectrics. I worked at designing electroencephalographs for awhile, and during the war I worked at Oak Ridge on nuclear physics. I'm a Jack-of-all-trades in the physics field. Lasker is a mathematician. He specializes in symbolic logic and is the only man I know who can really understand Tarski. He was the one who provided most of the theoretical background for our work. He says that the mathematics of what we are doing is not overly difficult, but we are held back by the language we think in and the unconscious assumptions we make. He has referred me to Korzybski's *Science and Sanity* a number of times, but so far I haven't had a chance to read it. Now I think I will. I *have* to know the meaning of our results. It's too important to let slide. Lasker and Dettner have both gone fishing. They said they would be back, but I'm not sure they will. I can't say I would blame them, but I've got to be more certain of what it means before I walk out of here for good.

We have been here over a year now—ever since they gave me that final lecture on Secrecy at Oak Ridge and let me go home. We have been working on the problem of time travel. When we took the job, they told us that they didn't expect any results for a long time, that we were on our own as far as working hours went, and that our main job was to clarify the problem and make preliminary experiments. Thanks to Lasker, we went ahead a lot faster than either they or we had expected. There was a professional philosopher working here with us at first. He taught philosophy at Columbia and was supposed to be an expert in his field. He quit after two months in a peeve. Couldn't stand it when Lasker would change the logic we were working with every few weeks. He had been pretty pessimistic about the whole thing from the first and couldn't understand how it was possible to apply scientific methods to a problem of this sort.

I still don't understand all the theory behind what we've done. The mathematics are a bit too advanced for me, but Lasker vouches for them.

Some of the problems we had should be fairly obvious. For instance, you can't introduce the concept "matter" into space-time mathematics without disrupting the space-time and working with Newtonian space *and* time mathematics. If you handle an "object"—as we sense it as a curvature of space-time—as Einstein does, it's pretty hard to do much with it theoretically. Lasker managed that by using Einstein formulations and manipulating them with several brands of Tarski's non-Aristotelian logic. As I said, we did it, although Dettner and I don't fully understand the mathematics and Lasker doesn't understand the gadget we used to produce the electrical fields.

There had been no hurry at all in our work up to the last month. At that time the Army wrote Dettner and myself and asked us to come back and work for them awhile. Neither of us wanted to refuse under the circumstances so we stalled them for thirty days and just twenty-two days later made our first test. The Army really wanted us badly and in a hurry, and it took a lot of talking to stall them.

What the Army wanted us for was to help find out about the cockroaches. That sounds funny, but it's true. It didn't make the newspapers, but about a year after the New Mexico atom-bomb test, the insect problem at the testing ground suddenly increased a hundred fold. Apparently the radiation did something to them and they came out in force one day against the control station. They finally had to dust the place with DDT to get rid of them.

Looking over the dead insects, all the government entomologists could say was that the radiation seemed to have increased their size about forty per cent and made them breed faster. They never did agree whether it was the intense radiation of the blast or the less intense, but longer continued, radiation from fused sand and quartz on the ground.

New Mexico was nothing to Hiroshima and Nagasaki. After all, there are comparatively few "true bugs" in the desert and a great many in a Japanese city. About a year and a half after Japan got A-bombed, they really swarmed on both cities at the same time. They came out suddenly one night by the millions. It's been estimated that they killed and ate several hundred people before they were brought under control. To stop them, MacArthur had his entire Chemical Warfare Service and a lot of extra units concentrated on the plague spots. They dusted with chemicals and even used some gas. At that, it was four days before the bugs were brought under control.

This time the government experts really went into the problem. They traced the insect tunnels about ten feet down and examined their breeding chambers and what not. According to their reports—all this is still kept strictly hush-hush by the Army, but we've seen all the data—the radiation seems to drive the insects down into the earth. They stay down for awhile and breed and then seem to have a "blind urge" to go to the surface. This urge "seems to affect the entire group made up of an immense number of connected colonies at the same time." That's a quote from their report. One other thing they mentioned is that there were large breeding chambers and some sort of communal life that—to their knowledge—had not been observed in these particular insects before. We told Lasker about it and showed him the reports. He was plenty worried, but he wouldn't say why.

Don't know why I wandered so far afield. I just wanted to explain that if this test wasn't successful, we would probably have to put things off for quite a while. We were interested in the beetle problem as it not only has some interesting implications, but the effect of radiation on protoplasm is a hard nut to crack. However, we had come so far on our time gadget that we wanted to finish it first. Well, we finished and tested it, and now Dettner and Lasker are out fishing. As I said, they probably won't come back.

It was the day before yesterday that we made the final test. Looked at one way, we had made tremendous progress. Looked at another, we had made very little. We had devised an electric field that would operate in the future. There were sixteen outlets forming the sides of a cube about four feet in diameter. When switched on, an electrical field was produced which "existed" at some future time. I know Lasker would say this was incorrect, but it gets the general idea over. He would say that instead of operating in "here-now", it operates in "here-then." He'd get angry every time we'd separate "space" and "time" in our talk and tell us that we weren't living in the eighteenth century.

"Newton was a great man," he'd say, "but he's dead now. If you talk as if it were 1750, you'll *think* and *act* as if it were 1750 and then we won't get anywhere. You use non-Newtonian formulations in your work, use them in everyday speech, too."

How far in the future our gadget would operate we had no way of knowing. Lasker said he would not even attempt to estimate "when" the field was active. When the power was turned off, anything that was in the cube of forces would be brought back to the present space-time. In other words, we had a "grab" that would reach out and drag something back from the future. Don't get the idea we were sending something into the future to bring something back with it, although that's what it amounts to for all practical purposes. We were warping space-time curvature so that anything "here-then" would be something "here-now."

We finished the gadget at three o'clock Tuesday morning. Lasker had been sleeping on the couch while we worked on it. He had checked and rechecked his formulae and said that, if we could produce the fields he'd specified, it would probably work. We tested each output separately and then woke him up. I can't tell you how excited we were as we stood there with everything ready. Finally Dettner said, "Let's get it done," and I pressed the start button.

The needles on our ammeters flashed over and back, the machine went dead as the circuit breakers came open, and there was an object in the cube.

We looked it over from all sides without touching it. Then the implications of it began to hit us. It's funny what men will do at a time like that. Dettner took out his watch, examined it carefully, as if he had never seen it before, and then went over and turned on the electric percolator. Lasker swore quietly in Spanish or Portuguese, I'm not sure which. I sat down and began a letter to my wife. I got as far as writing the date and then tore it up.

What was in the cube—it's still there, none of us have touched it—was a small statue about three feet high. It's some sort of metal that looks like silver. About half the height is pedestal and half is the statue itself. It's done in great detail and obviously by a skilled artist. The pedestal consists of a globe of the Earth with the continents and islands in relief. So far as I can determine it's pretty accurate, although I think the continents are a slightly different shape on most maps. But I may be wrong. The figure on top is standing up very straight and looking upwards. It's dressed only in a wide belt from which a pouch hangs on one side and a flat square box on the other. It looks intelligent and is obviously representing either aspiration or a religious theme, or maybe both. You can sense the dreams and ideals of the figure and the obvious sympathy and understanding of the artist with them. Lasker says he thinks the statue is an expression of religious feeling. Dettner and I both think it represents aspirations: *per adra ad astra,* or something of the sort. It's a majestic figure and it's easy to respond to it emphatically with a sort of "upward and onward" feeling. There is only one thing wrong. The figure is that of a beetle.

The Rag Thing

David Grinnell

It would have been all right if spring had never come. During the winter nothing had happened and nothing was likely to happen as long as the weather remained cold and Mrs. Larch kept the radiators going. In a way, though, it is quite possible to hold Mrs. Larch to blame for everything that happened. Not that she had what people would call malicious intentions, but just that she was two things practically every boarding-house landlady is—thrifty and not too clean.

She shouldn't have been in such a hurry to turn the heat off so early in March. March is a tricky month and she should have known that the first warm day is usually an isolated phenomenon. But then you could always claim that she shouldn't have been so sloppy in her cleaning last November. She shouldn't have dropped that rag behind the radiator in the third-floor front room.

As a matter of fact, one could well wonder what she was doing using such a rag anyway. Polishing furniture doesn't require a clean rag to start with, certainly not the rag you stick into the furniture polish, that's going to be greasy anyway—but she didn't have to use that particular rag. The one that had so much dried blood on it from the meat that had been lying on it in the kitchen.

On top of that, it is probable that she had spit into the filthy thing, too. Mrs. Larch was no prize package. Gross,

98

dull, unkempt, widowed, and careless, she fitted into the house—one of innumerable other brownstone fronts in the lower sixties of New York. Houses that in former days, fifty or sixty years ago, were considered the height of fashion and the residences of the well-to-do, now reduced to dingy rooming places for all manner of itinerants, lonely people with no hope in life other than dreary jobs, or an occasional young and confused person from the hinterland seeking fame and fortune in a city that rarely grants it.

So it was not particularly odd that when she accidentally dropped the filthy old rag behind the radiator in the room on the third-floor front late in November, she had simply left it there and forgotten to pick it up.

It gathered dust all winter, unnoticed. Skelty, who had the room, might have cleaned it out himself save that he was always too tired for that. He worked at some indefinite factory all day and when he came home he was always too tired to do much more than read the sports and comics pages of the newspapers and then maybe stare at the streaky brown walls a bit before dragging himself into bed to sleep the dreamless sleep of the weary.

The radiator, a steam one oddly enough (for most of these houses used the older hot-air circulation), was in none too good condition. Installed many, many years ago by the house's last Victorian owner, it was given to knocks, leaks, and cantankerous action. Along in December it developed a slow drip, and drops of hot water would fall to seep slowly into the floor and leave the rag lying on a moist hot surface. Steam was constantly escaping from a bad valve that Mrs. Larch would have repaired if it had blown off completely but, because the radiator always managed to be hot, never did.

Because Mrs. Larch feared drafts, the windows were rarely open in the winter, and the room would become oppressively hot at times when Skelty was away.

It is hard to say what is the cause of chemical reactions. Some hold that all things are mechanical in nature, others that life has a psychic side which cannot be duplicated in laboratories. The problem is one for metaphysicians; everyone knows that some chemicals are attracted to heat, others to light, and they may not necessarily be alive at all. Tropisms is the scientific term used, and if you want to believe that living matter is stuff with a great number of tropisms and dead matter is stuff with little or no tropisms, that's one way of looking at it. Heat and moisture and greasy chemical compounds were the sole ingredients of the birth of life in some ancient unremembered swamp.

Which is why it probably would have been all right if spring had never come. Because Mrs. Larch turned the radiators off one day early in March. The warm hours were but few. It grew cold with the darkness and by night it was back in the chill of February again. But Mrs. Larch had turned the heat off and, being lazy, decided not to turn it on again till the next morning, provided of course that it stayed cold the next day (which it did).

Anyway Skelty was found dead in bed the next morning. Mrs. Larch knocked on his door when he failed to come down to breakfast and when he hadn't answered, she turned the knob and went in. He was lying in bed, blue and cold, and he had been smothered in his sleep.

There was quite a to-do about the whole business but nothing came of it. A few stupid detectives blundered around the room, asked silly questions, made a few notes, and then left the matter to the coroner and the morgue. Skelty was a nobody, no one cared whether he lived or died, he had no enemies and no friends, there were no suspicious visitors, and he had probably smothered accidentally in the blankets. Of course the body was unusually cold when Mrs. Larch found it, as if the heat had been sucked out of him, but who notices a thing like that? They also discounted the grease smudge on the top sheet, the grease stains on the floor, and the slime on his face. Probably some grease he might have been using for some imagined skin trouble, though Mrs. Larch had not heard of his doing so. In any case, no one really cared.

Mrs. Larch wore black for a day and then advertised in the papers. She made a perfunctory job of cleaning the room. Skelty's possessions were taken away by a drab sister-in-law from Brooklyn who didn't seem to care much either, and Mrs. Larch was all ready to rent the room to someone else.

The weather remained cold for the next ten days and the heat was kept up in the pipes.

The new occupant of the room was a nervous young man from upstate who was trying to get a job in New York. He was a high-strung young man who entertained any number of illusions about life and society. He thought that people did things for the love of it and he wanted to find a job where he could work for that motivation rather than the sort of things he might have done back home. He thought New York was different, which was a mistake.

He smoked like fury which was something Mrs. Larch did not like because it meant ashes on the floor and burned spots on her furniture (not that there weren't plenty already), but there was nothing Mrs. Larch would do about it because it would have meant exertion.

After four days in New York, this young man, Gorman by name, was more nervous than ever. He would lie in bed nights smoking cigarette after cigarette thinking and thinking and getting nowhere. Over and over he was facing the problem of resigning himself to a life of gray drab. It was a thought he had tried not to face and now that it was thrusting itself upon him, it was becoming intolerable.

The next time a warm day came, Mrs. Larch left the radiators on because she was not going to be fooled twice. As a result, when the weather stayed warm, the rooms became insufferably hot because she was still keeping the windows down. So that when she turned the heat off finally, the afternoon of the second day, it was pretty tropical in the rooms.

When the March weather turned about suddenly again and became chilly about nine at night, Mrs. Larch was going to bed and figured that no one would complain and that it would be warm again the next day. Which may or may not be true, it does not matter.

Gorman got home about ten, opened the window, got undressed, moved a pack of cigarettes and an ash tray next to his bed on the floor, got into bed, turned out the light and started to smoke.

He stared at the ceiling, blowing smoke upwards into the darkened room trying to see its outlines in the dim light coming in from the street. When he finished one cigarette, he let his hand dangle out the side of the bed and picked up another cigarette from the pack on the floor, lit it from the butt in his mouth, and dropped the butt into the ash tray on the floor.

The rag under the radiator was getting cold, the room was getting cold, there was one source of heat radiation in the room. That was the man in the bed. Skelty had proven a source of heat supply once. Heat attraction was chemical force that could not be denied. Strange forces began to accumulate in the long-transformed fibers of the rag.

Gorman thought he heard something flap in the room but he paid it no attention. Things were always creaking in the house. Gorman heard a swishing noise and ascribed it to the mice.

Gorman reached down for a cigarette, fumbled for it, found the pack, deftly extracted a smoke in the one-handed manner chain smokers become accustomed to, lifted it to his mouth, lit it from the burning butt in his mouth, and reached down with the butt to crush it out against the tray.

He pressed the butt into something wet like a used handkerchief, there was a sudden hiss, something coiled and whipped about his wrist; Gorman gasped and drew his hand back fast. A flaming horror, twisting and writhing, was curled around it. Before Gorman could shriek, it had whipped itself from his hand and fastened over his face, over the warm, heat-radiating skin and the glowing flame of the cigarette.

Mrs. Larch was awakened by the clang of fire engines. When the fire was put out, most of the third floor had been gutted. Gorman was an unrecognizable charred mass.

The fire department put the blaze down to Gorman's habit of smoking in bed. Mrs. Larch collected on the fire insurance and bought a new house, selling the old one to a widow who wanted to start a boarding house.

The Good Provider

Marion Gross

Minnie Leggety turned up the walk of her Elm Street bun-
galow and saw that she faced another crisis. When Omar
sat brooding like that, not smoking, not "studying," but just
scrunched down inside of himself, she knew enough after
forty years to realize that she was facing a crisis. As though
it weren't enough just trying to get along on Omar's pension
these days, without having to baby him through another one
of his periods of discouragement! She forced a gaiety into her
voice that she actually didn't feel.

"Why, hello there, Pa, what are you doing out here? Did
you have to come up for air?" Minnie eased herself down beside Omar on the stoop and put the paper bag she had been
carrying on the sidewalk. Such a little bag, but it had taken
most of their week's food budget! Protein, plenty of lean,
rare steaks and chops, that's what that nice man on the radio
said old folks needed, but as long as he couldn't tell you how
to buy it with steak at $1.23 a pound, he might just as well
save his breath to cool his porridge. And so might she, for all
the attention Omar was paying her. He was staring straight
ahead as though he didn't even see her. This looked like one
of his real bad spells. She took his gnarled hand and patted it.

"What's the matter, Pa? Struck a snag with your gadget?"
The "gadget" filled three full walls of the basement and most

103

of the floor space besides, but it was still a "gadget" to Minnie—another one of his ideas that didn't quite work.

Omar had been working on gadgets ever since they were married. When they were younger, she hotly sprang to his defense against her sisters-in-law: "Well, it's better than liquor, and it's cheaper than pinochle; at least I know where he is nights." Now that they were older, and Omar was retired from his job, his tinkering took on a new significance. It was what kept him from going to pieces like a lot of men who were retired and didn't have enough activity to fill their time and their minds.

"What's the matter, Pa?" she asked again.

The old man seemed to notice her for the first time. Sadly he shook his head. "Minnie, I'm a failure. The thing's no good; it ain't practical. After all I promised you, Minnie, and the way you stuck by me and all, it's just not going to work."

Minnie never had thought it would. It just didn't seem possible that a body could go gallivanting back and forth the way Pa had said they would if the gadget worked. She continued to pat the hand she held and told him soothingly, "I'm not sure but it's for the best, Pa. I'd sure have gotten airsick, or timesick, or whatever it was. What're you going to work on now that you're giving up the time machine?" she asked anxiously.

"You don't understand, Min," the old man said. "I'm through. I've failed. I've failed at everything I've ever tried to make. They always *almost* work, and yet there's always something I can't get just right. I never knew enough, Min, never had enough schooling, and now it's too late to get any. I'm just giving up altogether. I'm through!"

This *was* serious. Pa with nothing to tinker at down in the basement, Pa constantly underfoot, Pa with nothing to keep him from just slipping away like old Mr. Mason had, was something she didn't like to think about. "Maybe it isn't as bad as all that," she told him. "All those nice parts you put into your gadget, maybe you could make us a television or something with them. Land, a television, that would be a nice thing to have."

"Oh, I couldn't do that, Min. I wouldn't know how to make a television; besides, I told you, it almost works. It's just that it ain't practical. It ain't the way I pictured it. Come down, I'll show you." He dragged her into the house and down into the basement.

The time machine left so little free floor space, what with the furnace and coal bin and washtubs, that Minnie had to stand on the stairway while Pa explained it to her. It needed explanation. It had more colored lights than a pinball machine, more plugs than the Hillsdale telephone exchange, and more levers than one of those newfangled voting booths.

"Now see," he said, pointing to various parts of the machine, "I rigged this thing up so we could move forward or back in time and space both. I thought we could go off and visit foreign spots, and see great things happening, and have ourselves an interesting old age."

"Well, I don't rightly know if I'd have enjoyed that, Pa," Minnie interrupted. "I doubt I'd know how to get along with all them foreigners, and their strange talk and strange ways and all."

Omar shook his head in annoyance. "The Holy Land. You'd have wanted to see the Holy Land, wouldn't you? You could have sat with the crowd at Galilee and listened to the Lord's words right from His lips. You'd have enjoyed that, wouldn't you?"

"Omar, when you talk like that you make the whole thing sound sacrilegious and against the Lord's ways. Besides, I suppose the Lord would have spoke in Hebrew, and I don't know one word of that and you don't either. I don't know but what I'm glad you couldn't get the thing to work," she said righteously.

"But Min, it does work!" Omar was indignant.

"But you said——"

"I never said it don't work. I said it ain't practical. It don't work good enough, and I don't know enough to make it work better."

Working on the gadget was one thing, but believing that it worked was another. Minnie began to be alarmed. Maybe folks had been right—maybe Omar had gone off his head at last. She looked at him anxiously. He seemed all right and, now that he was worked up at her, the depression seemed to have left him.

"What do you mean it works, but not good enough?" she asked him.

"Well, see here," Omar told her, pointing to an elaborate control board. "It was like I was telling you before you interrupted with your not getting along with foreigners, and your sacrilegion and all. I set this thing up to move a body in time and space any which way. There's a globe of the world worked in here, and I thought that by turning the globe and setting these time controls to whatever year you had in mind you could go wherever you had a mind to. Well, it don't work like that. I've been trying it out for a whole week and no matter how I set the globe, no matter how I set the time controls, it always comes out the same. It lands me over at Main and Center, right in front of Purdey's meat market."

"What's wrong with that?" Minnie asked. "That might be real convenient."

"You don't understand," Omar told her. "It isn't *now* when I get there, it's twenty years ago! That's the trouble, it don't take me none of the places I want to go, just Main and Center. And it don't take me none of the times I want to go, just twenty years ago, and I saw enough of the depression so I don't want to spend my old age watching people sell apples. Then on top of that, this here timer don't work." He pointed to another dial. "It's supposed to set to how long you want to stay, wherever you want to go, but it don't work at all. Twenty minutes, and then woosh, you're right back here in the basement. Nothing works like I want it to."

Minnie had grown thoughtful as Omar recounted the faults of the machine. Wasn't it a caution the way even a smart man like Pa, a man smart enough to make a time machine, didn't have a practical ounce to his whole hundred and forty-eight pounds? She sat down heavily on the cellar steps and, emptying the contents of her purse on her broad lap, began examining the bills.

"What you looking for, Min?" Omar asked.

Minnie looked at him pityingly. Wasn't it a caution. . .

Purdey the butcher was leaning unhappily against his chopping block. The shop was clean and shining, the floor was strewn with fresh sawdust, and Purdey himself, unmindful of the expense, had for the sake of his morale donned a fresh apron. But for all that, Purdey wished that he was hanging on one of his chromium-plated meat hooks.

The sky was blue and smogless, something it never was when the shops were operating and employing the valley's five thousand breadwinners. Such potential customers as were abroad had a shabby, threadbare look to them. Over in front of the Bijou old Mr. Ryan was selling apples.

While he watched, a stout, determined-looking woman appeared at the corner of Main and Center. She glanced quickly around, brushing old Mr. Ryan and his apples with her glance, and then came briskly toward Purdey's shop. Purdey straightened up.

"Afternoon, Ma'am, what can I do for you?" He beamed as though the light bill weren't three months overdue.

"I'll have a nice porterhouse," the lady said hesitantly. "How much is porterhouse?"

"Forty-five a pound, best in the house." Purdey held up a beauty, expecting her to change her mind.

"I'll take it," the lady said. "And six lamb chops. I want a rib roast for Sunday, but I can come back for that. No use carrying too much," she explained. "Could you please hurry with that? I haven't very much time."

"New in town?" Purdey asked as he turned to ring up the sale on the cash register.

"Yes, you might say so," the woman said. By the time Purdey turned back to ask her name, she was gone. But Purdey knew she'd be back. She wanted a rib roast for Sunday. "It just goes to show you," Purdey said to himself, surveying the satisfactory tab sticking up from the register, "there still is some money around. Two dollars, and she never even batted an eyelash. It goes to show you!"

Columbus Was a Dope

Robert A. Heinlein

"I do like to wet down a sale," the fat man said happily, raising his voice above the sighing of the air conditioner. "Drink up, Professor, I'm two ahead of you."

He glanced up from their table as the elevator door opposite them opened. A man stepped out into the cool dark of the bar and stood blinking, as if he had just come from the desert glare outside.

"Hey, Fred—Fred Nolan," the fat man called out. "Come over!" He turned to his guest. "Man I met on the hop from New York. Siddown, Fred. Shake hands with Professor Appleby, chief engineer of the star ship *Pegasus*—or will be when she's built. I just sold the professor an order of bum steel for his crate. Have a drink on it."

"Glad to, Mr. Barnes," Nolan agreed. "I've met Dr. Appleby. On business—Climax Instrument Company."

"Huh?"

"Climax is supplying us with precision equipment," offered Appleby.

Barnes looked surprised, then grinned. "That's one on me. I took Fred for a government man, or one of you scientific johnnies. What'll it be, Fred? Old fashioned? The same, Professor?"

"Right. But please don't call me 'Professor.' I'm not one and it ages me. I'm still young."

"I'll say you are, uh—Doc. Pete! Two old fashioneds and
108

another double Manhattan! I guess I expected a comic-book
scientist, with a long white beard. But now that I've met you,
I can't figure out one thing."

"Which is?"

"Well, at your age you bury yourself in this god-forsaken
place—"

"We couldn't build the *Pegasus* on Long Island," Appleby
pointed out, "and this is the ideal spot for the take off."

"Yeah, sure, but that's not it. It's—well, mind you, I sell
steel. You want special alloys for a star ship; I sell it to you.
But just the same, now that business is out of the way, why
do you want to do it? Why try to go to Proxima Centauri, or
any other star?"

Appleby looked amused. "It can't be explained. Why do
men try to climb Mount Everest? What took Peary to the
North Pole? Why did Columbus get the Queen to hock her
jewels? Nobody has ever been to Proxima Centauri—so we're
going."

Barnes turned to Nolan. "Do you get it, Fred?"

Nolan shrugged. "I sell precision instruments. Some people
raise chrysanthemums; some build star ships. I sell instruments."

Barnes's friendly face looked puzzled. "Well—" The bartender put down their drinks. "Say, Pete, tell me something.
Would you go along on the *Pegasus* expedition if you could?"

"Nope."

"Why not?"

"I like it here."

Dr. Appleby nodded. "There's your answer, Barnes, in re-
verse. Some have the Columbus spirit and some haven't."

"It's all very well to talk about Columbus," Barnes persisted, "but he expected to come back. You guys don't expect
to. Sixty years—you told me it would take sixty years. Why,
you may not even live to get there."

"No, but our children will. And our grandchildren will
come back."

"But—say, you're not *married?*"

"Certainly I am. Family men only on the expedition. It's a
two-to-three generation job. You know that." He hauled out

a wallet. "There's Mrs. Appleby, with Diane. Diane is three-and-a-half."

"She's a pretty baby," Barnes said soberly and passed it on to Nolan, who smiled at it and handed it back to Appleby. Barnes went on. "What happens to her?"

"She goes with us, naturally. You wouldn't want her put in an orphanage, would you?"

"No, but—" Barnes tossed off the rest of his drink. "I don't get it," he admitted. "Who'll have another drink?"

"Not for me, thanks," Appleby declined, finishing his more slowly and standing up. "I'm due home. Family man, you know." He smiled.

Barnes did not try to stop him. He said goodnight and watched Appleby leave.

"My round," said Nolan. "The same?"

"Huh? Yeah, sure." Barnes stood up. "Let's get up to the bar, Fred, where we can drink properly. I need about six."

"Okay," Nolan agreed, standing up. "What's the trouble?"

"Trouble? Did you see that picture?"

"Well?"

"Well, how do *you* feel about it? I'm a salesman, too, Fred. I sell steel. It don't matter what the customer wants to use it for; I sell it to him. I'd sell a man a rope to hang himself. But I do love kids. I can't stand to think of that cute little kid going along on that—that crazy expedition!"

"Why not? She's better off with her parents. She'll get as used to steel decks as most kids are to sidewalks."

"But look, Fred. You don't have any silly idea they'll make it, do you?"

"They might."

"Well, they won't. They don't stand a chance. I *know*. I talked it over with our technical staff before I left the home office. Nine chances out of ten they'll burn up on the take off. That's the best that can happen to them. If they get out of the solar system, which ain't likely, they'll still never make it. They'll never reach the stars."

Pete put another drink down in front of Barnes. He drained it and said:

"Set up another one, Pete. They can't. It's a theoretical

impossibility. They'll freeze—or they'll roast—or they'll starve. But they'll never get there."

"Maybe so."

"No maybe about it. They're *crazy*. Hurry up with that drink, Pete. Have one yourself."

"Coming up. Don't mind if I do, thanks." Pete mixed the cocktail, drew a glass of beer, and joined them.

"Pete, here, is a wise man," Barnes said confidentially. "You don't catch him monkeying around with any trips to the stars. Columbus—Pfui! Columbus was a dope. He shoulda stood in bed."

The bartender shook his head. "You got me wrong, Mr. Barnes. If it wasn't for men like Columbus, we wouldn't be here today—now, would we? I'm just not the explorer type. But I'm a believer. I got nothing against the *Pegasus* expedition."

"You don't approve of them taking kids on it, do you?"

"Well . . . there were kids on the *Mayflower*, so they tell me."

"It's not the same thing." Barnes looked at Nolan, then back to the bartender. "If the Lord had intended us to go to the stars, he would have equipped us with jet propulsion. Fix me another drink, Pete."

"You've had about enough for a while, Mr. Barnes."

The troubled fat man seemed about to argue, thought better of it.

"I'm going up to the Sky Room and find somebody that'll dance with me," he announced. "G'night." He swayed softly toward the elevator.

Nolan watched him leave. "Poor old Barnes." He shrugged. "I guess you and I are hard-hearted, Pete."

"No. I believe in progress, that's all. I remember my old man wanted a law passed about flying machines, keep 'em from breaking their fool necks. Claimed nobody ever could fly, and the government should put a stop to it. He was wrong. I'm not the adventurous type myself but I've seen enough people to know they'll try anything once, and that's how progress is made."

"You don't look old enough to remember when men couldn't fly."

"I've been around a long time. Ten years in this one spot."

"Ten years, eh? Don't you ever get a hankering for a job that'll let you breathe a little fresh air?"

"Nope. I didn't get any fresh air when I served drinks on Forty-second Street and I don't miss it now. I like it here. Always something new going on here, first the atom laboratories and then the big observatory and now the star ship. But that's not the real reason. I like it here. It's my home. Watch this."

He picked up a brandy inhaler, a great fragile crystal globe, spun it, and threw it straight up toward the ceiling. It rose slowly and gracefully, paused for a long reluctant wait at the top of its rise, then settled slowly, slowly, like a diver in a slow-motion movie. Pete watched it float past his nose, then reached out with thumb and forefinger, nipped it easily by the stem, and returned it to the rack.

"See that" he said. "One-sixty gravity. When I was tending bar on earth my bunions gave me the dickens all the time. Here I weigh only thirty-five pounds. I like it on the Moon."

Texas Week

Albert Hernhuter

The slick black car sped along the wide and straight street. It came to a smooth stop in front of a clean white house. A man got out of the car and walked briskly to the door. Reaching out with a pink hand, he pressed the doorbell with one well-manicured finger.

The door was answered by a housewife. She was wearing a white blouse, a green skirt, and a green apron trimmed with white. Her feet were tucked into orange slippers, her blonde hair was done up in a neat bun. She was dressed as the government had ordered for that week.

The man said, "You are Mrs. Christopher Nest?"

There was a trace of anxiety in her voice as she answered. "Yes. And you are . . . ?"

"My name is Maxwell Hanstark. As you may already know, I am the official psychiatrist for this district. My appointment will last until the end of this year."

Mrs. Nest invited him in. They stepped into a clean living room. At one end was the television set, at the other end were several chairs. There was nothing between the set and the chairs except a large grey rug which stretched from wall to wall. They walked to the chairs and sat down.

"Now, just what is the matter with your husband, Mrs. Nest?"

Mrs. Nest reached into a large bowl and absently picked

up a piece of stale popcorn. She daintily placed it in her mouth and chewed thoughtfully before she answered.

"I wish I knew. All he does all day long is sit in the backyard and stare at the grass. He insists that he is standing on top of a cliff."

Hanstark took out a small pad and a short ball-point pen. He wrote something down before he spoke again. "Is he violent? Did he get angry when you told him there was no cliff?"

Mrs. Nest was silent for a moment. A second piece of popcorn joined the first. Hanstark's pen was poised above the pad. "No. He didn't get violent."

Hanstark wrote as he asked the next question. "Just what *was* his reaction?"

"He said *I* must be crazy."

"Were those his exact words?"

"No. He said that I was"—she thought for a moment— "loco. Yes, that was the word."

"Loco?"

"Yes. He said it just like those cowboys on the television."

Hanstark looked puzzled. "Perhaps you had better tell me more about this. When did he first start acting this way?"

Mrs. Nest glanced up at the television set, then back at Hanstark. "It was right after Texas Week. You remember— they showed all of those old cowboy pictures."

Hanstark nodded.

"Well, he stayed up every night watching them. Some nights he didn't even go to sleep. Even after the set was off, he sat in one of the chairs, just staring at the screen. This morning, when I got up, he wasn't in the house. I looked all over but I couldn't find him. I was just about ready to phone the police when I glanced out the window into the backyard. And I saw him."

"What was he doing?"

"He was just sitting there in the middle of the yard, staring. I went out and tried to bring him into the house. He told me he had to watch for someone. When I asked him what he was talking about he told me that I was crazy. That was when I phoned you, Mr. Hanstark."

"A very wise move, Mrs. Nest. And would you show me where your husband is right now?"

She nodded her head and they both got up from the chairs. They walked through the dining room and kitchen. On the back porch Hanstark came to a halt.

"You'd better stay here, Mrs. Nest." He walked to the door and opened it.

"Mr. Hanstark," Mrs. Nest called.

Hanstark turned and saw her standing next to the automatic washing machine. "Yes?"

"Please be careful."

Hanstark smiled. "I shall be, Mrs. Nest."

He walked out the door and down three concrete steps. Looking a little to his right, he saw a man squatted on his heels. He walked up to the man. "You are Mr. Christopher Nest?"

The man looked up and stared for a moment at Hanstark. "Yep," he answered. Then he turned and stared at the grass again.

"And may I ask you what you are doing?"

Nest answered without looking up. "Guardin' the pass."

Hanstark scribbled something in his notebook. "And why are you guarding the pass?"

Nest rose to his feet and stared down at Hanstark. "Just what are you askin' all of these questions for, stranger?"

Hanstark saw Nest was bigger than he and decided to play along for awhile. After all, strategy . . .

"I'm just interested in your welfare, Mr. Nest."

Nest shrugged his shoulders. He reached into his shirt pocket and pulled out a sack of tobacco and some paper. Holding a piece of paper in one hand, he carefully poured a little tobacco onto it. In one quick movement he rolled the paper and tobacco into a perfect cylinder.

He put the sack of tobacco and paper back into his pocket and took out a wooden kitchen match. He scraped it to life on the sole of his shoe and applied the flame to the tip of the cigarette. He puffed it into life and threw the match away. It burned for a few moments in the moist grass, then went out. A thin trail of smoke rose from it, and then was gone.

"Why are you guarding the pass?" Hanstark asked again.

Nest resumed his crouch on the grass. "News is around that Dirty Dan the cattle rustler is gonna try to steal some of my cattle." He patted an imaginary holster at his side. "And I aim to stop him."

Hanstark thought for a moment. Strategy—he must use strategy . . . "Mr. Nest." He waited until Nest had turned to him. "Mr. Nest. What would you say if I told you that there was no pass down there."

"Why shucks, pardner. I'd say you'd been chewin' some loco weed."

"And if I could prove it?"

Nest answered after a moment's pause. "Why then, I guess I'd be loco."

Hanstark thought it was going to be easy. "Mr. Nest, it is a well known fact that no one can walk in mid-air. Is that not true?"

Nest took a deep drag on his cigarette and blew the smoke out of his nostrils. "Shore."

"Then if I were to walk out above your pass you'd have to admit there is no pass."

"Reckon so."

Hanstark began to walk in the direction of Nest's "cliff." Nest jumped to his feet and grabbed the official psychiatrist by the arm.

"What're you tryin' to do," Nest said angrily, "kill yourself?"

Hanstark shook free of his grasp. "Mr. Nest, I am not going to kill myself. I am merely going to walk in that direction." He pointed to where the cliff was supposed to be. "To you it will look as if I were walking in mid-air."

Nest dropped his hands to his sides. "Shucks, I don't care if you kill yourself. It's just that it's liable to make the cattle nervous."

Hanstark gave him a cold glare and began to walk. He took three paces and stopped. "You see, Mr. Nest. There is no cliff."

Nest looked at him and laughed. "You just take one more step and you'll find there *is* a cliff!"

Hanstark took another step—a long one. His face bore a surprised look as he disappeared beneath the grass. His screams could be heard for a moment before he landed on the rocks below.

Nest walked to the edge of the cliff and looked down at the mangled body. He took off his hat in respect.

"Little feller had a lotta guts." Then he added, "Poor little feller."

He put his hat back on and looked down at the entrance to the valley. A horse and rider appeared from behind several rocks.

"Dirty Dan!" Nest exclaimed. He reached down and picked up his rifle.

Hilda

H. B. Hickey

"Mmmm," said Mrs. Williams. "Kiss me again."

"Mmmm," said Roger. He kissed her again.

Stupid woman, he thought. Old enough, if not attractive enough, to be his mother. But rich. Mrs. Williams, Roger thought, could be worked for plenty.

They were on the balcony off Roger's bedroom. In the night sky, rockets traced paths of fire on their way to the Moon and Mars. Roger's shirt was open to the third button and Mrs. Williams was pressed tight against his broad, tanned chest.

"Ohhh," said Mrs. Williams. She was completely limp. "You're so strong, Roger. When you squeeze me like this it hurts."

"The strength of my desire," Roger said. He squeezed harder.

She was now in the bag, Roger knew from many such experiences, and good for anything from jeweled cuff links to an investment in a play starring Roger. A dozen women had made that same investment, but the only lines Roger had ever memorized were those of his love-making routine.

"You're hurting me," Mrs. Williams gasped.

"I can't help myself," said Roger, and squeezed her even harder, deliberately.

The door of his bedroom burst open and a man rushed in. He was middle-aged and he had a paunch and he was the chairman of the board of Tri-Planet Mining, with assets of over ten million.

He was also Mr. Williams.

"You skunk!" he shouted. "You dirty, wife-stealing—" He waved a gun at Roger.

"James!" shrieked Mrs. Williams.

"Hilda!" shouted Roger.

Something big and shiny, with arms of chrome steel and an alloy middle, came storming into the room. It took the gun away from Mr. Williams and tucked him under one arm. It scooped up Mrs. Williams, who had rushed to her husband's aid, and tucked her under the other arm.

It carried them from the apartment and slammed the door behind them.

"I will make you coffee," Hilda said metallically. "I will make you Swedish meatballs."

"Damn!" Roger cursed. He held up his cupped palm in a dramatic gesture. "I had her, damn it!"

"No food," said Hilda.

"Who said anything about no food?" Roger demanded.

Hilda marched toward the kitchen with measured tread. Over her shoulder she said, "The man was here for the rent today."

Roger cursed landlords in general and this one in particular. "What did you tell him?"

"You were not at home."

Hilda had paused and was regarding Roger with glowing plastic eyes. He tried to look melancholy.

"Hilda," he said, "we are broke."

"Broke," said Hilda. She had been through this before.

"It hurts me to ask this of you, Hilda. But there's a factory I know of, a place where they use leased robots—"

"A factory."

"Yes. Honestly, Hilda, it'll only be for a while. I know you need new rheostats and you haven't had a pressure check in a year—" He patted her shoulder. "Say you'll take the job."

"I will take the job," Hilda said. "I will make Swedish meatballs." She clumped into the kitchen.

What he would have done without Hilda, Roger didn't
know. He hated to think about it, even. You couldn't get
another one like her for love or money.

She was definitely a female robot, smaller than the all-
purpose kind, with real domestic aptitudes built in. She was a
fine cook, an excellent laundress, and she had a woman's
memory for trivia.

Hilda had been built by a Swedish firm for its president,
and Roger had got her from the president's widow. What had
become of the widow afterward, Roger was not sure. Maybe
she'd made good her threat to commit suicide.

One thing about Hilda, Roger thought. She'd never commit
suicide. And no matter how often he took advantage of her
she'd never threaten him with harm; the only emotion a robot
could have was love for its owner.

"More coffee, Hilda," Roger said, downing the last of the
meatballs. He felt much better. "And press my flannels. I'm
going out."

It was a bad night. The only likely woman Roger ran
across was with her husband, who watched her closely. And
recurring thoughts of the Williams fiasco made Roger drink
too much. He came home with a headache.

Hilda was already setting the table for breakfast. "A woman called."

Roger's nostrils flared. "Who was it?"

"Alice," she said.

"Hell," he said disgustedly. Alice Carter was only eighteen
and wouldn't have a dollar of her own for years. And the
young ones were so easy he couldn't even feel he was keeping
his hand in.

"She cried," Hilda said.

"They always cry."

He bit into a piece of toast that was done exactly to his
taste and picked up the facsimile newspaper Hilda had laid
beside his plate.

He said, "Oh, oh."

Mr. and Mrs. James Williams had crashed in their helicop-
ter. A 'copter control tower had overheard snatches of argument between them and Mr. Williams had forgotten to

set his automatic altitude controls. Mrs. Williams was in serious condition. "Too bad they weren't killed," Roger muttered.

Or too bad it wasn't Mr. Williams who was in serious condition. With the kind of childish reasoning of which husbands were capable, he was a sure bet to blame Roger for the crash. And ten million dollars could make trouble.

"Hilda," Roger said, "I think we'll go to Paris. You'd like that, wouldn't you?"

"Paris," Hilda said. She had been through this before too.

While she clumped off to begin packing, Roger stood and stared moodily out the window. Sometimes it seemed that no matter how hard a man tried he couldn't get a break. . . .

"Packed," Hilda said as she marched back into the living room.

Roger was sitting on the couch, his head in his hands. Hilda regarded him. "Packed," she said again.

"In a minute," Roger said. "I've got an awful headache."

"I will bring headache pills."

She clumped to the bathroom and clumped back, bearing the pills and a glass of water. After Roger had swallowed the pills Hilda brought the brandy from the sideboard and poured him a stiff drink.

"I will make more coffee," she said.

It was really wonderful, Roger thought, the way Hilda knew exactly what to do. Once she learned a routine she never forgot it.

Suddenly Roger felt much better. The brandy was warming his stomach and making his head swim. He ran after Hilda and flung his arms around her alloy middle and hugged her.

"Hilda," he said. "You're wonderful! I love you!"

"You only say that."

"No, I mean it. Honestly."

"Kiss me," Hilda said.

It was so vaguely familiar it puzzled him, and yet so funny he had to laugh. And because the brandy was making him feel so good he actually did plant a kiss on Hilda's faceplate.

"Mmmm," said Hilda. "Kiss me again."

"Hilda! Where did you ever learn such things?"

"I listened."

So that was why the routine seemed so familiar. What a robot!

"Hilda," Roger laughed, "there's nobody in the world like you." His laughter took on a twinge of pain. "Hilda! You forget those arms are steel. When you squeeze me like this it hurts."

"The strength of my desire," Hilda said metallically.

"You're hurting me!"

"I can't help myself," said Hilda. She squeezed harder.

Roger went limp in her arms. She let him go and he fell to the floor. He made a sound in his throat and blood ran from his nose. Then the sound stopped and the blood stopped too.

Hilda marched to the closet and got the cleaning things and wiped up the spots on the rug. She lifted Roger and laid him on the couch.

She put the cleaning things back and clumped to the kitchen.

"I will make you coffee," Hilda said.

The Choice

W. Hilton-Young

Before Williams went into the future he bought a camera and a tape recording machine and learned shorthand. That night, when all was ready, we made coffee and put out brandy and glasses against his return.

"Good-bye," I said. "Don't stay too long."

"I won't," he answered.

I watched him carefully, and he hardly flickered. He must have made a perfect landing on the very second he had taken off from. He seemed not a day older; we had expected he might spend several years away.

"Well?"

"Well," said he, "let's have some coffee."

I poured it out, hardly able to contain my impatience. As I gave it to him I said again, "Well?"

"Well, the thing is, I can't remember."

"Can't remember? Not a thing?"

He thought for a moment and answered sadly, "Not a thing."

"But your notes? The camera? The recording machine?"

The notebook was empty, the indicator of the camera rested at "1" where we had set it, the tape was not even loaded into the recording machine.

"But good heavens," I protested, "why? How did it happen? Can you remember nothing at all?"

123

"I can remember only one thing."

"What was that?"

"I was shown everything, and I was given the choice whether I should remember it or not after I got back."

"And you chose not to? But what an extraordinary thing to—"

"Isn't it?" he said. "One can't help wondering why."

Not with a Bang

Damon Knight

Ten months after the last plane passed over, Rolf Smith knew beyond doubt that only one other human being had survived. Her name was Louise Oliver, and he was sitting opposite her in a department-store cafe in Salt Lake City. They were eating canned Vienna sausages and drinking coffee.

Sunlight struck through a broken pane, lying like a judgment on the cloudy air of the room. Inside and outside, there was no sound; only a stifling rumor of absence. The clatter of dishware in the kitchen, the heavy rumble of streetcars—never again. There was sunlight, and silence, and the watery, astonished eyes of Louise Oliver.

He leaned forward, trying to capture the attention of those fishlike eyes for a second. "Darling," he said, "I respect your views, naturally. But I've got to make you see that they're impractical."

She looked at him with faint surprise, then away again. Her head shook slightly. No. *No, Rolf. I will not live with you in sin.*

Smith thought of the women of France, of Russia, of Mexico, of the South Seas. He had spent three months in the ruined studios of a radio station in Rochester, listening to the voices until they stopped. There had been a large colony in Sweden, including an English cabinet minister. They reported that Europe was gone. Simply gone; there was not an acre that had not been swept clean by radioactive dust. They had

125

two planes and enough fuel to take them anywhere on the
Continent; but there was nowhere to go. Three of them had
the plague; then eleven; then all.

There was a bomber pilot who had fallen near a government radio in Palestine. He did not last long because in the
crash he had broken some bones; but he had seen the vacant
waters where the Pacific Islands should have been. It was his
guess that the Arctic ice-fields had been bombed. He did not
know whether that had been a mistake or not.

There were no reports from Washington, from New York,
from London, Paris, Moscow, Chungking, Sydney. You could
not tell who had been destroyed by disease, who by the dust,
who by bombs.

Smith himself had been a laboratory assistant in a team
that was trying to find an antibiotic for the plague. His superiors had found one that worked sometimes, but it was a little
too late. When he left, Smith took along with him all there
was of it—forty ampoules, enough to last him for years.

Louise had been a nurse in a genteel hospital near Denver.
According to her, something rather odd had happened to the
hospital as she was approaching it the morning of the attack.
She was quite calm when she said this, but a vague look came
into her eyes and her shattered expression seemed to slip a
little more. Smith did not press her for an explanation.

Like himself, she had found a radio station which still
functioned, and when Smith discovered that she had not con-
tracted the plague, he agreed to meet her. She was, apparently, naturally immune. There must have been others, a few at
least; but the bombs and the dust had not spared them.

It seemed very awkward to Louise that not one Protestant
minister was left alive.

The trouble was, she really meant it. It had taken Smith a
long time to believe it, but it was true. She would not sleep
in the same hotel with him, either; she expected, and received,
the utmost courtesy and decorum. Smith had learned his lesson. He walked on the outside of the rubble-heaped sidewalks; he opened doors for her, when there were still doors;
he held her chair; he refrained from swearing. He courted
her.

Louise was forty or thereabouts, at least five years older

than Smith. He often wondered how old she thought she was. The shock of seeing whatever it was that had happened to the hospital, the patients she had cared for, had sent her mind scuttling back to her childhood. She tacitly admitted that everyone else in the world was dead, but she seemed to regard it as something one did not mention.

A hundred times in the last three weeks, Smith had felt an almost irresistible impulse to break her thin neck and go his own way. But there was no help for it; she was the only woman in the world, and he needed her. If she died, or left him, he died. *Old bitch!* he thought to himself furiously, and carefully kept the thought from showing on his face.

"Louise, honey," he told her gently, "I want to spare your feelings as much as I can. You know that."

"Yes, Rolf," she said, staring at him with the face of a hypnotized chicken.

Smith forced himself to go on. "We've got to face the facts, unpleasant as they may be. Honey, we're the only man and the only woman there are. We're like Adam and Eve in the Garden of Eden."

Louise's face took on a slightly disgusted expression. She was obviously thinking of fig leaves.

"Think of the generations unborn," Smith told her, with a tremor in his voice. *Think about me for once. Maybe you're good for another ten years, maybe not.* Shuddering, he thought of the second stage of the disease—the helpless rigidity, striking without warning. He'd had one such attack already, and Louise had helped him out of it. Without her, he would have stayed like that till he died, the hypodermic that would save him within inches of his rigid hand. He thought desperately, *If I'm lucky, I'll get at least two kids out of you before you croak. Then I'll be safe.*

He went on, "God didn't mean for the human race to end like this. He spared us, you and me, to——" He paused; how could he say it without offending her? "Parents" wouldn't do—too suggestive. "——to carry on the torch of life," he ended. There. That was sticky enough.

Louise was staring vaguely over his shoulder. Her eyelids blinked regularly, and her mouth made little rabbit-like motions in the same rhythm.

Smith looked down at his wasted thighs under the tabletop. *I'm not strong enough to force her,* he thought. *Christ, if I were strong enough!*

He felt the futile rage again and stifled it. He had to keep his head, because this might be his last chance. Louise had been talking lately, in the cloudy language she used about everything, of going up in the mountains to pray for guidance. She had not said, "alone," but it was easy enough to see that she pictured it that way. He had to argue her around before her resolve stiffened. He concentrated furiously and tried once more.

The pattern of words went by like a distant rumbling. Louise heard a phrase here and there; each of them fathered chains of thought, binding her revery tighter. "Our duty to humanity . . ." Mama had often said—that was in the old house on Waterbury Street of course, before Mama had taken sick—she had said, "Child, your duty is to be clean, polite, and God-fearing. Pretty doesn't matter. There's a plenty of plain women that have got themselves good, Christian husbands."

Husbands . . . to have and to hold . . . orange blossoms, and the bridesmaids; the organ music. Through the haze, she saw Rolf's lean, wolfish face. Of course, he was the only one she'd ever get; *she* knew that well enough. Gracious, when a girl was past twenty-five, she had to take what she could get.

But I sometimes wonder if he's really a nice *man*, she thought.

". . . in the eyes of God . . ." She remembered the stained-glass windows in the old First Episcopalian Church, and how she always thought God was looking down at her through that brilliant transparency. Perhaps He was still looking at her, though it seemed sometimes that He had forgotten. Well, of course she realized that marriage customs changed, and if you couldn't have a regular minister. . . . But it was really a shame, an outrage almost, that if she were actually going to marry this man, she couldn't have all those nice things . . . There wouldn't even be any wedding presents. Not even that. But of course Rolf would give her anything she wanted. She saw his face again, noticed the narrow black eyes staring at her with ferocious purpose, the thin mouth that jerked in a slow, regular tic, the hairy lobes of the ears below the tangle of black hair.

He oughtn't to let his hair grow so long, she thought, *it isn't quite decent.* Well, she could change all that. If she did marry him, she'd certainly make him change his ways. It was no more than her duty.

He was talking now about a farm he'd seen outside town— a good big house and a barn. There was no stock, he said, but they could get some later. And they'd plant things, and have their own food to eat, not go to restaurants all the time.

She felt a touch on her hand, lying pale before her on the table. Rolf's brown, stubby fingers, black-haired above and below the knuckles, were touching hers. He had stopped talking for a moment, but now he was speaking again, still more urgently. She drew her hand away.

He was saying, ". . . and you'll have the finest wedding dress you ever saw, with a bouquet. Everything you want, Louise, everything . . ."

A wedding dress! And flowers, even if there couldn't be any minister! Well, why hadn't the fool said so before?

Rolf stopped halfway through a sentence, aware that Louise had said quite clearly, "Yes, Rolf, I will marry you if you wish.

Stunned, he wanted her to repeat it, but dared not ask, "What did you say?" for fear of getting some fantastic answer, or none at all. He breathed deeply. He said, "Today, Louise?"

She said, "Well, *today* . . . I don't know quite . . . Of course, if you think you can make all the arrangements in time, but it does seem . . ."

Triumph surged through Smith's body. He had the advantage now, and he'd ride it. "Say you will, dear," he urged her; "say yes, and make me the happiest man. . . ."

Even then, his tongue balked at the rest of it; but it didn't matter. She nodded submissively. "Whatever you think best, Rolf."

He rose, and she allowed him to kiss her pale, sapless cheek. "We'll leave right away," he said. "If you'll excuse me for just a minute, dear?"

He waited for her "Of course" and then left her, making

footprints in the furred carpet of dust down toward the end of the room. Just a few more hours he'd have to speak to her like that, and then, in her eyes, she'd be committed to him forever. Afterwards, he could do with her as he liked— beat her when he pleased, submit her to any proof of his scorn and revulsion, use her. Then it would not be too bad, being the last man on Earth—not bad at all. She might even have a daughter. . . .

He found the washroom door and entered. He took a step inside, and froze, balanced by a trick of motion, upright but helpless. Panic struck at his throat as he tried to turn his head and failed; tried to scream, and failed. Behind him, he was aware of a tiny click as the door, cushioned by the hydraulic check, shut forever. It was not locked; but its other side bore the warning: MEN.

The Altar at Midnight

C. M. Kornbluth

He had quite a rum blossom on him for a kid, I thought at first. But when he moved closer to the light by the cash register to ask the bartender for a match or something, I saw it wasn't that. Not just the nose. Broken veins on his cheeks, too, and the funny eyes. He must have seen me look, because he slid back away from the light.

The bartender shook my bottle of ale in front of me like a Swiss bell ringer so it foamed inside the green glass.

"You ready for another, sir?" he asked.

I shook my head. Down the bar, he tried it on the kid—he was drinking scotch and water or something like that—and found out he could push him around. He sold him three scotch and waters in ten minutes.

When he tried for number four, the kid had his courage up and said, "I'll tell *you* when I'm ready for another, Jack." But there wasn't any trouble.

It was almost nine and the place began to fill up. The manager, a real hood type, stationed himself by the door to screen out the high school kids and give the big hello to conventioneers. The girls came hurrying in, too, with their little make up cases and their fancy hair piled up and their frozen faces with the perfect mouths drawn on them. One of them stopped to say something to the manager, some excuse about

131

something, and he said: "That's aw ri'; get inna dressing room."

A three-piece band behind the drapes at the back of the stage began to make warm-up noises and there were two bartenders keeping busy. Mostly it was beer—a midweek crowd. I finished my ale and had to wait a couple of minutes before I could get another bottle. The bar filled up from the end near the stage because all the customers wanted a good, close look at the strippers for their fifty-cent bottles of beer. But I noticed that nobody sat down next to the kid, or, if anybody did, he didn't stay long—you go out for some fun and the bartender pushes you around and nobody wants to sit next to you. I picked up my bottle and glass and went down on the stool to his left.

He turned to me right away and said: "What kind of a place is this, anyway?" The broken veins were all over his face, little ones, but so many, so close, that they made his face look something like marbled rubber. The funny look in his eyes was it—the trick contact lenses. But I tried not to stare and not to look away.

"It's okay," I said. "It's a good show if you don't mind a lot of noise from—"

He stuck a cigarette into his mouth and poked the pack at me. "I'm a spacer," he said, interrupting.

I took one of his cigarettes and said, "Oh."

He snapped a lighter for the cigarettes and said, "Venus."

I was noticing that his pack of cigarettes on the bar had some kind of yellow sticker instead of the blue tax stamp.

"Ain't that a crock?" he asked. "You can't smoke and they give you lighters for a souvenir. But it's a good lighter. On Mars last week, they gave us all some cheap pen-and-pencil sets."

"You get something every trip, hah?" I took a good, long drink of ale and he finished his scotch and water.

"Shoot. You call a trip a 'shoot.'"

One of the girls was working her way down the bar. She was going to slide onto the empty stool at his right and give him the business, but she looked at him first and decided not to. She curled around me and asked if I'd buy her a li'l ole drink. I said no and she moved on to the next. I could kind of feel the young fellow quivering. When I looked at him, he stood up. I followed him out of the dump. The manager grinned without thinking and said, "G'night, boys," to us.

The kid stopped in the street and said to me: "You don't have to follow me around, Pappy." He sounded like one wrong word and I would get socked in the teeth.

"Take it easy. I know a place where they won't spit in your eye."

He pulled himself together and made a joke of it. "This I have to see," he said. "Near here?"

"A few blocks."

We started walking. It was a nice night.

"I don't know this city at all," he said. "I'm from Covington, Kentucky. You do your drinking at home there. We don't have places like this." He meant the whole Skid Row area.

"It's not so bad," I said. "I spend a lot of time here."

"Is that a fact? I mean, down home a man your age would likely have a wife and children."

"I do. The hell with them."

He laughed like a real youngster and I figured he couldn't even be twenty-five. He didn't have any trouble with the broken curbstones in spite of his scotch and waters. I asked him about it.

"Sense of balance," he said. "You have to be tops for balance to be a spacer—you spend so much time outside in a suit. People don't know how much. Punctures. And you aren't worth a damn if you lose your point."

"What's that mean?"

"Oh. Well, it's hard to describe. When you're outside and you lose your point, it means you're all mixed up, you don't know which way the can—that's the ship—which way the can is. It's having all that room around you. But if you have a good balance, you feel a little tugging to the ship, or maybe you just *know* which way the ship is without feeling it. Then you have your point and you can get the work done."

"There must be a lot that's hard to describe."

He thought that might be a crack and he clammed up on me.

"You call this Gandytown," I said after a while. "It's where the stove-up old railroad men hang out. This is the place."

It was the second week of the month, before everybody's pension check was all gone. Oswiak's was jumping. The Grandsons of the Pioneers were on the juke singing the *Man from Mars Yodel* and old Paddy Shea was jigging in the middle of the floor. He had a full seidel of beer in his right hand and his empty left sleeve was flapping.

The kid balked at the screen door. "Too damn bright," he said.

I shrugged and went on in and he followed. We sat down at a table. At Oswiak's you can drink at the bar if you want to, but none of the regulars do.

Paddy jigged over and said: "Welcome home, Doc." He's a Liverpool Irishman; they talk like Scots, some say, but they sound almost like Brooklyn to me.

"Hello, Paddy. I brought somebody uglier than you. Now what do you say?"

Paddy jigged around the kid in a half-circle with his sleeve flapping and then flopped into a chair when the record stopped. He took a big drink from the seidel and said: "Can he do this?" Paddy stretched his face into an awful grin that showed his teeth. He had three of them. The kid laughed and asked me: "What the hell did you drag me into here for?"

"Paddy says he'll buy drinks for the house the day anybody uglier than he is comes in."

Oswiak's wife waddled over for the order and the kid asked us what we'd have. I figured I could start drinking, so it was three double scotches.

After the second round, Paddy started blowing about how they took his arm off without any anesthetics except a bottle of gin because the red-ball freight he was tangled up in couldn't wait.

That brought some of the other old gimps over to the table with their stories.

Blackie Bauer had been sitting in a boxcar with his legs sticking through the door when the train started with a jerk.

Wham, the door closed. Everybody laughed at Blackie for being that dumb in the first place, and he got mad.

Sam Fireman has palsy. This week he was claiming he used to be a watchmaker before he began to shake. The week before, he'd said he was a brain surgeon. A woman I didn't know, a real old Boxcar Bertha, dragged herself over and began some kind of story about how her sister married a Greek, but she passed out before we found out what happened.

Somebody wanted to know what was wrong with the kid's face—Bauer, I think it was, after he came back to the table.

"Compression and decompression," the kid said. "You're all the time climbing into your suit and out of your suit. Inboard air's thin to start with. You get a few red lines—that's these ruptured blood vessels—and you say the hell with the money; all you'll make is just one more trip. But, God, it's a lot of money for anybody my age! You keep saying that until you can't be anything but a spacer. The eyes are hard-radiation scars."

"You like dot all ofer?" asked Oswiak's wife politely.

"All over, ma'am," the kid told her in a miserable voice. "But I'm going to quit before I get a Bowman head."

"I don't care," said Maggie Rorty. "I think he's cute."

"Compared with—" Paddy began, but I kicked him under the table.

We sang for a while, and then we told gags and recited limericks for a while, and I noticed that the kid and Maggie had wandered into the back room—the one with the latch on the door.

Oswiak's wife asked me, very puzzled: "Doc, w'y dey do dot flyink by planyets?"

"It's the damn govermint," Sam Fireman said.

"Why not?" I said. "They got the Bowman Drive, why the hell shouldn't they use it? Serves 'em right." I had a double scotch and added, "Twenty years of it and they found out a few things they didn't know. Red lines are only one of them. Twenty years more, maybe they'll find out a few more things they didn't know. Maybe by the time there's a bathtub in every American home and an alcoholism clinic in every American town, they'll find out a whole *lot* of things they didn't know. And every American boy will be a pop-eyed, blood-raddled wreck, like our friend here, from riding the Bowman Drive."

"It's the damn govermint," Sam Fireman repeated.

"And what the hell did you mean by that remark about alcoholism?" Paddy said, real sore. "Personally, I can take it or leave it alone."

So we got to talking about that and everybody there turned out to be people who could take it or leave it alone.

It was maybe midnight when the kid showed at the table again, looking kind of dazed. I was drunker than I ought to be by midnight, so I said I was going for a walk. He tagged along and we wound up on a bench at Screwball Square. The soapboxers were still going strong. Like I said, it was a nice night. After a while, a pot-bellied old auntie who didn't give a damn about the face sat down and tried to talk the kid into going to see some etchings. The kid didn't get it and I led him over to hear the soapboxers before there was trouble.

One of the orators was a mush-mouthed evangelist. "And oh, my friends," he said, "when I looked through the porthole of the space ship and beheld the wonder of the firmament—"

"You're a stinkin' Yankee liar!" the kid yelled at him. "You say one damn more word about can shootin' and I'll ram your space ship down your lyin' throat! Wheah's your red lines if you're such a hot spacer?"

The crowd didn't know what he was talking about, but "wheah's your red lines" sounded good to them, so they heckled mush-mouth off his box with it.

I got the kid to a bench. The liquor was working in him all of a sudden. He simmered down after a while and asked: "Doc, should I've given Miz Rorty some money? I asked her afterward and she said she'd admire to have something to remember me by, so I gave her my lighter. She seem' to be real pleased with it. But I was wondering if maybe I embarrassed her by asking her right out. Like I tol' you, back in Covington, Kentucky, we don't have places like that. Or maybe we did and I just didn't know about them. But what do you think I should've done about Miz Rorty?"

"Just what you did," I told him. "If they want money, they ask you for it first. Where you staying?"

"YMCA," he said, almost asleep. "Back in Covington, Kentucky, I was a member of the Y and I kept up my membership. They have to let me in because I'm a member. Spacers have all kinds of trouble, Doc. Woman trouble. Hotel trouble. Fam'ly trouble. Religious trouble. I was raised a Southern Baptist, but wheah's Heaven, anyway? I ask' Doctor Chitwood las' time home before the red lines got so thick— Doc, you aren't a minister of the Gospel, are you? I hope I di'n' say anything to offend you."

"No offense, son," I said. "No offense."

I walked him to the avenue and waited for a fleet cab. It was almost five minutes. The independents that roll drunks dent the fenders of fleet cabs if they show up in Skid Row and then the fleet drivers have to make reports on their own time to the company. It keeps them away. But I got one and dumped the kid in.

"The Y hotel," I told the driver. "Here's five. Help him in when you get there."

When I walked through Screwball Square again, some college kids were yelling "wheah's your red lines" at old Charlie, the last of the Wobblies.

Old Charlie kept roaring, "The hell with your bread lines! I'm talking about atomic bombs. *Right—up—there!*" And he pointed at the Moon.

It was a nice night, but the liquor was dying in me.

There was a joint around the corner, so I went in and had a drink to carry me to the club; I had a bottle there. I got into the first cab that came.

"Athletic Club," I said.

"Inna dawghouse, harh?" the driver said, and he gave me a big personality smile.

I didn't say anything and he started the car.

He was right, of course. I was in everybody's doghouse. Some day I'd scare hell out of Tom and Lise by going home and showing them what their daddy looked like.

Down at the Institute, I was in the doghouse.

"Oh, dear," everybody at the Institute said to everybody, "I'm sure I don't know what ails the man. A lovely wife and two lovely grown children and she had to tell him 'either you go or I go.' And *drinking!* And this is rather subtle, but it's a well-known fact that neurotics seek out low company to compensate for their guilt feelings. The *places* he frequents. Doctor Francis Bowman, the man who made space flight a reality. The man who put the Bomb Base on the Moon! Really, I'm sure I don't know what ails him."

The hell with them all.

A Bad Day for Sales

Fritz Leiber

The big bright doors of the office building parted with a
pneumatic *whoosh* and Robie glided onto Times Square. The
crowd that had been watching the fifty-foot-tall girl on the
clothing billboard get dressed, or reading the latest news about
the hot truce scrawl itself in yard-high script, hurried to look.

Robie was still a novelty. Robie was fun. For a little while
yet, he could steal the show. But the attention did not make
Robie proud. He had no more emotions than the pink plastic
giantess, who dressed and undressed endlessly whether there
was a crowd or the street was empty, and who never once
blinked her blue mechanical eyes. But she merely drew business while Robie went out after it.

For Robie was the logical conclusion of the development
of vending machines. All the earlier ones had stood in one
place, on a floor or hanging on a wall, and blankly delivered
merchandise in return for coins, whereas Robie searched for
customers. He was the demonstration model of a line of sales
robots to be manufactured by Shuler Vending Machines,
provided the public invested enough in stocks to give the company capital to go into mass production.

The publicity Robie drew stimulated investments hand-
somely. It was amusing to see the TV and newspaper coverage
of Robie selling, but not a fraction as much fun as being approached personally by him. Those who were usually bought

anywhere from one to five hundred shares, if they had any money and foresight enough to see that sales robots would eventually be on every street and highway in the country.

Robie radared the crowd, found that it surrounded him solidly, and stopped. With a carefully built-in sense of timing, he waited for the tension and expectation to mount before he began talking.

"Say, Ma, he doesn't look like a robot at all," a child said. "He looks like a turtle."

Which was not completely inaccurate. The lower part of Robie's body was a metal hemisphere hemmed with sponge rubber and not quite touching the sidewalk. The upper was a metal box with black holes in it. The box could swivel and duck.

A chromium-bright hoopskirt with a turret on top.

"Reminds me too much of the Little Joe Paratanks," a legless veteran of the Persian War muttered, and rapidly rolled himself away on wheels rather like Robie's.

His departure made it easier for some of those who knew about Robie to open a path in the crowd. Robie headed straight for the gap. The crowd whooped.

Robie glided very slowly down the path, deftly jogging aside whenever he got too close to ankles in skylon or sockassins. The rubber buffer on his hoopskirt was merely an added safeguard.

The boy who had called Robie a turtle jumped in the middle of the path and stood his ground, grinning foxily.

Robie stopped two feet short of him. The turret ducked. The crowd got quiet.

"Hello, youngster," Robie said in a voice that was smooth as that of a TV star, and was, in fact, a recording of one.

The boy stopped smiling. "Hello," he whispered.

"How old are you?" Robie asked.

"Nine. No, eight."

"That's nice," Robie observed. A metal arm shot down from his neck, stopped just short of the boy.

The boy jerked back.

"For you," Robie said.

The boy gingerly took the red polly-lop from the neatly

fashioned blunt metal claws, and began to unwrap it.

"Nothing to say?" asked Robie.

"Uh—thank you."

After a suitable pause, Robie continued, "And how about a nice refreshing drink of Poppy Pop to go with your polly-lop?" The boy lifted his eyes, but didn't stop licking the candy. Robie waggled his claws slightly. "Just give me a quarter and within five seconds—"

A little girl wriggled out of the forest of legs. "Give me a polly-lop, too, Robie," she demanded.

"Rita, come back here!" a woman in the third rank of the crowd called angrily.

Robie scanned the newcomer gravely. His reference silhouettes were not good enough to let him distinguish the sex of children, so he merely repeated, "Hello, youngster."

"Rita!"

"Give me a polly-lop!"

Disregarding both remarks, for a good salesman is single-minded and does not waste bait, Robie said winningly, "I'll bet you read *Junior Space Killers*. Now I have here—"

"Uh-uh, I'm a girl. *He* got a polly-lop."

At the word "girl," Robie broke off. Rather ponderously, he said, "I'll bet you read *Gee-Gee Jones, Space Stripper*. Now I have here the latest issue of that thrilling comic, not yet in the stationary vending machines. Just give me fifty cents and within five—"

"Please let me through. I'm her mother."

A young woman in the front rank drawled over her pow-der-sprayed shoulder, "I'll get her for you," and slithered out on six-inch platform shoes. "Run away, children," she said nonchalantly. Lifting her arms behind her head, she pir-ouetted slowly before Robie to show how much she did for her bolero half-jacket and her form-fitting slacks that melted into skylon just above the knees. The little girl glared at her. She ended the pirouette in profile.

At this age level, Robie's reference silhouettes permitted him to distinguish sex, though with occasional amusing and embarrassing miscalls. He whistled admiringly. The crowd cheered.

Someone remarked critically to a friend, "It would go over better if he was built more like a real robot. You know, like a man."

The friend shook his head. "This way it's subtler."

No one in the crowd was watching the newscript overhead as it scribbled, "Ice pack for hot truce? Vanadin hints Russ may yield on Pakistan."

Robie was saying, ". . . in the savage new glamor-tint we have christened Mars Blood, complete with spray applicator and fit-all fingerstalls that mask each finger completely except for the nail. Just give me five dollars—uncrumpled bills may be fed into the revolving rollers you see beside my arm—and within five seconds—"

"No, thanks, Robie," the young woman yawned.

"Remember," Robie persisted, "for three more weeks, seductivizing Mars Blood will be unobtainable from any other robot or human vendor."

"No, thanks."

Robie scanned the crowd resourcefully. "Is there any gentleman here . . ." he began just as a woman elbowed her way through the front rank.

"I told you to come back!" she snapped at the little girl.

"But I didn't get my polly-lop!"

". . . who would care to . . ."

"Rita!"

"Robie cheated. Ow!"

Meanwhile, the young woman in the half-bolero had scanned the nearby gentlemen on her own. Deciding that there was less than a fifty-per-cent chance of any of them accepting the proposition Robie seemed about to make, she took advantage of the scuffle to slither gracefully back into the ranks. Once again the path was clear before Robie.

He paused, however, for a brief recapitulation of the more magical properties of Mars Blood, including a telling phrase about "the passionate claws of a Martian sunrise."

But no one bought. It wasn't quite time. Soon enough silver coins would be clinking, bills going through the rollers faster than laundry, and five hundred people struggling for the privilege of having their money taken away from them by America's first mobile sales robot.

But there were still some tricks that Robie had to do free, and one certainly should enjoy those before starting the more expensive fun.

So Robie moved on until he reached the curb. The variation in level was instantly sensed by his under-scanners. He stopped. His head began to swivel. The crowd watched in eager silence. This was Robie's best trick.

Robie's head stopped swiveling. His scanners had found the traffic light. It was green. Robie edged forward. But then the light turned red. Robie stopped again, still on the curb. The crowd softly *ahhed* its delight.

It was wonderful to be alive and watching Robie on such an exciting day. Alive and amused in the fresh, weather-controlled air between the lines of bright skyscrapers with their winking windows and under a sky so blue you could almost call it dark.

(But way, way up, where the crowd could not see, the sky was darker still. Purple-dark, with stars showing. And in that purple-dark, a silver-green something, the color of a bud, plunged down at better than three miles a second. The silver-green was a newly developed paint that foiled radar.)

Robie was saying, "While we wait for the light, there's time for you youngsters to enjoy a nice refreshing Poppy Pop. Or for you adults—only those over five feet tall are eligible to buy—to enjoy an exciting Poppy Pop fizz. Just give me a quarter or—in the case of adults, one dollar and a quarter; I'm licensed to dispense intoxicating liquors—and within five seconds . . ."

But that was not cutting it quite fine enough. Just three seconds later, the silver-green bud bloomed above Manhattan into a globular orange flower. The skyscrapers grew brighter and brighter still, the brightness of the inside of the Sun. The windows winked blossoming white fire-flowers.

The crowd around Robie bloomed, too. Their clothes puffed into petals of flame. Their heads of hair were torches.

The orange flower grew, stem and blossom. The blast came.

The winking windows shattered tier by tier, became black holes. The walls bent, rocked, cracked. A stony dandruff flaked from their cornices. The flaming flowers on the sidewalk were all leveled at once. Robie was shoved ten feet. His metal hoopskirt dimpled, regained its shape.

The blast ended. The orange flower, grown vast, vanished overhead on its huge, magic beanstalk. It grew dark and very still. The cornice-dandruff pattered down. A few small fragments rebounded from the metal hoopskirt.

Robie made some small, uncertain movements, as if feeling for broken bones. He was hunting for the traffic light, but it no longer shone either red or green.

He slowly scanned a full circle. There was nothing anywhere to interest his reference silhouettes. Yet whenever he tried to move, his under-scanners warned him of low obstructions. It was very puzzling.

The silence was disturbed by moans and a crackling sound, as faint at first as the scampering of distant rats.

A seared man, his charred clothes fuming where the blast had blown out the fire, rose from the curb. Robie scanned him.

"Good day, sir," Robie said. "Would you care for a smoke? A truly cool smoke? Now I have here a yet-unmarketed brand . . ."

But the customer had run away, screaming, and Robie never ran after customers, though he could follow them at a medium-brisk roll. He worked his way along the curb where the man had sprawled, carefully keeping his distance from the low obstructions, some of which writhed now and then, forcing him to jog. Shortly he reached a fire hydrant. He scanned it. His electronic vision, though it still worked, had been somewhat blurred by the blast.

"Hello, youngster," Robie said. Then, after a long pause, "Cat got your tongue? Well, I have a little present for you. A nice, lovely polly-lop.

"Take it, youngster," he said after another pause. "It's for you. Don't be afraid."

His attention was distracted by other customers, who began to rise up oddly here and there, twisting forms that confused his reference silhouettes and would not stay to be scanned properly. One cried, "Water," but no quarter clinked in Robie's claws when he caught the word and suggested, "How about a nice refreshing drink of Poppy Pop?"

The rat-crackling of the flames had become a jungle muttering. The blind windows began to wink fire again.

A little girl marched, stepping neatly over arms and legs she did not look at. A white dress and the once taller bodies around her had shielded her from the brilliance and the blast. Her eyes were fixed on Robie. In them was the same imperious confidence, though none of the delight, with which she had watched him earlier.

"Help me, Robie," she said. "I want my mother."

"Hello, youngster," Robie said. "What would you like? Comics? Candy?"

"Where is she, Robie? Take me to her."

"Balloons? Would you like to watch me blow up a balloon?"

The little girl began to cry. The sound triggered off another of Robie's novelty circuits, a service feature that had brought in a lot of favorable publicity.

"Is something wrong?" he asked. "Are you in trouble? Are you lost?"

"Yes, Robie. Take me to my mother."

"Stay right here," Robie said reassuringly, "and don't be frightened. I will call a policeman." He whistled shrilly, twice.

Time passed. Robie whistled again. The windows flared and roared. The little girl begged, "Take me away, Robie," and jumped onto a little step in his hoop skirt.

"Give me a dime," Robie said.

The little girl found one in her pocket and put it in his claws.

"Your weight," Robie said, "is fifty-four and one-half pounds."

"Have you seen my daughter, have you seen her?" a woman was crying somewhere. "I left her watching that thing while I stepped inside—*Rita!*"

"Robie helped me," the little girl began babbling at her. "He knew I was lost. He even called the police, but they didn't come. He weighed me, too. Didn't you, Robie?"

But Robie had gone off to peddle Poppy Pop to the members of a rescue squad which had just come around the corner, more robot-like in their asbestos suits than he in his metal skin.

Who's Cribbing?

Jack Lewis

April 2, 1952

Mr. Jack Lewis
90-26 219 St.
Queens Village, N.Y.

Dear Mr. Lewis:

We are returning your manuscript "The Ninth Dimension." At first glance, I had figured it a story well worthy of publication. Why wouldn't I? So did the editors of *Cosmic Tales* back in 1934 when the story was first published.

As you no doubt know, it was the great Todd Thromberry who wrote the story you tried to pass off on us as an original. Let me give you a word of caution concerning the penalties resulting from plagiarism.

It's not worth it. Believe me.

Sincerely,

Doyle P. Gates
Science Fiction Editor
Deep Space Magazine

April 5, 1952

Mr. Doyle P. Gates, Editor
Deep Space Magazine
New York, N.Y.

Dear Mr. Gates:

I do not know, nor am I aware of the existence of any
Todd Thromberry. The story you rejected was submitted in
good faith, and I resent the inference that I plagiarized it.

"The Ninth Dimension" was written by me not more than
a month ago, and if there is any similarity between it and the
story written by this Thromberry person, it is purely coin-
cidental.

However, it has set me thinking. Some time ago, I submitted another story to *Stardust Scientifiction* and received a
penciled notation on the rejection slip stating that the story
was, "too thromberrish."

Who in the hell is Todd Thromberry? I don't remember
reading anything written by him in the ten years I've been interested in science fiction.

Sincerely,
Jack Lewis

April 11, 1952

Mr. Jack Lewis
90-26 219 St.
Queens Village, N.Y.

Dear Mr. Lewis:

Re: Your letter of April 5.

While the editors of this magazine are not in the habit of
making open accusations and are well aware of the fact in
the writing business there will always be some overlapping of

plot ideas, it is very hard for us to believe that you are not familiar with the works of Todd Thromberry.

While Mr. Thromberry is no longer among us, his works, like so many other writers', only became widely recognized after his death in 1941. Perhaps it was his work in the field of electronics that supplied him with the bottomless pit of new ideas so apparent in all his works. Nevertheless, even at this stage of science fiction's development it is apparent that he had a style that many of our so called contemporary writers might do well to copy. By "copy," I do not mean rewrite word for word one or more of his works, as you have done. For while you state this has been accidental, surely you must realize that the chance of this phenomenon actually happening is about a million times as great as the occurrence of four pat royal flushes on one deal.

Sorry, but we're not that naive.

Sincerely yours,
Doyle P. Gates
Science Fiction Editor
Deep Space Magazine

April 14, 1952

Mr. Doyle P. Gates, Editor
Deep Space Magazine
New York, N.Y.

Sir:

Your accusations are typical of the rag you publish. Please cancel my subscription immediately.

April 14, 1952

Science Fiction Society
144 Front Street
Chicago, Ill.

Gentlemen:

I am interested in reading some of the works of the late
Todd Thromberry.

I would like to get some of the publications that feature
his stories.

Respectfully,
Jack Lewis

April 22, 1952

Mr. Jack Lewis
90-26 219 St.
Queens Village, N.Y.

Dear Mr. Lewis:

So would we. All I can suggest is that you contact the publishers if any are still in business, or haunt your second-hand
bookstores.

If you succeed in getting any of these magazines, please let
us know. We'll pay you a handsome premium on them.

Yours,
Ray Albert
President
Science Fiction Society

May 11, 1952

Mr. Sampson J. Gross, Editor
Strange Worlds Magazine
St. Louis, Mo.

Dear Mr. Gross:

I am enclosing the manuscript of a story I have just completed. As you see on the title page, I call it "Wreckers of Ten Million Galaxies." Because of the great amount of research that went into it, I must set the minimum price on this one at not less than two cents a word.

Hoping you will see fit to use it for publication in your magazine, I remain,

Respectfully,
Jack Lewis

May 19, 1952

Mr. Jack Lewis
90-26 219 St.
Queens Village, N.Y.

Dear Mr. Lewis:

I'm sorry, but at the present time we won't be able to use "Wreckers of Ten Million Galaxies." It's a great yarn though, and if at some future date we decide to use it we will make out the reprint check directly to the estate of Todd Thromberry.

That boy sure could write.

Cordially,
Sampson J. Gross
Editor
Strange Worlds Magazine

May 23, 1952

Mr. Doyle P. Gates, Editor
Deep Space Magazine
New York, N.Y.

Dear Mr. Gates:

While I said I would never have any dealings with you or your magazine again, a situation has arisen which is most puzzling.

It seems all my stories are being returned to me by reason of the fact that except for the byline, they are exact duplicates of the works of this Todd Thromberry person.

In your last letter you aptly described the odds on the accidental occurrence of this phenomenon in the case of one story. What would you consider the approximate odds on no less than half a dozen of my writings?

I agree with you—astronomical!

Yet in the interest of all mankind, how can I get the idea across to you that every word I have submitted was actually written *by me!* I have never copied any material from Todd Thromberry, nor have I ever seen any of his writings. In fact, as I told you in one of my letters, up until a short while ago I was totally unaware of his very existence.

An idea has occurred to me however. It's a truly weird theory, and one that I probably wouldn't even suggest to anyone but a science fiction editor. But suppose—just suppose—that this Thromberry person, what with his experiments in electronics and everything, had in some way managed to crack through this time-space barrier mentioned so often in your magazine. And suppose—egotistical as it sounds—he had singled out my work as being the type of material he had always wanted to write.

Do you begin to follow me? Or is the idea of a person from a different time cycle looking over my shoulder while I write too fantastic for you to accept?

Please write and tell me what you think of my theory?

Respectfully,
Jack Lewis

May 25, 1952

Mr. Jack Lewis
90-26 219 St.
Queens Village, N.Y.

Dear Mr. Lewis:

We think you should consult a psychiatrist.

Sincerely,
Doyle P. Gates
Science Fiction Editor
Deep Space Magazine

June 3, 1952

Mr. Sam Mines
Science Fiction Editor
Standard Magazines Inc.
New York 16, N.Y.

Dear Mr. Mines:

While the enclosed is not really a manuscript at all, I am submitting this series of letters, carbon copies, and correspondence, in the hope that you might give some credulity to this seemingly unbelievable happening.

The enclosed letters are all in proper order and should be self-explanatory. Perhaps if you publish them, some of your readers might have some idea how this phenomenon could be explained.

I call the entire piece "Who's Cribbing?"

Respectfully,
Jack Lewis

June 10, 1952

Mr. Jack Lewis
90-26 219 St.
Queens Village, N.Y.

Dear Mr. Lewis:

Your idea of a series of letters to put across a science-fiction idea is an intriguing one, but I'm afraid it doesn't quite come off.

It was in the August 1940 issue of *Macabre Adventures* that Mr. Thromberry first used this very idea. Ironically enough, the story title also was "Who's Cribbing?"

Feel free to contact us again when you have something more original.

Yours,
Samuel Mines
Science Fiction Editor
Standard Magazines Inc.

Spectator Sport

John D. MacDonald

Dr. Rufus Maddon was not generally considered to be an impatient man—or addicted to physical violence.

But when the tenth man he tried to stop on the street brushed by him with a mutter of annoyance Rufus Maddon grabbed the eleventh man, swung him around and held him with his shoulders against a crumbling wall.

He said, "You will listen to me, sir! I am the first man to travel into the future and I will not stand—"

The man pushed him away, turned around and said, "You got this dust on my suit. Now brush it off."

Rufus Maddon brushed mechanically. He said, with a faint uncontrollable tremble in his voice, "But nobody seems to care."

The man peered back over his shoulder. "Good enough, chum. Better go get yourself lobed. The first time I saw the one on time travel it didn't get to me at all. Too hammy for me. Give me those murder jobs. Every time I have one of those I twitch for twenty hours."

Rufus made another try. "Sir, I am physical living proof that the future is predetermined. I can explain the energy equations, redesign the warp projector, send myself from your day further into the future—"

The man walked away. "Go get a lobe job," he said.

"But don't I look different to you?" Rufus called after him, a plaintive note in his voice.

The man, twenty feet away, turned and grinned at him. "How?"

When the man had gone Rufus Maddon looked down at his neat grey suit, stared at the men and women in the street. It was not fair of the future to be so—so dismally normal.

Four hundred years of progress? The others had resented the experience that was to be his. In those last few weeks there had been many discussions of how the people four hundred years in the future would look on Rufus Maddon as a barbarian.

Once again he continued his aimless walk down the streets of the familiar city. There was a general air of disrepair. Shops were boarded up. The pavement was broken and pot-holed. A few automobiles traveled on the broken streets. They, at least, appeared to be of a slightly advanced design but they were dented, dirty and noisy.

The man who had spoken to him had made no sense. "Lobe job?" And what was "the one on time travel?"

He stopped in consternation as he reached the familiar park. His consternation arose from the fact that the park was all too familiar. Though it was a tangle of weeds the equestrian statue of General Murdy was still there in deathless bronze, liberally decorated by pigeons.

Clothes had not changed nor had common speech. He wondered if the transfer had gone awry, if this world were something he was dreaming.

He pushed through the knee-high tangle of grass to a wrought-iron bench. Four hundred years before he had sat on that same bench. He sat down again. The metal powdered and collapsed under his weight, one end of the bench dropping with a painful thump.

Dr. Rufus Maddon was not generally considered to be a man subject to fits of rage. He stood up rubbing his bruised elbow, and heartily kicked the offending bench. The part he kicked was all too solid.

He limped out of the park, muttering, wondering why the park wasn't used, why everyone seemed to be in a hurry.

It appeared that in four hundred years nothing at all had been accomplished. Many familiar buildings had collapsed. Others still stood. He looked in vain for a newspaper or a magazine.

One new element of this world of the future bothered him considerably. That was the number of low-slung white-panel delivery trucks. They seemed to be in better condition than the other vehicles. Each bore in fairly large gilt letters the legend WORLD SENSEWAYS. But he noticed that the smaller print underneath the large inscription varied. Some read, *Feeder Division*—others, *Hookup Division*.

The one that stopped at the curb beside him read, *Lobotomy Division*. Two husky men got out and smiled at him and one said, "You've been taking too much of that stuff, Doc."

"How did you know my title?" Rufus asked, thoroughly puzzled.

The other man smiled wolfishly, patted the side of truck. "Nice truck, pretty truck. Climb in, bud. We'll take you down and make you feel wonderful, hey?"

Dr. Rufus Maddon suddenly had a horrid suspicion that he knew what a lobe job might be. He started to back away. They grabbed him quickly and expertly and dumped him into the truck.

The sign on the front of the building said WORLD SENSEWAYS. The most luxurious office inside was lettered, *Regional Director—Roger K. Handriss*.

Roger K. Handriss sat behind his handsome desk. He was a florid grey-haired man with keen grey eyes. He was examining his bank book thinking that in another year he'd have enough money with which to retire and buy a permanent hookup. Permanent was so much better than the Temp stuff you could get on the home sets. The nerve ends was what did it, of course.

The girl came in and placed several objects on the desk in front of him. She said, "Mr. Handriss, these just came up from LD. They took them out of the pockets of a man reported as wandering in the street in need of a lobe job."

She had left the office door open. Cramer, deputy chief of LD, sauntered in and said, "The guy was really off. He was yammering about being from the past and not to destroy his mind."

Roger Handriss poked the objects with a manicured finger. He said, "Small pocket change from the twentieth century, Cramer. Membership cards in professional organizations of that era. Ah, here's a letter."

As Cramer and the girl waited Roger Handriss read the letter through twice. He gave Cramer an uncomfortable smile and said, "This appears to be a letter from a technical publishing house telling Mr.—ah—Maddon that they intend to reprint his book, *Suggestions on Time Focus* in February of 1950. Miss Hart, get on the phone and see if you can raise anyone at the library who can look this up for us. I want to know if such a book was published."

Miss Hart hastened out of the office.

As they waited Handriss motioned to a chair. Cramer sat down. Handriss said, "Imagine what it must have been like in those days, Al. They had the secrets but they didn't begin to use them until—let me see—four years later. Aldous Huxley had already given them their clue with his literary invention of the Feelies. But they ignored him.

"All their energies went into wars and rumors of wars and random scientific advancement and sociological disruptions. Of course, with Video on the march at that time, they were beginning to get a little preview. Millions of people were beginning to sit in front of the Video screens, content even with that crude excuse for entertainment."

Cramer suppressed a yawn. Handriss was known to go on like that for hours.

"Now," Handriss continued, "all the efforts of a world society are channeled into World Senseways. There is no waste of effort changing a perfectly acceptable status quo. Every man can have Temp and if you save your money you can have Permanent, which they say, is as close to heaven as man can get. Uh—what was that, Miss Hart?"

"There is such a book, Mr. Handriss, and it was published at that time. A Dr. Rufus Maddon wrote it."

Handriss sighed and clucked. "Well," he said, "have Maddon brought up here."

Maddon was brought into the office by an attendant. He

wore a wide foolish smile and a tiny bandage on his temple. He walked with the clumsiness of an overgrown child.

"Blast it, Al," Handriss said, "why couldn't your people have been more careful! He looks as if he might have been intelligent."

Al shrugged. "Do they come here from the past every couple of minutes? He didn't look any different than any other lobey to me."

"I suppose it couldn't be helped," Handriss said. "We've done this man a great wrong. We can wait and re-educate, I suppose. But that seems to be treating him rather shabbily."

"We can't send him back," Al Cramer said.

Handriss stood up, his eyes glowing. "But it is within my authority to grant him one of the Perm setups given me. World Senseways knows that Regional Directors make mistakes. This will rectify any mistake to an individual."

"Is it fair he should get it for free?" Cramer asked. "And besides, maybe the people who helped send him up here into the future would like to know what goes on."

Handriss smiled shrewdly. "And if they knew, what would stop them from flooding in on us? Have Hookup install him immediately."

The subterranean corridor had once been used for underground trains. But with the reduction in population it had ceased to pay its way and had been taken over by World Senseways to house the sixty-five thousand Perms.

Dr. Rufus Maddon was taken, in his new shambling walk, to the shining cubicle. His name and the date of installation were written on a card and inserted in the door slot. Handriss stood enviously aside and watched the process.

The bored technicians worked rapidly. They stripped the unprotesting Rufus Maddon, took him inside his cubicle, forced him down onto the foam couch. They rolled him over onto his side, made the usual incision at the back of his neck, carefully slit the main motor nerves, leaving the senses, the heart and lungs intact. They checked the air conditioning and plugged him into the feeding schedule for that bank of Perms.

Next they swung the handrods and the footplates into

position, gave him injections of local anesthetic, expertly flayed the palms of his hands and the soles of his feet, painted the raw flesh with the sticky nerve graft and held his hands closed around the rods, his feet against the plates until they adhered in the proper position.

Handriss glanced at his watch.

"Guess that's all we can watch, Al. Come along."

The two men walked back down the long corridor. Handriss said, "The lucky so and so. We have to work for it. I get my Perm in another year—right down here beside him. In the meantime we'll have to content ourselves with the hand sets, holding onto those blasted knobs that don't let enough through to hardly raise the hair on the back of your neck."

Al sighed enviously. "Nothing to do for as long as he lives except twenty-four hours a day of being the hero of the most adventurous and glamorous and exciting stories that the race has been able to devise. No memories. I told them to dial him in on the Cowboy series. There's seven years of that now. It'll be more familiar to him. I'm electing Crime and Detection. Eleven years of that now, you know."

Roger Handriss chuckled and jabbed Al with his elbow. "Be smart, Al. Pick the Harem series."

Back in the cubicle the technicians were making the final adjustments. They inserted the sound buttons in Rufus Maddon's ears, deftly removed his eyelids, moved his head into just the right position and then pulled down the deeply concave shining screen so that Rufus Maddon's staring eyes looked directly into it.

The elder technician pulled the wall switch. He bent and peered into the screen. "Color okay, three dimensions okay. Come on, Joe, we got another to do before quitting."

They left, closed the metal door, locked it.

Inside the cubicle Dr. Rufus Maddon was riding slowly down the steep trail from the mesa to the cattle town on the plains. He was trail-weary and sun-blackened. There was an old score to settle. Feeney was about to foreclose on Mary Ann's spread and Buck Hoskie, Mary Ann's crooked foreman, had threatened to shoot on sight.

Rufus Maddon wiped the sweat from his forehead on the back of a lean hard brown hero's hand.

The Cricket Ball

Avro Manhattan

The ferrous-liquid substance crashed to the ground with a heavy thud, concentrated itself into the shape of a ball, rolled slowly out of the shed, reached the middle of the road, then stopped. Its path across the reinforced concrete was marked by a deep furrow, as though it had rolled through clay.

Professor Lay looked at his watch. 3:33 p.m. His experiment had succeeded. He had created a substance of unknown specific gravity which now, by an unfortunate chance, was lying in the middle of the road.

"Here," said P. C. Jelks, "what's this?"

The Professor and the policeman looked at the ball. "It's gone and ploughed up the road," said Jelks. He looked uneasy. "What is it?"

"In certain stars," the Professor said, "the atoms are squeezed in such a way that the matter of which they are composed is unusually heavy. In Van Maanen, for instance, a star where matter is 300,000 times the density of water, a pinhead would shoot through your hand like a bullet."

"I see," said P. C. Jelks. He seemed to be about to examine his hand, as though this might clarify the situation. "You know best, sir, I'm sure," he said. "Better get it back into your workshop. We don't want to hold up the traffic." P. C. Jelks wished to have nothing more to do with the object.

"I don't think I can," the Professor said. He bent down and tried to pick up the ball. It would not move.

"Is it stuck?" P. C. Jelks asked. He raised his large boot and kicked the ball, then staggered back, clutching his foot. The ball had not moved.

Nobby Clark, from the garage, pulled up in his van. "No football here, mate," he told P. C. Jelks, an old enemy.

"It's stuck," Jelks said, too surprised to retaliate.

Nobby got out of the van. He shoved the ball with his foot. "What is it?" he asked the Professor.

"An experiment," Professor Lay said. "Have you any tools? I'd like to get it back into my workshop."

Nobby produced a seven-pound hammer. He swung it sideways at the ball, giving it all he'd got. The hammer bounced back. Nobby gave a roar, dropped the hammer, and sucked his fingers.

"That blow would have dislocated at least three hundred pounds," Professor Lay said. "Most interesting. The ball must weigh more."

The local fire engine swept round the corner, summoned by P. C. Jelks. The firemen looked at the ball. As usual, their talent for improvisation came to the rescue. They laid the loop of a wire hawser round the ball and fastened the other end of the hawser to the fire engine. The driver of the fire engine started off slowly in first gear. The hawser snapped a minute later, making a considerable mess of the fire engine.

A police car drew up. Four policemen in flat caps jumped out. Soon afterwards the road was cordoned off, and a screen of sacking was erected round the ball. The Prime Minister was informed, and a guarded statement given to the newspapers, to the effect that a mishap in the neighborhood of a War Office experimental station had placed a small area out of bounds to the general public. There was, however, no cause for alarm, as no radioactive materials were involved.

The three War Office brass hats arrived in time for tea, which was provided by local representatives of the Women's Institute and served in the screened-off space by P. C. Jelks.

"Professor Lay," the General said, "we don't like this publicity. Most unbecoming."

"The ball rolled out of my workshop," the Professor explained. "Some sudden, extragravitational pull. I was unable to stop it."

"Get a tank crane," the General snapped.

It was some time before the crane crew could get a satisfactory grip on the object. They tried digging out the concrete around it but as they did so the ball seemed to sink further in. Eventually they modified a grab to grip the ball as a vise.

The crane's engine roared. The hawsers hummed. The crane visibly vibrated with the vast effort it was making. The ball did not move.

"Give it full throttle, man!" the General shouted. "It's government property."

The grab broke. So did the crane boom. They had to send to Aldershot for another crane to remove the first one. The General and the other brass hats returned to the War Office to write reports about faulty equipment now being provided for Her Majesty's Forces by civilian concerns which should certainly be brought under immediate military discipline.

Next morning the national newspapers—their source of inspiration being Nobby Clark—had whipped the nation into such a state of anxiety about Professor Lay's object that crowds gathered outside Downing Street shortly after breakfast. Everyone present—men, women, and children—were insistent that something must be done. There had even been a cable from the Australian Premier asking what steps were being taken to prevent the ball falling right through the center of the Earth and coming out the other side, possibly wrecking the wicket so carefully prepared for the Fourth Test.

The Prime Minister himself appeared several times on the steps of No. 10, giving the V sign. As a method of raising the ball, however, it seemed to be inadequate.

By lunch time there were even more dramatic developments. The extremist wing of the Opposition, at the same time as demanding the resignation of the Government, suggested that Britain's hydrogen bomb should be dropped on the offending ball, thus removing it and a predominantly Tory constituency at the same time.

The American Air Force, using jet bombers from Greenham Common, flew in the world's biggest crane in sections—

a 250 tonner. Krupps, of Essen, phoned to say that in another hour's time they would have completed a 500-ton crane.

After lunch the Prime Minister left Downing Street by car to examine the problem on the spot. He was now seen to be giving the V sign with a ping-pong ball held between the fingers.

The site by now was a maze of temporary railway lines, cranes, fire engines, troops, trades union representatives and, on the outskirts, grandstands erected by Butlin's Holiday Camps, Ltd. The P.M. made his way through to the inner screens with difficulty.

"I'm sorry about this, sir," the Professor said. "Somewhat unforeseen complications."

The P.M. grunted. He looked at the ball, which by now had become highly polished by the various lifting devices which had been clamped round it. He poked at it angrily with his walking stick. The ball jumped out of the groove in which it lay, and rolled gently down the camber of the road, to come to rest in the gutter.

Professor Lay laughed. He looked at his watch. 3:33 p.m. "I should have thought of that," he said, "An unstable compound. Its molecular structure deteriorates after—" he looked at his watch again—"twenty-four hours. I must see what I can do about it."

He picked up the ball and put it in his pocket. "A scientist's work is never done," he said. He went into his workshop and shut the door.

Double-Take

*Winston K. Marks**

Paul made good in Hollywood, all right, but not the way many people predicted. I wish the bastard *had* turned actor. He could have easily enough. The 1966 trend to picture heroes was back on the pale, frail, mother-me-baby cycle, and Paul Conrad's tall slenderness fit the casting specifications to the droop of a pathetic shoulder.

His deep eyes and pallid brow had every female on the set quivering for one of the rare glimpses of him. Glimpses were rare, because when he came to me out of Cal. Tech. as a stereophysicist he buried himself in the camera sound lab and wouldn't even come out for lunch.

We men were interested in Paul, too. I was technical director at Medoc Studios, and I hired him because he claimed to have a patent on a special lens that solved the only remaining problem we had before launching a colossal new projection technique. The industry needed something to drag itself out of its latest slump. The novelty had worn off the 3-D and stereo projections that hit so hard in the fifties, and television was pulling theater box office out by its screaming roots again.

Paul was such a shy guy, I thought, that I had to coddle him and make much over him just to be safe. I passed the

---

* Originally published under the pseudonym "Ken Winney."

word on to all the important people on the lot to do likewise.
We didn't want this cookie leaving us for *any* reason.

He didn't take to the assortment of glamor girls that I introduced to him, and this worried me. If some other studio
got to him with the right babe—well, it was a chance I
couldn't take. So I went all out. I persuaded Gloria Breen to
befriend Paul. This was a rough decision for me, because I
was crazy about her.

She was a starlet who was graduating fast. She was so
beautiful and talented that she didn't have to accept dates
from producers to get parts, which is real talent even in
Hollywood. In fact so far I was the only guy in the studio
she'd even had lunch with, and I figured I was on the way
in with her at the time I got this damned fool notion of hanging her on Paul as a company anchor.

I introduced them at the cafeteria, and that was the last
time I had her with me. From then on they went out together
almost every night. At the spots she would fend off the agents,
predatory females and rival casting directors who stared at
Paul hungrily from every corner. And Paul would sit there
and talk with her.

Talk, talk, talk. That's all they did. Never even held hands.
Hopper couldn't make much out of it, but she said whatever
was going on it couldn't happen to a couple of nicer people.

Soon everyone wondered why they didn't get married. Oh,
everybody was so happy for them, the shy inventor and the
ambitious young actress. And I couldn't complain, because
Gloria was only doing the job I asked her to.

Then I started getting uneasy about Paul on another score.
His invention was the McCoy, and soon I didn't have to go
around getting people to be nice to him. Our new secret
process was mostly my idea, but it was beginning to appear
that it was all Paul's baby. I had planned to make Paul my
first assistant when I thought the front office would hold still
for it, so it was a little shock when *they* told *me* to promote
him. They intimated I was trying to hide his light under a
bushel.

Well, we shot that first picture under tight wraps, and by
the time the preview was ready, tension was so great around

town that nobody less than a director, first vice president, or an arrived star could get a ticket to Grauman's for that night.

It was a flesh-potty little picture done on a B budget which we spent mainly on exotic lounging pajamas and interestingly designed chaise longues. The critics shook their heads on the way in when we handed them spectacles in the foyer. I stood by and listened to their remarks.

"I thought Polaroids went out two years ago."

"This is new? Nuts, I knew Medoc was bluffing!"

"Like I was saying at Rotary this noon, pictures gotta go forward or they go backwards. Medoc's slipping."

But Alf Moccho, president of Medoc, stood at the door and beamed, insisting that each couple get the right glasses. "Pink rims for the little girls, blue for the little boys," he repeated over and over with a smugness that stank of confidence.

We had the ushers double-check as they seated the patrons to be sure the men and women had the right color goggles.

Two hours later I wiped the sweat off my face and watched our distinguished audience do the same. They were bright-eyed and enthusiastic, but none stopped to fill out the audience-reaction cards. A few ducked their heads together to exchange remarks. I managed to catch a few of the whispers.

"Not much plot, but my God, what characterization!"

"Well, that *was* something!"

"Incredible! I had her on my lap!"

"Why, darling, when he leaned over me I thought I'd faint!"

Gloria came out on Paul's arm. I stuck out my hand to him expecting to exchange congratulations. They brushed by me with little nods as if I was the doorman. I almost clobbered the slob right there and then. If I had I would have been better off. At least I would have made the morning editions.

As it happened, our little bomb exploded the headlines, all right, but whose picture and whose name got the credit?

A dozen columnists ran interviews under Paul's quotes. They were his usual stuffy, reserved line of guff. So reserved that he forgot to mention me.

Then it came to big stupid me. He wasn't shy at all. I had been trying to build up the most egotistical character in the colony. And all the time he was slipping the knife to me so gently I never felt it.

His steel got into my guts but good that same day when I showed up for a scheduled victory conference. After lunch he hailed me with a small, generous smile and turned to the gathered officials. "I want you to know, gentlemen, that I am grateful for this appointment, but I accept only on the stipulation that you allow me to keep Jake, here, as my assistant."

That's right. He had my girl. Now he had my job. And he was insisting that I take his old job. I've done a little acting in my time, and I managed to paste a big, wet smile on my face and make the honor seem overwhelming.

It wasn't easy to get to a guy whose success depended upon an invention. Not only did he have a top salary—my salary—but within six months every studio in town was paying him a licensing fee to use his special lens. It's hard to undermine a man with a million dollars in the bank. I needed a break, and I finally got it.

Paul and Gloria were still inseparable. They were addicts for the "double-takes." They were called this because our new technique consisted of filming our pictures twice: once from the point of view of the heroine, through whose eyes the lady customers enjoyed the picture, and then again through the hero's eyes. The men never saw the hero, just the heroine as he leaned over to kiss her, etc. Likewise, the ladies *lived* the part of the female lead. The two pictures, projected simultaneously, were separated for customers of the proper sex by the pink- and blue-rimmed polarized spectacles.

Without the restriction of having to satisfy both sexes with the same point of view, our producers went wild with their scenarios. As Fiddler put it, they leaned over forward on the love scenes. Another critic put it, "Why get married?"

Everybody liked them.

Well, as I said, Paul and Gloria were two of the best customers in town for the "horrid-torrids." So I wasn't too amazed to see them sit down in front of me one night for a repeat showing of *Come With Me*. It was dark, and I leaned forward to make sure it was them, but they didn't notice me. I leaned forward just in time to catch them—

   —Holding hands? Playing footsie or something? Sniffing heroin? No, Hedda. *They were trading spectacles.*

Prolog

John P. McKnight

A sharp sound crackled in the quiet of the morning, and the hairy man-creature drowsing before his cave came abruptly awake.

In one swift movement, he was on his feet. He swung to the young one, where it lay on the deerskin at the cave mouth. But the child slept peacefully, no danger near it.

Ungainly, the man shambled then to the lip of the narrow stone ledge and, blinking against the spring sunlight, peered out across the tall trees to the river below. There at dawn and at dusk the animals came to drink. But now, its bank was deserted. In the glade . . .

In the glade a sapling bent. A moment after, the crack of its breaking reached the man. A great, dark shape bulked momentarily in the dappled shade. The biggest beast was feeding.

Instinctively, the man reached for the sharp stone he had found at the river bank two winters ago. He cuddled it in his hand; his palm fitted snugly against it; his fingers found good purchase. It was a good thing, this stone. With it, he had flayed the deer the evening before, and killed the creeping thing coiled before the cave this morning. In some ways, it was a better thing than a club. If he had a club, with a stone like this at its end . . .

The man looked about him once more, and went back to

his place near the child. He squatted there; and almost at once his eyes closed again.

The man idled in the sun because he had fed to his full the night before, and there was yet meat in the cave. Coming back empty handed from the hunt, he had chanced upon a saber-toothed tiger's leavings a moment after the gorged killer lazed off to a canebrake to sleep. He had packed the torn carcass of the deer up to the cave, and the woman had charred gobbets of the sweet tender flesh over the fire they kept always burning, and they had eaten until their swollen stomachs would hold no more.

Awaking in the bright dawn, the man was still surfeited. A cold marrow bone and some grubs he found under stones at the brookside had sufficed to break the fast of the night. So he sat somnolent in the sunshine, motionless but for his fingers that ceaselessly explored the mat of hair covering his chest and belly. Now and then the searching fingers routed out lice; and these the man, grunting in sleepy triumph, cracked between powerful jaws and ate: despite his satiety, the morsel was tasty; and satisfaction at disposing of an old enemy sauced the titbit.

Beside him, now, the young one woke. It moved on the deerskin, waving its hands and kicking its feet. It made little gurgling sounds. Across the man's mind, as he listened sleepily to the liquid syllables, there flitted pictures of the brook that bubbled from the hillside high above the cave to go chuckling down to the river. "Wa, wa, wa," the child babbled: the man thought of the clear cool water plashing over the big rock where he sometimes sat to watch the slender fish skittering about the green depths of the pool below. "Coo, coo," the child piped; the man thought of the birds in the tall trees calling to each other at nightfall.

But then, the child's noises changed. They grew fretful. Its lips, moving loosely against toothless gums, made the sound, "Ma, ma." Over and over, it whimpered, "Ma, ma; ma, ma."

Disturbed, the man made to rise. But the woman was there before him, swift and silent on bare feet, taking the child up from the skin, holding it to her breast. At once, the child's wails stopped: there was the soft slup-slup of its lips as it suckled.

In the man's brain, memory stirred. Dimly, he recalled another child—the child that the great soft-padding saber-tooth had carried off before their eyes. That child, too, had fretted and whimpered, and made the sound "ma, ma" when it hungered. And at the sound, he remembered, the woman, leaving her tasks in the cave, had gone to it and given it suck.

The man took up the sharp stone again and began scratching aimlessly at the rock of the ledge. Something about the pictures his brain made excited and disturbed him. They roused in him the same vague uneasiness he had known the day he climbed all alone to the top of the highest hill and gazed out across the unimagined vastness of the plains beyond the river. In his perturbation, he got to his feet, tossing lank black hair back from his sloping forehead, and went to the rim of the ledge to stare down toward the river. But its bank was deserted; the glade too was empty, the saplings still in the tranquil morning; in the canebrake, nothing moved.

Behind him, the woman put the child down and, noiselessly, went back into the cave. The child cooed, and burbled, and was at last silent. The man turned to look at it. It was sleeping again.

In the growing warmth, the man mused. On a time many winters past, memory told him, he himself had been a child; and so he must once have been a tiny helpless creature like this one, that wailed when it was hungry and fed at a woman's breast. He wondered idly if he had made the same noises that this baby, and the other, made when they hungered. Tentatively, silently, he shaped his thick lips to form the sounds. . . .

A leaf rustled behind him. He wheeled, in sudden prescience of danger.

In a low thicket beside the cave mouth, a great wild dog crouched. It was mangy, gaunt from hunger. Its red-rimmed eyes were fixed on the sleeping child.

Stealthily, belly to ground, the dog inched upon its tiny prey. In the instant after the man turned to see, it was near enough. It gathered for the spring.

The man's eyes measured quickly. He was too far away.

He could not reach the child in time.

Before he could traverse half the distance, the dog would pounce, clamp slavering jaws on the infant, and be off into the underbrush.

A moment the man stood frozen, in the paralysis of helplessness.

Then his lips shaped to remembered sounds. To his surprise the great roar of his voice shattered the stillness. "Ma, ma!" he bellowed. "Ma, ma!"

The dog started. It jerked bared fangs at the man. Then its eyes went back to the child; it tensed again.

But as it did, the woman appeared in the cave mouth. Old practice of peril schooled her. In an instant, she scooped up the child and stepped back to safety.

The dog's spring fell on the empty deerskin, and at the man's rush it skulked off into the thicket.

Carrying the child, the woman came back.

The man's brain at last reached the end of the thing that had disturbed it.

He put out one hand and pointed it at the woman. "Mama," he said. "Mama."

The Available Data on the Worp Reaction

Lion Miller

The earliest confirmed data on Aldous Worp, infant, indicates that, while apparently normal in most physical respects, he was definitely considered by neighbors, playmates, and family as a hopeless idiot. We know, too, that he was a quiet child, of extremely sedentary habits. The only sound he was ever heard to utter was a shrill monosyllable, closely akin to the expression "Whee!" and this only when summoned to meals or, less often, when his enigmatic interest was aroused by an external stimulus, such as an odd-shaped pebble, a stick, or one of his own knuckles.

Suddenly this child abandoned his accustomed inactivity. Shortly after reaching his sixth birthday—the time is unfortunately only approximate—Aldous Worp began a series of exploratory trips to the city dump which was located to the rear of the Worp premises.

After a few of these tours, the lad returned to his home one afternoon dragging a large cogwheel. After lengthy deliberation, he secreted said wheel within an unused chicken coop.

Thus began a project that did not end for nearly twenty years. Young Worp progressed through childhood, boyhood, and young manhood, transferring thousands of metal objects, large and small, of nearly every description, from the dump to the coop. Since any sort of formal schooling was apparently beyond his mental capacity, his parents were pleased by the activity that kept Aldous happy and content. Presumably they did not trouble themselves with the aesthetic problems involved.

As suddenly as he had begun it, Aldous Worp abandoned his self-imposed task. For nearly a year—again, the time is approximate due to insufficient data—Aldous Worp remained within the confines of the Worp property. When not occupied with such basic bodily needs as eating and sleeping, he moved slowly about his pile of debris with no apparent plan or purpose.

One morning he was observed by his father (as we are told by the latter) to be selecting certain objects from the pile and fitting them together.

It should be noted here, I think, that no account of the Worp Reaction can be complete without certain direct quotations from Aldous' father, Lambert Simnel Worp. Concerning the aforementioned framework the elder Worp has said, "The thing that got me, was every (deleted) piece he picked up fit with some other (deleted) piece. Didn't make no (deleted) difference if it was a (deleted) bedspring or a (deleted) busted egg beater, if the (deleted) kid stuck it on another (deleted) part, it stayed there."

Concerning usage of tools by Aldous Worp, L. S. Worp has deposed: "No tools."

A lengthier addendum is offered us by L. S. Worp in reply to a query which I quote direct: "How in God's name did he manage to cause separate parts to adhere to each other to make a whole?" (Dr. Palmer) A. "The (deleted) stuff went together tighter'n a mallard's (deleted), and nobody—but *nobody*—Mister, could get 'em apart."

It was obviously quite stable, since young Aldous frequently clambered into the maze to add another "part," without disturbing its equilibrium in the slightest.

The foregoing, however sketchy, is all the background we have to the climactic experiment itself. For an exact report of the circumstances attendant upon the one "controlled" demonstration of the Worp Reaction we are indebted to Major Herbert R. Armstrong, U. S. Army Engineers, and

Dr. Philip H. Eustace Cross, AEC, who were present.

It seems that, at exactly 10:46 a.m., Aldous Worp picked up a very old and very rusty cogwheel . . . the very first object he had retrieved from oblivion on the junk-pile, so long ago when he was but a tad of six. After a moment's hesitation, he climbed to the top of his jerry-built structure, paused, then lowered himself into its depths. He disappeared from the sight of these trained observers for several minutes. (Dr. Cross: four minutes, fifty-nine seconds; Major Armstrong: five minutes, two seconds.) Finally Aldous reappeared, climbed down, and stared fixedly at his creation.

We now quote from the combined reports of Major Armstrong and Dr. Cross: "After standing dazedlike for a few minutes, Worp finally came very close to his assembly. There was a rod sticking out with the brass ball of a bedpost fastened to it. Aldous Worp gave this a slight tug. What happened then was utterly fantastic. First, we heard a rushing sound, something like a waterfall. This sound grew appreciably louder and, in about fifteen seconds, we saw a purplish glow emanate from *beneath* the contraption. Then, the whole congeries of rubbish arose into the air for a height of about three meters and hung there, immobile. The lad Aldous jumped around with every semblance of glee and we distinctly heard him remark 'Whee!' three times. Then he went to one side of the phenomenon, reached down and turned over the rusty wheel of a coffee mill and his 'machine' slowly settled to earth."

There was, of course, considerable excitement. Representatives of the armed services, the press services, the AEC, various schools for advanced studies, *et al.*, arrived in droves. Communication with Aldous Worp was impossible since the young man had never learned to talk. L. S. Worp, however profane, was an earnest and sincere gentleman, anxious to be of service to his country; but the above quotations from his conversations will indicate how little light he was able to shed on the problem. Efforts to look inside the structure availed little, since the closest and most detailed analysis could elicit no other working hypothesis than "it's all nothing but a bunch of junk" (Dr. Palmer). Further, young Worp obviously resented such investigations.

However, he took great delight in operating his machine and repeatedly demonstrated the "reaction" to all beholders.

The most exhaustive tests, Geiger, electronic, Weisendonk, litmus, et al., revealed nothing.

Finally, the importunities of the press could no longer be denied and early in the afternoon of the second day, telecasters arrived on the scene.

Aldous Worp surveyed them for a moment, then brought his invention back to earth. With a set look on his face, he climbed to its top, clambered down into its bowels and, in due course, reappeared with the ancient cogwheel. This he carefully placed in its original resting place in the chicken coop. Systematically, and in order of installation, he removed each part from his structure and carefully returned it to its original place in the original heap by the chicken coop.

Today, the component parts of the whole that was Worp's Reaction are scattered. For, silently ignoring the almost hysterical pleas of the men of science and of the military, Aldous Worp, after dismantling his machine completely and piling all parts in and over the chicken coop, then took upon himself the onerous task of transporting them, one by one, back to their original place in the city dump.

Now, unmoved by an occasional berating by L. S. Worp, silent before an infrequent official interrogation, Aldous Worp sits on a box in the back yard of his ancestral home, gazing serenely out over the city dump. Once in a very great while his eyes light up for a moment and he says "Whee!" very quietly.

Narapoia

Alan Nelson

"I don't know exactly how to explain it to you, Doctor," the young man began. He smoothed back his slick black hair that shone like a phonograph record and blinked his baby-blue eyes. "It seems to be the opposite of a persecution complex."

Dr. Manly J. Departure was a short severe man who made a point of never exhibiting surprise. "The opposite of a persecution complex?" he said, permitting one eyebrow to elevate. "How do you mean—the opposite of a persecution complex, Mr. McFarlane?"

"Well, for one thing, I keep thinking that I'm following someone." McFarlane sat placidly in the big easy chair, hands folded, pink cheeks glowing, the picture of health and tranquility. Dr. Departure stirred uneasily.

"You mean you think someone is following *you*, don't you?" the doctor corrected.

"No. No, I don't! I mean that while I'm walking along the street, suddenly I have this feeling there is somebody just ahead of me. Somebody I'm after. Someone I'm following. Sometimes I even begin to run to catch up with him! Of course—there's no one there. It's inconvenient. Damned inconvenient. And I hate to run."

Dr. Departure fiddled with a pencil. "I see. Is there anything else?"

"Well, yes. I keep having this feeling that people . . . that people . . . well, it's really very silly . . ."

"It's quite all right," Dr. Departure purred. "Feel free to tell me anything."

"Well, I keep having this strange feeling that people are plotting to do me good. That they're trying to be benevolent and kind toward me. I don't know exactly who they are, or why they wish me all this kindness, but . . . it's all very fantastic, isn't it?"

It had been a long hard day for Dr. Departure. Somehow he did not feel up to any more symptoms. He busied himself the rest of the hour obtaining factual background. McFarlane was thirty-two; happily married; healthy, normal childhood; satisfactorily employed as a radio repairman; no physical complaints; no bad dreams; no drinking; no history of parental discord; no financial worries. Nothing.

"Shall we say Thursday at ten, then?" he smiled, ushering McFarlane out.

At ten minutes to ten on Thursday, Dr. Departure looked at his appointment book and frowned. Well, maybe he wouldn't show up. Very often that happened. He certainly hoped that this would be one of the occasions. Opposite of a persecution complex! Delusions of beneficence! Indeed! The man must be . . . he checked himself hastily. He'd almost said *mad*. At that moment the door buzzer sounded, and McFarlane was grinning and shaking his hand.

"Well, well." Dr. Departure's affability seemed somewhat hollow. "Any new developments?"

"Seems to me I'm getting worse," McFarlane beamed. "This business of following someone, I mean. Yes sir. Yesterday, I must have walked five miles!"

Dr. Departure relaxed into his chair across the desk.

"Well, now, suppose you tell me more about it. *All* about it. Just *anything* that comes to mind."

McFarlane frowned.

"What do you mean, Doctor, just anything that comes to mind?"

"Just ramble on—about anything—whatever comes into your head."

"I'm not sure I understand. Could you show me what you mean, Doctor? Just by way of illustration?"

The doctor permitted himself a little chuckle.

"Why, it's very simple. . . . Well . . . like right now I'm thinking how one time I stole some money out of mother's purse . . . and now I'm thinking about my wife, wondering what to get her for our wedding anniversary . . ." The doctor looked up hopefully. "See? Just anything like that."

"Anything like what? I still don't quite understand." But McFarlane's face was not puzzled; it was eager. "Could you give me just a couple more illustrations? They're very interesting."

The doctor found himself relating disconnected, half-forgotten images. McFarlane sat back with a strangely contented expression.

At the end of the hour, Dr. Departure was quite exhausted. His voice was hoarse; his collar and tie askew. ". . . and well, my wife—she completely dominates me . . . I always was very sensitive that my eyes are slightly crossed . . . I never will forget—that time in the attic, with the little girl across the street . . . I was only eleven I guess . . ." Reluctantly, he broke off, wiped his eyes and glanced at his watch.

"I feel much better," he heard McFarlane say. "Shall we say Tuesday at ten?"

Next Tuesday at ten, Dr. Departure inwardly braced himself.

"There'll be no more nonsense like last Thursday's session," he assured himself, but he had no cause for concern. McFarlane was strangely silent and preoccupied. He carried a large cardboard box, which he carefully set upon the floor before seating himself in the leather chair. The doctor prodded him with a few preliminary questions.

"I'm afraid I'm beginning to be troubled with hallucinations, Doctor," McFarlane finally volunteered.

Dr. Departure mentally rubbed his hands. He was back on old familiar territory now. He felt more comfortable.

"Ah, hallucinations!"

"Rather, they're not really hallucinations, Doctor. You might say they were the *opposite* of hallucinations."

Dr. Departure rested his eyes a moment. The smile disappeared from his face. McFarlane continued:

"Last night, for instance, Doctor, I had a nightmare. Dreamed there was a big ugly bird perched on my shortwave set waiting for me to wake up. It was a hideous thing—a fat bulbous body and a huge beak that turned upward like a sickle. Blood-shot eyes with pouches under them. And ears, Doctor. Ears! Did you ever hear of a bird with ears? Little tiny, floppy ears, something like a cocker spaniel's. Well, I woke up, my heart pounding, and what do you think? There actually *was* an ugly fat bird with ears sitting on the short-wave set."

Dr. Departure perked up again. A very simple case of confusing the real with the unreal. Traditional. Almost classical.

"A real bird on the short-wave set?" he asked gently. "With blood-shot eyes?"

"Yes," McFarlane replied. "I know it sounds silly. I know it's hard to believe."

"Oh, not at all. Not at all. That type of visual aberration is a common enough phenomenon." The doctor smiled soothingly. "Nothing to . . ."

McFarlane interrupted him by reaching down and hoisting the carton onto the desk. "You don't understand, Doctor," he said. "Go ahead. Open it."

The doctor looked at McFarlane a moment, then at the brown box which was punctured with air holes and tied with heavy twine. Disconcertedly, the doctor cut the string and folded back the top flaps. He leaned over and peered in— then sucked in his breath. Pouchy, blood-shot eyes leered up at him. Floppy ears. The up-side-down beak. An obscene-looking bird.

"His name is Lafayette," McFarlane said, tossing a few bread crumbs into the carton which were quickly devoured with a noisy, repulsive gulp. "He rather grows on you after awhile, don't you think?"

After McFarlane left with his hallucination, the doctor sat a few moments meditating. He felt a little dizzy and lightheaded as though he had just emerged from a ride through the Tunnel of Horrors at the beach.

Maybe I *am* witnessing an entirely new psychosis, he told himself. Funny things are happening in the world today. He saw himself before the American Psychiatric Congress delivering a monograph: "The Emergence of a New Psychosis." This new disorder apparently had symptoms opposite from paranoia—he would call it "narapoia." Hopefully, Dr. Departure foresaw the possibility that some of his colleagues would insist on naming it after its discoverer: "Departureomania." He would be famous; his name linked with Freud. A sickening thought struck him. Supposing this man McFarlane were a malingerer! A fake! By God, he'd find out! Quickly, he buzzed his secretary, Miss Armstrong, and instructed her to cancel all appointments for the rest of the day. Then he reached for his hat and fled from the building.

Three days later the telephone in Dr. Departure's office rang. Miss Armstrong answered it. It was Mrs. Departure.

"No, he isn't here," Miss Armstrong said. "As a matter of fact he hasn't been here for three days except to bounce in and out for his mail."

"I don't know what's the matter with that man." Mrs. Departure's exasperated voice rattled the receiver. "He's gone half the night, too. Comes home utterly exhausted. What do you suppose he's writing in that little notebook?"

"Frankly, I'm worried about him," Miss Armstrong replied. "He's so irritable. And in such a frightful rush all the time."

"You're looking peaked, Doc," McFarlane said, at his next meeting a week later. It was the first time the doctor had sat behind the desk for many days. His legs ached. Stealthily, beneath the desk, he slipped off both scuffed shoes to relieve the pressure from his blistered feet.

"Never mind about me," the doctor snapped. "How are *you*?" The doctor's fingers twitched. He was much thinner and his face was pale and drawn.

"I think I must be getting better," McFarlane announced. "I have the feeling lately that someone is following *me*."

"Nonsense!" Dr. Departure snapped at him irritably. "It's just your imagination." He squinted his eyes and gazed at McFarlane. If only he could be sure this McFarlane was not faking. So far there was nothing to indicate he was. After all, his sudden urge on the streets to overtake someone seemed perfectly genuine. McFarlane would raise his head, his pace would quicken, and away he would go. "Well, I'll just have to watch him a little while longer," the doctor told himself. He closed his eyes a moment, reviewing his activities for the previous week: the long cross-city jaunts in which he had almost lost McFarlane a dozen times; the long, long waits outside restaurants and bars waiting for McFarlane to emerge. "I'll just have to keep going until I get all the facts," he thought. But he was a little concerned with the weight he'd lost, and with the strange ringing noises in his head which had recently developed. . . .

At the end of the hour, McFarlane tiptoed out of the office. Dr. Departure was snoring fuzzily.

On the day of McFarlane's next appointment with the doctor, he was met at the door by Miss Armstrong. "Doctor isn't here," she informed him. "He's taken a leave of absence for three months—possibly a year."

"Oh, I'm sorry to hear it," McFarlane said. "He *was* looking done in, though. Where is he, on vacation?"

"As a matter of fact, he's at Marwood Sanitarium."

A strange puzzled look suddenly settled over McFarlane's face and he gazed into space a moment. Presently, he smiled at the secretary.

"I just had the funniest feeling," he said. "Suddenly I feel like I'm completely cured. All of a sudden. Just when you told me about Dr. Departure."

The doctors had quite a time with Dr. Departure at the sanitarium.

"Just tell us anything that comes into your mind," they urged. Departure's eyes were glazed and he was very excited.

"I've got to follow him, I tell you! I can't let him get out of sight. Not for an instant. He's got a bird with baggy eyes and floppy ears."

"Very interesting. *All* very interesting!" The doctors gloomed among themselves, shaking their heads scientifically:

"Something entirely new!"

"It's rather like a persecution complex—isn't it?—only the opposite!"

"He seems to have the delusion he is following someone. Amazing, isn't it?"

"Probably the emergence of a brand new psychosis. I suggest that we observe him very closely."

And here one of the doctors went so far as to suggest further that they allow Dr. Departure to move about the city at will—closely watched, of course, by alternately selected members of their staff—so that all his actions could be carefully noted. . . .

Tiger by the Tail

Alan E. Nourse

The department store was so crowded with the post season rush, it was surprising that they spotted her at all. The salesgirl at the counter was busy at the far end, and the woman was equally busy at her own end, slipping goods from the counter into the large black purse. Kearney watched for several minutes in growing alarm before he motioned over the other section manager.

"Watch that woman for a minute," he said in an offhand whisper. "She's sorting that hardware like she owns the store!"

"A klepto? What are you waiting for?" asked the other. "Let's have a talk with her—"

Kearney scratched his head. "Watch her for a moment. There's something damned fishy—"

They watched. She was standing at the kitchenware counter, her hands running over the merchandise on the shelf. She took three cookie cutters and popped them into the pocketbook. Two large cake tins and a potato masher followed. Then a small cake safe and two small pots. Then a large aluminum skillet.

The second man stared in disbelief. "She's taken enough junk there to stock a store. And she's putting it all into that pocketbook. Kearney, *she couldn't get all that junk into a pocketbook!*"

"I know," said Kearney. "Let's go."

They moved in on her from opposite sides, and Kearney took her gently by the arm. "We'd like to speak to you, madam. Please come with us quietly."

She looked up blankly, then shrugged and followed them into a small office. "I don't know what this means—"

"We've been watching you for fifteen minutes." Kearney took the pocketbook from her arm, unsnapped it, glanced inside, and shook it in alarm.

He looked up, eyes wide and puzzled. "Jerry, *look at this*."

Jerry looked. When he tried to speak, there just weren't any words.

The pocketbook was empty.

Frank Collins parked his car in front of the Institute of Physics and was passed by fingerprint into the lab wing. Evanson met him in the corridor.

"Glad you got here," Evanson said grimly.

"Listen, John, what *is* this about a pocketbook? I hope it's not your idea of a joke."

"Not this gadget," Evanson promised. "Wait till you see it."

He led the way into one of the large lab sections. Collins eyed the shiny control panels uneasily, the giant generators and boosters, the duocalc relay board with its gleaming tubes and confused wiring. "I can't see what you want with me here. I'm a mechanical engineer."

Evanson walked into a small office off the lab. "You're also a trouble shooter from way back. Meet the research team, Frank."

The research team wore smocks, glasses, and a slouch. Collins nodded, and looked at the pocketbook lying on the table.

"Looks just like any other pocketbook to me," he said. He picked it up. It felt like a pocketbook. "What's in it?"

"You tell us," Evanson said.

Collins opened it up. It was curiously dark inside, with a dull metallic ring around the inside, near the top. He turned it upside down and shook it. Nothing came out.

"Don't reach around inside," Evanson cautioned. "It's not safe. One fellow tried, and lost a wristwatch."

Collins looked up, his bland, full face curious. "Where did you get this?"

"A couple of section managers spotted a shoplifter down in the Taylor-Hyden store a couple of days ago. She was helping herself to kitchen hardware and was stuffing anything and everything into the pocketbook. They nabbed her, but when they tried to get the hardware back out of the pocketbook they couldn't find any. One of them lost a wristwatch groping around in it."

"Yes, but how did *you* wind up with the purse?"

Evanson shrugged. "Ever since the end of the war in '71, when they organized Psych, they've turned shoplifters over to them. This woman was taken to Psych, but when they jarred her into remembering who she was, she couldn't recall having the purse. After Psych had looked at the pocketbook, they naturally sent it over to us. Here, I'll show you why."

Evanson picked up a meter stick and began to push it into the pocketbook. It went in about ten centimeters, to the bottom of the purse—

And kept on going.

It didn't poke out the bottom. It didn't even bulge the purse.

Collins goggled at it. "Holy smoke, how'd you do that?"

"Maybe it's going somewhere else. Fourth dimension. I don't know."

"Nuts!"

"Where else, then?" Evanson laid the meter stick down. "Another thing about that pocketbook," he added. "No matter what you do, you *can't* turn it inside out."

Collins looked at the dark inside of the pocketbook. Gingerly he stuck his finger in, rubbed the metallic ring, scratched it with his nail. A shiny line appeared. "That's aluminum in there," he said. "An aluminum circle."

Evanson took it and looked. "All the stuff she was stealing was aluminum," he said. "That's one reason we called you. You know your mechanics and you know your metals. We've been trying for three days to figure out what happens here. We can't. Maybe you can."

"What have you been doing?"

"Pushing stuff in. Checking it with all the instruments, X-ray, everything. Didn't tell us a thing. We'd like to know where that stuff goes that we push in."

Collins dropped an aluminum button into the purse. It went through the aluminum circle and vanished. "Say," he asked suddenly, scowling, "what do you mean, you can't turn this thing inside out?"

"It's a second-order geometric form." Evanson lit a cigarette carefully. "You can turn a first-order form, like a sphere or rubber ball, inside out through a small hole in the surface. But you *can't* turn an inner tube inside out, no matter what you do."

"Why not?"

"Because it's got a hole in it. And you can't pull a hole through a hole. Not even an infinitesimal hole."

"Well?" said Collins, frowning.

"It's the same thing with that purse. We think it's wrapped around a chunk of another universe. A four-dimensional universe. And you can't pull a chunk of another universe through this one without causing a lot of trouble."

"But you *can* turn an inner tube inside out," Collins protested. "It may not look like an inner tube any more, but it will all come through the hole."

Evanson eyed the pocketbook on the table. "Maybe so. A second-order geometric under condition of stress. But there's one hitch to that. *It won't be an inner tube any more.*"

Evanson pushed the fourth item made of aluminum into the purse. He shook his head tiredly. "I don't know. *Something* is taking that aluminum—" He pushed in a wooden ruler; it popped right out again. "And it wants *only* aluminum. Nothing else. That detective had an aluminum military watch, which disappeared from his wrist, but he had two gold rings on that hand, and neither one was touched."

"Let's play some thinking games," Collins said.

Evanson looked up sharply. "What do you mean?"

Collins grinned. *"Whatever* is on the other side of that pocketbook seems to want aluminum. Why? There's an aluminum ring around the mouth of the purse—all around it. Like a portal. But it isn't very big, and it doesn't use much aluminum. They seem to want lots more."

"They?"

"Whatever takes the metal but pushes back the wood."

"Why?"

"We could venture a guess. Maybe they're building *another* opening. A large one."

Evanson stared at him. "Don't be silly," he said. "Why—"

"I was just thinking out loud," said Collins mildly. He picked up a steel meter stick. Taking a firm grip on one end, he pushed the other end into the purse.

Evanson watched, puzzled. "They don't want it. They're trying to push it back."

Collins continued to insert the stick, with pressure, and suddenly the end appeared, curving back out. Like a flash Collins grabbed it and began tugging both ends at once.

"Watch it, watch it!" Evanson snapped. "You're making their universe conform to our geometry!" The purse seemed to sag inward.

One end of the rod suddenly slipped out of Collins' hand. He fell back, grasping the stick. It was straight.

"Evanson!" he snapped excitedly. "Can you get a winch up here?"

Evanson blinked dully, and nodded.

"Good," said Collins. "I think I know how we can hook onto their universe."

The big three-inch steel bar rolled easily into the lab on a dolly. The end of the bar, for six inches, was covered with shiny aluminum tubing and bent into a sharp hook.

"Is the winch ready?" Collins asked excitedly.

Evanson told him it was.

"Then slide the purse onto the end of the bar."

The end of the bar disappeared into the pocketbook.

"What are you trying to do?" Evanson asked uneasily.

"They seem to want aluminum, so we're going to give them some. If they're building another opening through with it, I want to hook onto the opening and pull it out into this lab. They'll be putting the aluminum on this bar with the rest. If we can hook onto that aluminum, they'll either have to cut it free and let us retrieve it, or open it into this lab."

Evanson scowled. "But what if they don't do either?"

"They *have* to. If we pull a nonfree section of their universe through the purse, it will put a terrific strain on their whole geometric pattern. Their whole universe will be twisted. Just like an inner tube."

The winch squeaked as Collins worked the bar to and fro inside the purse.

"Up a little," he said to the operator.

Evanson shook his head sourly. "I don't see—" he began. The bar twanged under sudden pressure.

"Hold it! You've got it hooked!" Collins shouted.

The winch squealed noisily, the motor whining under the strain. The steel bar slid slowly out of the purse, millimeter by millimeter, pulled as taut as a piano wire. Every ten minutes one of the technicians made a chalk mark on the bar by the mouth of the purse.

Frank Collins filled a pipe and puffed nervously. "The way I see it," he said, "these beings pried a small fourth-dimension hole into our universe, and somehow got that woman under a suggestive trance. They made her collect aluminum so they could build a bigger opening."

"But why?" Evanson poured coffee out of a thermos. It was late, and the whole building was silent and deserted except for this one lab section. The only noise in the room was the whine of the winch, straining at the other universe.

"Who knows? To get more and more aluminum? Whatever the reason, they want to get through to our universe. Maybe theirs is in some danger or other. Hell, the reason may be so alien that we couldn't possibly understand it."

"But what's the idea of hooking onto them?" Evanson's eyes were worried.

"Control. We pull a nonfree chunk of their universe into ours, and they can't use the opening. It'll be plugged up. The more we pull through, the more strain on the structure of their universe. They'll have to listen to *our* terms then. They'll have to give us their information so that we can build openings and examine them properly. If they don't, we'll wreck their universe."

"But you don't even know what they're *doing* in there!"

Collins shrugged, made another chalk mark on the bar. The bar was humming.

"I don't think we should take the risk," Evanson complained. "I didn't have permission to try this. I just let you go ahead on my own authority, on data—" he shuddered suddenly—"that's so damned vague, it makes no sense at all."

Collins knocked out his pipe sharply. "It's all the data we have."

"I say it's wrong. I think we should release the bar right now and wait till Chalmers gets here in the morning."

Collins eyed the winch with growing uneasiness, lighting his pipe with a match held in unsteady fingers. "We *can't* release the bar now. The tapered sheaves are under too much tension. We couldn't even burn through that rod with an oxytorch in less than twenty minutes—and it would jolt the whole building apart when it broke."

"But the danger—" Evanson stood up, his forehead beaded with perspiration. He nodded toward the creaking winch. "You might be gambling our whole universe."

"Oh, calm down!" Collins said angrily. "We don't have any choice now, or even time to talk it over. We're *doing* it, and that's all there is to it. When you grab a tiger by the tail, you've got to hang on."

Evanson crossed the room excitedly. "It seems to me," he said tensely, "that the tiger might have the advantage. If it went the wrong way, think what *they* could do to *our* universe!"

Collins blew smoke from the corner of his mouth. "At any rate, I'm glad we thought of it first—" He trailed off, his face slowly turning white.

Evanson followed his stare, and his breath came in a sharp gasp. The thermos clattered noisily to the floor. He pointed at the second chalk mark, sliding *into* the pocketbook.

"You mean you hope we did," he said.

Counter Charm

Peter Phillips

Shavallan adjusted the burden on his old, bony shoulders and toiled on. Loose shale slid from under his plodding feet. The journey to the Silent Lands had been weary, but his goal was nearly in sight. Cloud mist wreathed the upper slopes of Slieve-na-mona; but the summit of the mountain was clear, and as he emerged from the mist, Shavallan saw the throne of the King of the Shee.

The court was in full session, awaiting his return; and a burden heavier even than that which weighted his shoulders lifted from his heart as he saw his own folk, and their many cousins and relatives gathered here from distant lands.

Two northern trolls hurried forward to help him, but Shavallan waved them away and came to the foot of the throne before he put down his offering with a sigh of relief. The package was almost as big as himself.

Three pixies started plucking at the paper and string with quick mischievous fingers. "Whatisit, whatisit, whatisit?" Shavallan shooed them away and bowed to the King of the Shee.

"Sit down," said the King. "And let's be having some silence from the rest of ye. Give the feller time to find his breath."

"All the time in the world," muttered a kobold. "All the time in the great wide world."

192

Shavallan sat down thankfully and leaned against his package.

"How was it?" asked the King.

Shavallan took a pinch of snuff, sneezed once, and shivered. "Great magic," he said. "Greater magic than even you can make, Sire, with all respect to ye. There is silence everywhere: not even the song of birds or the squeaking of rats."

"And Those-Who-See-Us-Not?"

"The fields are yellow," said Shavallan, pretending not to hear. "Even the weeds barely grow. The trees are without leaf. The rivers are sullen and there are no fish."

"But Those-Who-See-Us-Not?"

"See-Us-Never," said Shavallan simply. He knelt and began to untie the string round his package. The King leaned forward and the others clustered round excitedly.

"This," said Shavallan with a trace of pride, "is a great charm, a Counter-Magic. With it, we may go freely and unharmed into their houses and palaces, wear their clothes and dance in their streets."

He took his time in revealing his gift to the Little Folk.

"All the time in the world," grumbled the kobold again. "All the time in the great wide world."

"Well, what *is* it?" asked the King impatiently.

"It is," said Shavallan, turning back the wrappings, "a *Geiger counter for the detection of residual radioactivity.*"

The Fly

Arthur Porges

Shortly after noon the man unslung his Geiger counter and placed it carefully upon a flat rock by a thick, inviting patch of grass. He listened to the faint, erratic background ticking for a moment, then snapped off the current. No point in running the battery down just to hear stray cosmic rays and residual radioactivity. So far he'd found nothing potent, not a single trace of workable ore.

Squatting, he unpacked an ample lunch of hard-boiled eggs, bread, fruit, and a thermos of black coffee. He ate hungrily, but with the neat, crumbless manners of an outdoorsman; and when the last bite was gone, he stretched out, braced on his elbows, to sip the remaining drops of coffee. It felt mighty good, he thought, to get off your feet after a six-hour hike through rough country.

As he lay there, savoring the strong brew, his gaze suddenly narrowed and became fixed. Right before his eyes, artfully spun between two twigs and a small, mossy boulder, a cunning snare for the unwary spread its threads of wet silver in a network of death. It was the instinctive creation of a master engineer, a nearly perfect logarithmic spiral, stirring gently in a slight updraft.

He studied it curiously, tracing with growing interest the special cable, attached only at the ends, that led from a silk cushion at the web's center up to a crevice in the boulder.

He knew that the mistress of this snare must be hidden there, crouching with one hind foot on her primitive telegraph wire and awaiting those welcome vibrations which meant a victim thrashing hopelessly among the sticky threads.

He turned his head and soon found her. Deep in the dark crevice the spider's eyes formed a sinister, jeweled pattern. Yes, she was at home, patiently watchful. It was all very efficient and, in a reflective mood, drowsy from his exertions and a full stomach, he pondered the small miracle before him: how a speck of protoplasm, a mere dot of white nerve tissue which was a spider's brain, had antedated the mind of Euclid by countless centuries. Spiders are an ancient race; ages before man wrought wonders through his subtle abstractions of points and lines, a spiral not to be distinguished from this one winnowed the breezes of some prehistoric summer.

Then he blinked, his attention once more sharpened. A glowing gem, glistening metallic blue, had planted itself squarely upon the web. As if manipulated by a conjurer, the bluebottle fly had appeared from nowhere. It was an exceptionally fine specimen, he decided, large, perfectly formed, and brilliantly rich in hue.

He eyed the insect wonderingly. Where was the usual panic, the frantic struggling, the shrill, terrified buzzing? It rested there with an odd indifference to restraint that puzzled him.

There was at least one reasonable explanation. The fly might be sick or dying, the prey of parasites. Fungi and the ubiquitous roundworms shattered the ranks of even the most fertile. So unnaturally still was this fly that the spider, wholly unaware of its feathery landing, dreamed on in her shaded lair.

Then, as he watched, the bluebottle, stupidly perverse, gave a single sharp tug; its powerful wings blurred momentarily and a high-pitched buzz sounded. The man sighed, almost tempted to interfere. Not that it mattered how soon the fly betrayed itself. Eventually the spider would have made a routine inspection; and unlike most people, he knew her for a staunch friend of man, a tireless killer of insect pests. It was not for him to steal her dinner and tear her web.

But now, silent and swift, a pea on eight hairy, agile legs, she glided over her swaying net. An age-old tragedy was about to be enacted, and the man waited with pitying interest for the inevitable denouement.

About an inch from her prey, the spider paused briefly, estimating the situation with diamond-bright, soulless eyes. The man knew what would follow. Utterly contemptuous of a mere fly, however large, lacking either sting or fangs, the spider would unhesitatingly close in, swathe the insect with silk, and drag it to her nest in the rock, there to be drained at leisure.

But instead of a fearless attack, the spider edged cautiously nearer. She seemed doubtful, even uneasy. The fly's strange passivity apparently worried her. He saw the needle-pointed mandibles working, ludicrously suggestive of a woman wringing her hands in agonized indecision.

Reluctantly she crept forward. In a moment she would turn about, squirt a preliminary jet of silk over the bluebottle, and by dexterously rotating the fly with her hind legs, wrap it in a gleaming shroud.

And so it appeared, for satisfied with a closer inspection, she forgot her fears and whirled, thrusting her spinnerets towards the motionless insect.

Then the man saw a startling, an incredible thing. There was a metallic flash as a jointed, shining rod stabbed from the fly's head like some fantastic rapier. It licked out with lightning precision, pierced the spider's plump abdomen, and remained extended, forming a terrible link between them.

He gulped, tense with disbelief. A bluebottle fly, a mere lapper of carrion, with an extensible, sucking proboscis! It was impossible. Its tongue is only an absorbing cushion, designed for sponging up liquids. But then was this really a fly after all? Insects often mimic each other and he was no longer familiar with such points. No, a bluebottle is unmistakable; besides, this was a true fly, two wings and everything. Rusty or not, he knew that much.

The spider had stiffened as the queer lance struck home. Now she was rigid, obviously paralyzed. And her swollen abdomen was contracting like a tiny fist as the fly sucked its juices through that slender, pulsating tube.

He peered more closely, raising himself to his knees and longing for a lens. It seemed to his straining gaze as if that gruesome beak came not from the mouth region at all, but through a minute, hatchlike opening between the faceted eyes, with a nearly invisible square door ajar. But that was absurd; it must be the glare, and—ah! Flickering, the rod retracted; there was definitely no such opening now. Apparently the bright sun was playing tricks. The spider stood shriveled, a pitiful husk, still upright on her thin legs.

One thing was certain, he must have this remarkable fly. If not a new species, it was surely very rare. Fortunately it was stuck fast in the web. Killing the spider could not help it. He knew the steely toughness of those elastic strands, each a tight helix filled with superbly tenacious gum. Very few insects, and those only among the strongest, ever tear free. He gingerly extended his thumb and forefinger. Easy now; he had to pull the fly loose without crushing it.

Then he stopped, almost touching the insect, and staring hard. He was uneasy, a little frightened. A brightly-glowing spot, brilliant even in the glaring sunlight, was throbbing on the very tip of the blue abdomen. A reedy, barely audible whine was coming from the trapped insect. He thought momentarily of fireflies, only to dismiss the notion with scorn for his own stupidity. Of course, a firefly is actually a beetle, and this thing was—not that, anyway.

Excited, he reached forward again, but as his plucking fingers approached, the fly rose smoothly in a vertical ascent, lifting a pyramid of taut strands and tearing a gap in the web as easily as a falling stone. The man was alert, however. His cupped hand, nervously swift, snapped over the insect, and he gave a satisfied grunt.

But the captive buzzed in his eager grasp with a furious vitality that appalled him, and he yelped as a searing, slashing pain scalded the sensitive palm. Involuntarily he relaxed his grip. There was a streak of electric blue as his prize soared, glinting in the sun. For an instant he saw that odd glowworm taillight, a dazzling spark against the darker sky, then nothing.

He examined the wound, swearing bitterly. It was purple, and already little blisters were forming. There was no sign of a puncture. Evidently the creature had not used its lancet, but merely spurted venom—acid, perhaps—on the skin. Certainly the injury felt very much like a bad burn. Damn and blast! He'd kicked away a real find, an insect probably new to science. With a little more care he might have caught it.

Stiff and vexed, he got sullenly to his feet and repacked the lunch kit. He reached for the Geiger counter, snapped on the current, took one step towards a distant rocky outcrop—and froze. The slight background noise had given way to a veritable roar, an electronic avalanche that could mean only one thing. He stood there, scrutinizing the grassy knoll and shaking his head in profound mystification. Frowning, he put down the counter. As he withdrew his hand, the frantic chatter quickly faded out. He waited, half stooped, a blank look in his eyes. Suddenly they lit with doubting, half-fearful comprehension. Catlike, he stalked the clicking instrument, holding one arm outstretched, gradually advancing the blistered palm.

And the Geiger counter raved anew.

The Business, As Usual

Mack Reynolds

"Listen," the time traveler said to the first pedestrian who came by, "I'm from the Twentieth Century. I've only got fifteen minutes and then I'll go back. I guess it's too much to expect you to understand me, eh?"

"Certainly, I understand you."

"Hey! You talk English fine. How come?"

"We call it Amer-English. I happen to be a student of dead languages."

"Swell! But, listen, I only got a few minutes. Let's get going."

"Get going?"

"Yeah, yeah. Look, don't you get it? I'm a time traveler. They picked me to send to the future. I'm important."

"Ummm. But you must realize that we have time travelers turning up continuously these days."

"Listen, that rocks me, but I just don't have time to go into it, see? Let's get to the point."

"Very well. What have you got?"

"What d'ya mean, what've I got?"

The other sighed. "Don't you think you should attempt to acquire some evidence that you have been in the future? I can warn you now, the paradoxes involved in time travel prevent you from taking back any knowledge which might alter the past. On your return, your mind will be blank in regard to what happened here."

The time traveler blinked. "Oh?"

"Definitely. However, I shall be glad to make a trade with you."

"Listen, I get the feeling I came into this conversation half a dozen sentences too late. What'd'ya mean, a trade?"

"I am willing to barter something of your century for something of mine, although, frankly, there is little in your period that is of other than historical interest to us." The pedestrian's eyes held a gleam now. He cleared his throat. "However, I have here an atomic pocket knife. I hesitate to even tell you of the advantages it has over the knives of your period."

"Okay. I got only ten minutes left, but I can see you're right. I've got to get something to prove I was here."

"My knife would do it," the pedestrian nodded.

"Yeah, yeah. Listen, I'm a little confused, like. They picked me for this job the last minute—didn't want to risk any of these professor guys, see? That's the screwiest knife I ever saw, let me have it for my evidence."

"Just a moment, friend. Why should I give you my knife? What can you offer in exchange?"

"But I'm from the Twentieth Century."

"Ummm. And I'm from the Thirtieth."

The time traveler looked at him for a long moment. Finally, "Listen, pal, I don't have a lot of time. Now, for instance, my watch—"

"Ummm. And what else?"

"Well, my money, here."

"Of interest only to a numismatist."

"Listen, I *gotta* have some evidence I been in the Thirtieth Century!"

"Of course. But business is business as the proverb goes."

"I wish the hell I had a gun."

"I have no use for a gun in this age," the other said primly.

"No, but I have," the time traveler muttered. "Look, fella, my time is running out by the second. What d'ya want? You see what I got, clothes, my wallet, a little money, a key ring, a pair of shoes."

"I'm willing to trade, but your possessions are of small

value. Now some art object—an original Al Capp or something."

The time traveler was plaintive. "Do I look like I'd be carrying around art objects? Listen, I'll give you everything I got but my pants for that screwy knife."

"Oh, you want to keep your pants, eh? What're you trying to do, Anglo me down?—Or does your period antedate the term?"

"Anglo . . . what? I don't get it."

"Well, I'm quite an etymologist—"

"That's too bad, but—"

"Not at all, a fascinating hobby," the pedestrian said. "Now as to the phrase *Anglo me down*. The term Anglo first came into popular use during the 1850—1950 period. It designated persons from the eastern United States, English descent principally, who came into New Mexico and Arizona shortly after the area was liberated—I believe that was the term used at the time—from Mexico. The Spanish and Indians came to know the easterners as Anglos."

The time traveler said desperately, "Listen, *pal*, we get further and further from—"

"Tracing back the derivation of the phrase takes us along two more side trails. It goes back to the fact that these Anglos became the wealthiest businessmen of the Twentieth Century. So much so that they soon dominated the world with their dollars."

"Okay, okay. I know all about that. Personally I never had enough dollars to dominate anybody, but—"

"Very well, the point is that the Anglos became the financial wizards of the world, the most clever dealers, the sharpest bargainers, the most competent businessmen."

The time traveler shot a quick despairing look at his watch. "Only three—"

"The third factor is one taken from still further in the past. At one time there was a racial minority, which many of the Anglos held in disregard, called the Joos. For many years the term had been used, to *Joo you down*—meaning to make the price lower. As the Anglos assumed their monetary dominance, the term evolved from *Joo you down* to *Anglo you down;* and thus it has come down to our own day, although neither Anglo nor Joo still exists as a separate people."

The time traveler stared at him. "And I won't be able to take the memory of this story back with me, eh? And me a guy named Levy." He darted another look at his watch and groaned. "Quick!" he said, "Let's make this trade; everything I got for that atomic knife!"

The deal was consummated. The citizen of the Thirtieth Century stood back, his loot in his arms, and watched as the citizen of the Twentieth, nude but with the knife grasped tightly and happily in hand, faded slowly from view.

The knife poised momentarily in empty air, then dropped to the ground as the time traveler completely disappeared.

The other stooped, retrieved it, and stuck it back in his pocket. "Even more naive than usual," he muttered. "Must have been one of the very first. I suppose they'll never reconcile themselves to the paradoxes. Obviously, you can carry things *forward* in time, since that's the natural flow of the dimension; but you just can't carry anything, not even memory, *backward* against the current."

He resumed his journey homeward.

Marget, hands on hips, met him at the door. "Where in *kert* have you been?" she snapped.

"You mustn't swear, darling," he said. "I met another time traveler on the way home."

"You didn't—"

"Certainly, why not? If I didn't somebody else would."

"But you've already got the closet overflowing with—"

"Now Marget, don't look that way. One of these days some museum or collector—"

She grunted skeptically and turned back into the house.

Two Weeks in August

Frank M. Robinson

I suppose there's a guy like McCleary in every office.

Now I'm not a hard man to get along with and it usually takes quite a bit more than overly bright remarks from the office boy to bother me. But try as I might, I could never get along with McCleary. To be as disliked as he was, you have to work at it.

What kind of guy was he? Well, if you came down to the office one day proud as Punch because of something little Johnny or Josephine had said, it was a sure cinch that McCleary would horn in with something his little Louie had spouted off that morning. At any rate, when McCleary got through, you felt like taking Johnny to the doctor to find out what made him subnormal.

Or maybe you happened to buy a new super-eight that week and were bragging about the mileage, the terrific pickup, and how quickly it responded to the wheel. Leave it to McCleary to give a quick rundown on his own car that would make you feel like selling yours for junk at the nearest scrap heap.

Well, you see what I mean.

But by far the worst of it was when vacation time rolled around. You could forgive a guy for topping you about how brainy his kids are, and you might even find it in your heart to forget the terrific bargain he drove to work in. But vaca-

tion time was when he'd really get on your nerves. *You* could
pack the wife and kids in Old Reliable and roll out to the lake
for your two weeks in August. You might even break the
bank and spend the two weeks at a poor man's Sun Valley.
But no matter where you went, when you came back, you'd
have to sit in silence and listen to McCleary's account of his
Vacation in the Adirondacks, or his Tramp in the Canadian
Wilds, or maybe even the Old French Quarter.

The trouble was he always had the photographs, the ticket
stubs, and the souvenirs to prove it. Where he got the money,
I'll never know. Sometimes I'd tell the wife about it and she'd
sniff and wonder what kind of shabby house they lived in that
they could afford all the other things. I never looked him up
myself. Tell you the truth, I was afraid I'd find the McClearys
lived on Park Avenue.

Now you look forward to a vacation all year, but particularly during the latter part of July, when, what with the
heat and the stuffy office, you begin to feel like a half-done
hotdog at a barbecue. I was feeling even worse than usual as
I was faced with spending my two weeks in my own backyard,
most of my vacation dough having gone to pay the doctor.
The only thing I minded was having McCleary find out about
it and seeing that phony look of sympathy roll across his fat
face while he rambled on about the vacation *he* was going to
have.

It was lunch time and we had just finished talking about
the latest on television and what was wrong with the Ad-
ministration and who'd win the pennant when Bob Young
brought up the subject of vacations. It turned out he was due
for a trip to the Ozarks and Donley was going after walleyed
pike in northern Wisconsin. I could sense McCleary prick
up his ears clear across the room.

"How about you, Bill?" Donley asked me. "Got any
plans?"

I winked heavily and jerked a thumb warningly toward
McCleary, making sure McCleary couldn't see the gesture.

"My vacation is really going to be out of the world this
time," I said. "Me and the wife are going to Mars. Dry, you
know. Even better than Arizona for her sinus."

Even with the wink they were caught off guard for a minute.

"Mars?" Donley said feebly, edging his chair away. "Yeah, sure. Great place. Never been there myself, though."

Young just gaped, then grinned as he caught on. "I understand it's a wonderful spot," he chipped in.

I casually peeled a hard-boiled egg the wife had packed in my lunch bucket and leaned back in my swivel chair. "It's really swell," I said dreamily, but loud enough so McCleary couldn't help but overhear. "Drifting down the Grand Canal at evening, the sun a faint golden disk behind the crystal towers of Marsport . . ." I let my voice drift into a long sigh and reached for Donley's sack of grapes.

About this time McCleary had gnawed his way through a big pastrami sandwich and waddled over. He stood there expectantly, but we carefully ignored him.

"Always wanted to go myself," Donley said in the same tone of voice he would have used to say he'd like to go to California someday. "Pretty expensive, though, isn't it?"

"Expensive?" I raised a studiedly surprised eyebrow. "Oh, I suppose a little, but it's worth it. The wife and I got a roomette on the *Princess of Mars* for $139.50. That's one way, of course."

"Mars!" Young sighed wistfully.

There was a moment of silence, with all three of us paying silent tribute to the ultimate in vacations. McCleary slowly masticated a leaf of lettuce, his initial look of suspicion giving way to half-belief.

"Let's hear some more about it," Young said enthusiastically, suddenly recovering from his reverie.

"Oh, there isn't much more," I said indifferently. "We plan to stay at the Redsands Hotel in Marsport—American plan. Take in Marsport, with maybe a side trip to Crystallite. If we have time we might even take a waterway cruise to the North Pole. . . ."

I broke off and dug Donley in the ribs.

"Man, you never fished until you have a Martian flying fish at the end of the line!" I grabbed a ruler off the desk and began using it as an imaginary rod and reel. "Talk about fight . . . oh, sorry, Mac." My ruler had amputated part of a floppy lettuce leaf that hung from McCleary's sandwich.

I settled down in my chair again and started paying attention to my lunch. "Nothing like it," I added between mouthfuls of liverwurst.

"How about entertainment?" Young winked slyly.

"Well, you know—the wife will be along," I said. "But some of the places near the Grand Canal—and those Martian mist maidens! Brother, if I was unattached . . ."

"There ain't any life on Mars," McCleary said, suspicious again.

All three of us looked at him in shocked silence.

"He says there's no life on Mars!" Donley repeated.

"You ever been there, McCleary?" I asked sarcastically.

"No, but just the same . . ."

"All right," I cut in, "then you don't know whether there is or isn't. So kindly reserve your opinion until you know a little about the subject under discussion."

I turned back to Donley and Young.

"Really a wonderful place for your health. Dry, thin air, nice and cool at night. And beautiful! From Marsport you can see low-slung mountains in the distance, dunes of soft, red sand stretching out to them. If I were you, Bob, I'd forget all about the Ozarks and sign up on the rocket."

"There ain't any rockets going to Mars," McCleary said obstinately.

"Isn't," I corrected. "I mean, there is. Besides, McCleary, just because you never heard of something doesn't mean it doesn't exist."

"The government's still working on V-2," McCleary said flatly. "They haven't even reached the moon yet."

I sighed softly, acting disgusted at having to deal with somebody as stupid as McCleary. "Mac, that's the government and besides they're dealing with military rockets. And did you ever hear of the government perfecting something before private industry? Who perfected the telephone, the radio, television? The government? No, private industry, of course! Private industry has always been ahead of the government on everything, including rockets. Get on the stick, Mac."

McCleary started in on his lettuce leaf again, looking very shrewd.

"How come I never heard of it before now?" he asked, springing the clincher argument.

"Look, Mac, this is relatively new. The company's just starting, can't afford to take full-page ads and that sort of thing. Just give 'em time, that's all. Why, a couple of years from now you'll be spending your vacation on Venus or Jupiter or some place like that. From now on, California and the Bahamas will be strictly old hat."

McCleary looked half-believing.

"Where'd you get your tickets?"

I waved vaguely in the direction of downtown. "Oh, there must be at least a couple of agencies downtown. Might even be able to find them in the phone book. Look under *Interplanetary Rocket Lines* or something like that. You might have a little difficulty, of course. Like I say, they're not too well advertised."

McCleary was about to say something more, but then the one o'clock bell rang and we went back to the office grind.

Well, McCleary didn't say anything more about it the next day, even though we'd throw in a chance comment about Mars every now and then, as if it were the most natural thing in the world, but Mac didn't rise to the bait. We gradually forgot about it.

The next couple of weeks came and went and then my two weeks in August. As I said before, my vacation dough had gone to pay the doctor, so I stayed at home and watered the begonias.

The Monday morning after vacation, we were all back in the office, if anything looking more fagged than we had when we left. When lunch time rolled around, Donley and Young and I piled our lunches on Donley's desk—his desk was near a window on the north side of the building so we could get the breeze—and talked about what we had done during vacation.

McCleary ambled up and like it usually does after McCleary comes around, the conversation just naturally died down. After a two minute silence I finally took the hook.

"Okay, Mac," I said, "I know you're just dying to tell us. Where did you go?"

He almost looked surprised. "To Mars," he said, like he might have said Aunt Minnie's.

The three of us looked blank for a minute and then we caught on. It took us a while to recover from laughing and my sides were still aching when I saw McCleary's face. It definitely had a hurt look on it.

"You don't think I did," he accused us.

"Oh, come off it, McCleary," I said crossly. "A gag's a gag, but it can be carried too far. Where'd you go? California, Oregon, some place like that?"

"I said I went to Mars," McCleary repeated hotly, "and I can prove it!"

"Sure," I said. "Like I can prove the world's flat and it's supported by four elephants standing on a turtle's back like the old Greeks . . ."

I cut off. McCleary had thrown a couple of pasteboards on the desk and I picked them up. The printing on them was like you see on a Pullman ticket. It said something about a roomette, first-class passage on the *Martian Prince*, for $154.75, and there was even a place where they had the tax figured. In two blanks at the top of the ticket, they had it filled out to *E. C. McCleary and wife*. The bottom half was torn off, just like they do with train tickets.

"Very clever," I said, "but you shouldn't have gone to all that trouble to have these printed up."

McCleary scowled and dropped a little bunch of koda-chrome slides on the desk. I took one and held it up to the light. It showed Mac and his wife mounted on something that looked like a cross between a camel and a zebra. They were at the top of a sand dune and in the distance you could see the towers of a city. The funny thing was the towers looked a little—but not much—like minarets and the sand dunes were colored a beautiful pink.

I passed it on to Donley and Young and started leafing through the rest. They were beautiful slides. McCleary and spouse in front of various structures in a delicately tinted marble and crystal city. McCleary in a pink and black boat on a canal that looked as wide as the Mississippi. McCleary standing on a strangely carved sandstone parapet, admiring a sunset caused by a sun looking half as big as ours. And everywhere were the dunes of pink sand.

"Pictures can be faked, Mac," I said.

He looked hurt and got some things out of his desk—a sateen pillow with scenes like those on his snapshots, an urn filled with pink sand, a tiny boat like a gondola, only different, a letter opener made out of peculiar bubbly pink glass. They were all stamped "Souvenir of Mars" and that kind of junk you don't have made up for a gag. I know mass-produced articles when I see them.

"We couldn't afford the first-class tour," McCleary said expansively, "but I figure we can cover that next year." He turned to me puzzledly. "I asked the passenger agent about the *Princess of Mars* and he said he had never heard of the ship. And it's Mars City, not Marsport. Couldn't understand how you made a mistake."

"It was easy," I said weakly. I pointed to the pasteboard ducats. "Where'd you get these, Mac?"

He waved generously in the direction of downtown. "Like you said, there's a couple of agencies downtown. . . ."

You know, sometimes I think we misjudged McCleary. It takes a while to get to know a guy like Mac. Maybe his Louie *is* brighter than Johnny, and maybe his chugmobile *is* something terrific.

For the last few years, all on account of Mac, my two weeks in August have really been well spent. Beautiful! Why, from Mars City you can see low-slung mountains in the distance and dunes of soft, red sand stretching out to them. And the sunsets when you're standing on the parapets of that delicate crystal city . . . And, man, fishing in the Grand Canal . . .

How do you get to Mars? There's probably a couple of agencies in your own town. You can look them up in your phone book under "Vacation at the Planets of Pleasure" or something like that. They might be a little difficult to find, though.

You see, they're not very well advertised yet.

See?

Edward G. Robles, Jr.

Well, there was this song a few years back. You know the one. Phil Harris singing about a thing that you couldn't get rid of, no matter what you did, a thing so repulsive it made you a social outcast. Never thought I'd see one, though. Dirty Pete found it.

Don't rush me. I'll tell you about it.

We're hobos, understand? Now a hobo is a different breed of cat than you think. Oh, people are getting educated to the idea that a hobo will work and move on, whereas a tramp will mooch and move on, and a bum will mooch and hang around, but you still find folks who are ignorant enough to call us bums.

We're aristocrats, yes sir. If it wasn't for us, you wouldn't enjoy half the little luxuries you do. Oh, don't believe me—talk to your experts. They know that, without the migratory worker, most of the crops wouldn't get harvested. And, if I talk high-falutin' once in a while, don't blame me. Associating with the Professor improves any man's vocabulary, in spite of themselves.

There was the four of us, see? We'd been kicking around together for longer than I care to think about. There was the Professor and Dirty Pete and Sacks and Eddie. I'm Eddie. Nicknames are funny things. Take the Professor—he was a real professor once, until he began hitting the bottle. Well, he lost his job, his home, his family, and his reputation.

One morning, he wakes up on Skid Row without a nickel in his jeans and the great-granddaddy of all hangovers. He comes to a decision. Either he could make a man out of himself, or he could die. Right then, dying looked like the easiest thing to do, but it took more guts than he had to jump off a bridge, so he went on the Road instead.

After he got over his shakes—and he sure had 'em bad—he decided that, if he never took another drink, it'd be the best thing for him. So he didn't. He had a kind of dignity, though, and he could really talk, so he and I teamed up during the wheat harvest in South Dakota. We made all the stops, and when we hit the peaches in California we picked up Sacks and Dirty Pete.

Sacks got his monicker because he never wore shoes. He claimed that gunny-sacks, wrapped around his feet and shins, gave as much protection and more freedom, and they were more comfortable, besides costing nix. Since we mostly bought our shoes at the dumps, at four bits a pair, you might say he was stretching a point, but that's one of the laws of the Road. You don't step on the other guy's corns, and he don't step on yours.

So guess why Dirty Pete was called that. Yeah. He hadn't taken a bath since 'forty-six, when he got out of the army, and he didn't figger on ever takin' another. He was a damn' good worker, though, and nobody'd ever try anything with him around. He wasn't any bigger than a Mack truck. Besides, he was quiet.

Oh, sure. You wanna know why I'm on the Road. Well, it happens I like whiskers. Trouble is, they're not fashionable, unless you're some kind of an artist, which I'm not. You know, social disapproval. I didn't have the guts to face it, so I lit out. Nobody cares on the Road what you do, so I was okay with my belt-length beard.

A beard's an enjoyable thing, too. There's a certain kind of thrill you get from stroking it, and feeling its silkiness run through your fingers. And besides, combing it, and keeping it free of burrs, snarls and tangles, sort of keeps your spare

moments so full that the devil don't find any idle time to put
your hands to work in. If you ask me, I think that the razor
has been the downfall of society. And I'm willing to bet I
have plenty of company with the same opinion.

Show me a man who doesn't let his beard grow once in a
while, even if it's only for a day or so, and you've shown me
a man who thinks more of social pressure than he does of
his own comfort. And show me a man who says he likes to
shave, and you've shown me a man who is either a liar or is
asking for punishment.

That's enough about us. Now to get on with the story.
You know, if the Professor hadn't been around, there would
probably have been murder done over the Thing, or at least
our little group would've split up, 'cause none of us had the
brains to figure it out.

Pete's an expert scrounger. His eyes are sharp, and he's always on the lookout for a salable piece of goods, even if he
can only get a nickel for it. One night, we're sitting in a
jungle near Sacramento, trying to figure out whether to go
north for the grapes, or south for the grapes. They're all
over California, you know, and they pay pretty well.

Pete, as usual, is out looking, and pretty soon he comes
back into camp with this Thing in his hand. He handles it
like it was hot, but he's pleased he's found it, because he hopes
to merchandise it. So he walks up to me, and says, "Hey,
Eddie. What'll you gimme for this, huh?"

I say, "Get that to hell away from me! I'll give you a swift
kick in the pants if you don't."

He looks real surprised. He says, "Huh, I thought maybe
you could use it."

I get up on my feet. I say, real low and careful, because
maybe he's joking, "Look, Pete—you oughtta know by this
time, I *like* my beard. Now will you go away?"

He mooches off, looking like I'd kicked him, and goes over
to the Professor. I figure maybe the Professor could use it,
so I listen. The Prof looks like he was being offered a live
rattlesnake.

"No, thanks, really, Pete. I have resolved never to touch
it again. I hope you don't mind."

Well, for some reason Pete don't look pleased, and he's real unhappy by this time, but he tries again.

"Hey, Sacks, what'll you gimme for—"

He don't get a chance to finish. I'm only listening with half an ear, but I'm so surprised I stand up like I been stuck with a pin. Sacks says, "Whatinell would I do with a left shoe? You know I don't use 'em."

Pete looks at the Thing in his hand, and the Prof and I go over there.

The Professor looks at the Thing real carefully and speaks up. "Say, Pete, look at that Thing and tell me what it is."

"Why, it's a brand new bar of soap, of course. I don't use it, but one of you might want to. What's all the beef about?"

"Soap?" I say. "Why, you poor fish, something must have happened to your eyes. When you offered me that straight razor, I thought you'd gone off your nut. Now I *know* it."

The Professor interrupts. He looks excited. "Wait a minute, Eddie. To me that item looks exactly like a full fifth of Old Harvester, 100 proof. Used to be my favorite, before I became an abstainer. To Pete, it looks like soap. To you, it looks like a straight razor while, to Sacks, it resembles a shoe. Does that give you any ideas?"

"Means we're all having hallucinations," I grunts.

"Exactly. Pete, was there anything else in the location where you found this thing?"

"Nothing but some scrap tin."

"Show us."

So, the four of us wander across the field and, sure enough, there was this silly looking object lying there. It was about eighteen or twenty feet across, and two feet thick, and I nearly made a fool of myself. I almost screamed when I saw six straight razors *crawling* out of a hole in its side.

The Professor whistled. "Grab them, boys. We want them."

Well, Sacks sacrifices one of his sacks, and we rounded up fifteen of the useless things. We went back to the jungle, where the Prof explained it.

"Look, fellows, suppose you were a being from another planet that wanted to take over here. Suppose, further, that you were rather small and relatively defenseless. To finish the suppositions, suppose you were a positive telepath, with not only the ability to read minds, but also the ability to create visual and tactile hallucinations. How would you protect yourself?"

A light began to dawn, but I didn't say a word about it.

The Professor continued. "If you could do all this, you'd make yourself look just as useless as possible. To Pete, you'd look like a bar of soap, because he never uses the stuff. To Sacks, you'd look like a shoe, because his dislike for shoes is evident in his mind. To Eddie, who is proud of his beard, you'd look like a razor, while to me, you'd look like a bottle of booze, because I dislike its effects intensely. In other words, you would assume an imposture that would assure you'd never be picked up, except by someone like Pete, who would see in you a salable item, even though not a usable one. It may be, Pete, that you have saved the world."

So, that's the story. We're all still on the Road, of course, but now we are the "Commission for the Investigation of Extraterrestrial Invasion." Congress named us as that, when we got the data to them.

Now, Mr. Mayor, you see our problem. Have your citizens seen anything around that they don't want? If they have, we want to look at it.

Appointment at Noon

Eric Frank Russell

Henry Curran was big, busy, and impatient of triflers. He had the build of a wrestler, the soul of a tiger, and his time was worth a thousand bucks an hour. He knew of nobody who rated more.

And crime did not pay? Bah!

Jungle tactics paid off. The entire opposition had been conditioned out of men by what is called civilization.

Entering his spacious office with the swift, heavy tread of a large man in fighting trim, Henry slung his hat onto a hook, glanced at the wall clock, noted that it registered ten minutes to twelve.

Planting himself in the seat behind his desk, he kept his expectant gaze upon the door through which he had entered. His wait lasted about ten seconds. Scowling at the thought of it, Curran reached over and thumbed a red stud on his big desk.

"What's wrong with you?" he snapped when Miss Reed came in. "You get worse every day. Old age creeping over you or something?"

She posed, tall, neat, and precise, facing him across the desk, her eyes wearing a touch of humility born of fear. Curran employed only those about whom he knew too much.

"I'm sorry, Mr. Curran, I was—"

"Never mind the alibi. Be faster—or else! Speed's what I like. *Speed*—see?"

215

216

"Yes, Mr. Curran."

"Has Lolordo phoned in yet?"

"No, Mr. Curran."

"He should be through by now if everything went all right." He viewed the clock again, tapped irritably on his desk. "If he's made a mess of it and the mouthpiece comes on, tell him to let Lolordo stew. He's in no position to talk, anyway. A spell in jail will teach him not to be stupid."

"Yes, Mr. Curran. There's an old—"

"Shut up till I've finished. If Michaelson calls up and says the *Firefly* got through, ring Voss and tell him without delay! And I mean without delay! That's important!" He mused a moment, finished, "There's that meeting downtown at twelve-twenty. God knows how long it will go on but if they want trouble they can have it aplenty. If anyone asks, you don't know where I am and you don't expect me back before four."

"But, Mr. Curran—"

"You heard what I said. Nobody sees me before four."

"There's a man already here," she got out with a sort of apologetic breathlessness. "He said you have an appointment with him at two minutes to twelve."

"And you fell for a gag like that?" He studied her with open contempt.

"I can only repeat what he said. He seemed quite sincere."

"That's a change," scoffed Curran. "Sincerity in the outer office. He's got the wrong address. Go tell him to spread himself across the tracks."

"I said you were out and didn't know when you would return. He took a seat and said he'd wait because you would be back at ten to twelve."

Involuntarily, both stared at the clock. Curran bent an arm, eyed his wristwatch by way of checking the accuracy of the instrument on the wall.

"That's what the scientific bigbrains would call precognition. I call it a lucky guess. One minute either way would have made him wrong. He ought to back horses." He made a gesture of dismissal. "Push him out—or do I have to get the boys to do it for you?"

"That wouldn't be necessary. He is old and blind."

"I don't give a damn if he's armless and legless—that's *his* tough luck. Give him the rush."

Obediently she left. A few moments later she was back with the martyred air of one compelled to face his wrath.

"I'm terribly sorry, Mr. Curran, but he insists that he has a date with you for two minutes to twelve. He is to see you about a personal matter of major importance."

Curran scowled at the wall. The clock said four minutes to twelve. He spoke with sardonic emphasis.

"I know no blind man and I don't forget appointments. Throw him down the stairs."

She hesitated, standing there wide-eyed. "I'm wondering whether—"

"Out with it!"

"Whether he's been sent to you by someone who'd rather he couldn't identify you by sight."

He thought it over, said, "Could be. You use your brains once in a while. What's his name?"

"He won't say."

"Nor state his business?"

"No."

"H'm! I'll give him two minutes. If he's panhandling for some charity he'll go out through the window. Tell him time is precious and show him in."

She went away, brought back the visitor, gave him a chair. The door closed quietly behind her. The clock said three minutes before the hour.

Curran lounged back and surveyed his caller, finding him tall, gaunt, and white-haired. The oldster's clothes were uniformly black, a deep, somber, solemn black that accentuated the brilliance of the blue, unseeing eyes staring from his colorless face.

Those strange eyes were the other's most noteworthy feature. They held a most curious quality of blank penetration as if somehow they could look *into* the things they could not look *at*. And they were sorry—sorry for what they saw.

For the first time in his life feeling a faint note of alarm, Curran said, "What can I do for you?"

"Nothing," responded the other. "Nothing at all."

His low, organlike voice was pitched at no more than a whisper and with its sounding a queer coldness came over the room. He sat there unmoving and staring at whatever a blind man can see. The coldness increased, became bitter. Curran shivered despite himself. He scowled and got a hold on himself.

"Don't take up my time," advised Curran. "State your business or get to hell out."

"People don't take up time. Time takes up people."

"What the blazes do you mean? Who are you?"

"You know who I am. Every man is a shining sun unto himself until dimmed by his dark companion."

"You're not funny," said Curran, freezing.

"I am never funny."

The tiger light blazed in Curran's eyes as he stood up, placed a thick, firm finger near his desk stud.

"Enough of this tomfoolery! What d'you want?"

Suddenly extending a lengthless, dimensionless arm, Death whispered sadly, "You!"

And took him.

At exactly two minutes to twelve.

We Don't Want Any Trouble

James H. Schmitz

"Well, that wasn't a very long interview, was it?" asked the professor's wife. She'd discovered the professor looking out of the living room window when she'd come home from shopping just now. "I wasn't counting on having dinner before nine," she said, setting her bundles down on the couch. "I'll get at it right away."

"No hurry about dinner," the professor replied without turning his head. "I didn't expect we'd be through there before eight myself."

He had clasped his hands on his back and was swaying slowly, backward and forward on his feet, staring out at the street. It was a favorite pose of his, and she never had discovered whether it indicated deep thought or just daydreaming. At the moment, she suspected uncomfortably it was very deep thought, indeed. She took off her hat.

"I suppose you could call it an interview," she said uneasily. "I mean you actually talked with it, didn't you?"

"Oh, yes, we talked with it," he nodded. "Some of the others did, anyway."

"Imagine *talking* with something like that! It really *is* from another world, Clive?" She laughed uneasily, watching the back of his head with frightened eyes. "But, of course, you can't violate the security rules, can you? You can't tell me anything about it at all. . . ."

219

He shrugged, turning around. "There'll be a newscast at six o'clock. In ten minutes. Wherever there's a radio or television set on Earth, everybody will hear what we found out in that interview. Perhaps not quite everything, but almost everything."

"Oh?" she said in a surprised, small voice. She looked at him in silence for a moment, her eyes growing more frightened. "Why would they do a thing like that?"

"Well," said the professor, "it seemed like the right thing to do. The best thing, at any rate. There may be some panic, of course." He turned back to the window and gazed out on the street, as if something there were holding his attention. He looked thoughtful and abstracted, she decided. But then a better word came to her, and it was "resigned."

"Clive," she said, almost desperately, "what happened?"

He frowned absently at her and walked to the radio. It began to make faint, humming noises as the professor adjusted dials unhurriedly. The humming didn't vary much.

"They've cleared the networks, I imagine," he remarked.

The sentence went on repeating itself in his wife's mind, with no particular significance at first. But then a meaning came into it and grew and swelled swiftly, until she felt her head would burst with it. They've cleared the networks. All over the world this evening, they've cleared the networks. Until the newscast comes on at six o'clock . . .

"As to what happened," she heard her husband's voice saying, "that's a little difficult to understand or explain. Even now. It was certainly amazing—" He interrupted himself. "Do you remember Milt Caldwell, dear?"

"Milt Caldwell?" She searched her mind blankly. "No," she said, shaking her head.

"A rather well-known anthropologist," the Professor informed her, with an air of faint reproach. "Milt got himself lost in the approximate center of the Australian deserts some two years ago. Only we have been told he didn't get lost. They picked him up—"

"*They?*" she said. "You mean there's more than one?"

"Well, there would be more than one, wouldn't there?" he asked reasonably. "That explains, at any rate, how they learned to speak English. It made it seem a little more reasonable, anyhow," he added, "when it told us that. Seven minutes to six . . ."

"What?" she said faintly.

"Seven minutes to six," the Professor repeated. "Sit down, dear. I believe I can tell you, in seven minutes, approximately what occurred. . . ."

The Visitor from Outside sat in its cage, its large gray hands slackly clasping the bars. Its attitudes and motions, the professor had noted in the two minutes since he had entered the room with the other men, approximated those of a rather heavily built ape. Reporters had called it "the Toad from Mars," on the basis of the first descriptions they'd had of it—the flabby shape and loose, warty skin made that a vaguely adequate identification. The round, horny head almost could have been that of a lizard.

With a zoologist's fascination in a completely new genus, the professor catalogued these contradicting physical details in his mind. Yet something somewhat like this might have been evolved on Earth, if Earth had chosen to let the big amphibians of its Carboniferous Period go on evolving.

That this creature used human speech was the only almost-impossible feature.

It had spoken as they came in. "What do you wish to know?" it asked. The horny, toothed jaws moved, and a broad yellow tongue became momentarily visible, forming the words. It was a throaty, deliberate "human" voice.

For a period of several seconds, the human beings seemed to be shocked into silence by it, though they had known the creature had this ability. Hesitantly, then, the questioning began.

The professor remained near the back of the room, watching. For a while, the questions and replies he heard seemed to carry no meaning to him. Abruptly he realized that his thoughts were fogged over with a heavy, cold, physical dread of this alien animal. He told himself that under such circumstances fear was not an entirely irrational emotion, and his understanding of it seemed to lighten its effects a little.

But the scene remained unreal to him, like a badly lit stage on which the creature in its glittering steel cage stood out in sharp focus, while the humans were shadow-shapes stirring restlessly against a darkened background.

"This won't do!" he addressed himself, almost querulously, through the fear. "I'm here to observe, to conclude, to report—I was selected as a man they could trust to think and act rationally!"

He turned his attention deliberately away from the cage and what it contained, and he directed it on the other human beings, to most of whom he had been introduced only a few minutes before. A young, alert-looking Intelligence major, who was in some way in charge of this investigation; a sleepy-eyed general; a very pretty Wac captain acting as stenographer, whom the major had introduced as his fiancée. The handful of other scientists looked for the most part like brisk business executives, while the two Important Personages representing the government looked like elderly professors.

He almost smiled. They were real enough. This was a human world. He returned his attention again to the solitary intruder in it.

"Why shouldn't I object?" the impossible voice was saying with a note of lazy good humor. "You've caged me like—a wild animal! And you haven't even informed me of the nature of the charges against me. Trespassing, perhaps—eh?"

The wide mouth seemed to grin as the Thing turned its head, looking them over one by one with bright black eyes. The grin was meaningless; it was the way the lipless jaws set when the mouth was closed. But it gave expression to the pleased malice the professor sensed in the voice and words.

The voice simply did not go with that squat animal shape.

Fear surged up in him again. He found himself shaking.

If it looks at me now, he realized in sudden panic, I might start to scream!

One of the men nearest the cage was saying something in low, even tones. The Wac captain flipped over a page of her shorthand pad and went on writing, her blonde head tilted to one side. She was a little pale, but intent on her work. He had a moment of bitter envy for their courage and self-control. But they're insensitive, he tried to tell himself; they don't know Nature and the laws of Nature. They can't feel as I do how *wrong* all this is!

Then the black eyes swung around and looked at him.
Instantly, his mind stretched taut with blank, wordless terror. He did not move, but afterward he knew he did not
faint only because he would have looked ridiculous before
the others, and particularly in the presence of a young woman. He heard the young Intelligence officer speaking sharply;
the eyes left him unhurriedly, and it was all over.

"You indicate," the creature's voice was addressing the
major, "that you can force me to reveal matters I do not
choose to reveal at this time. However, you are mistaken.
For one thing, a body of this type does not react to any of
your drugs."

"It will react to pain!" the major said, his voice thin and
angry.

Amazed by the words, the professor realized for the first
time that he was not the only one in whom this being's presence had aroused primitive, irrational fears. The other men
had stirred restlessly at the major's threat, but they made no
protest.

The Thing remained silent for a moment, looking at the
major.

"This body will react to pain," it said then, "only when I
choose to let it feel pain. Some of you here know the effectiveness of hypnotic blocks against pain. My methods are not
those of hypnosis, but they are considerably more effective.
I repeat, then, that for me there is no pain, unless I choose
to experience it."

"Do you choose to experience the destruction of your
body's tissues?" the major inquired, a little shrilly.

The Wac captain looked up at him quickly from the chair
where she sat, but the professor could not see her expression.
Nobody else moved.

The Thing, still staring at the major, almost shrugged.

"And do you choose to experience death?" the major
cried, his face flushed with excitement.

In a flash of insight, the Professor understood why no one
was interfering. Each in his own way, they had felt what
he was feeling: that here was something so outrageously
strange and new that no amount of experience, no rank,
could guide a human being in determining how to deal with

it. The major was dealing with it—in however awkward a fashion. With no other solution to offer, they were, for the moment, unable or unwilling to stop him.

The Thing then said slowly and flatly, "Death is an experience I shall never have at your hands. That is a warning. I shall respond to no more of your threats. I shall answer no more questions.

"Instead, I shall tell you what will occur now. I shall inform my companions that you are as we judged you to be—foolish, limited, incapable of harming the least of us. Your world and civilization are of very moderate interest. But they are a novelty which many will wish to view for themselves. We shall come here and leave here, as we please. If you attempt to interfere again with any of us, it will be to your own regret."

"Will it?" the major shouted, shaking. "Will it now?"

The professor jerked violently at the quick successive reports of a gun in the young officer's hand. Then there was a struggling knot of figures around the major, and another man's voice was shouting hoarsely, "You fool! You damned hysterical fool!"

The Wac captain had dropped her notebook and clasped her hands to her face. For an instant, the professor heard her crying, "Jack! Jack! Stop—don't—"

But he was looking at the thing that had fallen on its back in the cage, with the top of its skull shot away and a dark-brown liquid staining the cage floor about its shoulders.

What he felt was an irrational satisfaction, a warm glow of pride in the major's action. It was as if he had killed the Thing himself.

For that moment, he was happy.

Because he stood far back in the room, he saw what happened then before the others did.

One of the Personages and two of the scientists were moving excitedly about the cage, staring down at the Thing. The others had grouped around the chair into which they had forced the major. Under the babble of confused, angry voices, he could sense the undercurrent of almost joyful relief he felt himself.

The Wac captain stood up and began to take off her clothes.

She did it quickly and quietly. It was at this moment, the professor thought, staring at her in renewed terror, that the height of insanity appeared to have been achieved in this room. He wished fervently that he could keep that sense of insanity wrapped around him forevermore, like a protective cloak. It was a terrible thing to be rational! With oddly detached curiosity, he also wondered what would happen in a few seconds when the others discovered what he already knew.

The babbling voices of the group that had overpowered the major went suddenly still. The three men at the cage turned startled faces toward the stillness. The girl straightened up and stood smiling at them.

The major began screaming her name.

There was another brief struggling confusion about the chair in which they were holding him. The screaming grew muffled as if somebody had clapped a hand over his mouth.

"I warned you," the professor heard the girl say clearly, "that there was no death. Not for us."

Somebody shouted something at her, like a despairing question. Rigid with fear, his own blood a swirling roar in his ears, the professor did not understand the words. But he understood her reply.

"It could have been any of you, of course," she nodded. "But I just happened to like *this* body."

After that, there was one more shot.

The professor turned off the radio. For a time, he continued to gaze out the window.

"Well, they know it now!" he said. "The world knows it now. Whether they believe it or not—At any rate . . ." His voice trailed off. The living room had darkened and he had a notion to switch on the lights, but decided against it. The evening gloom provided an illusion of security.

He looked down at the pale oval of his wife's face, almost featureless in the shadows.

"It won't be too bad," he explained, "if not too many of them come. Of course, we don't know how many there are of them, actually. Billions, perhaps. But if none of our people try to make trouble—the aliens simply don't want any trouble."

He paused a moment. The death of the young Intelligence major had not been mentioned in the broadcast. Considering the issues involved, it was not, of course, a very important event and officially would be recorded as a suicide. In actual fact, the major had succeeded in wresting a gun from one of the men holding him. Another man had shot him promptly without waiting to see what he intended to do with it.

At all costs now, every rational human being must try to prevent trouble with the Visitors from Outside.

He felt his face twitch suddenly into an uncontrollable grimace of horror.

"But there's no way of being absolutely sure, of course," he heard his voice tell the silently gathering night about him, "that they won't decide they just happen to like *our* kind of bodies."

Built Down Logically

Howard Schoenfeld

Hillburt Hooper Aspasia sat in his baby buggy in a lecture hall at Harvard University where he was scheduled to deliver an address at commencement exercises. Seated in front of him were several thousand students. They whispered excitedly as they wondered what topic the young genius had chosen for his talk.

Hooper, leaning forward in his buggy, raised his hand for silence.

"I will discuss the origin of human intelligence today," Hooper said. "Does heredity determine the intelligence of human beings, or does environment? Or do both play a part in the development of this highly overrated phenomenon?

"My contention is that intelligence is the result of the type of food we receive at a given time. My own case history proves it. I've become the world's most brilliant baby by living on a diet of crib slats and turnips."

Hooper paused. In the back of the hall two students fell to discussing Hooper's point.

"If what he says is true, then neither heredity nor environment plays a part in developing human intelligence," said one student.

"That's right," said the other.

It was natural for these two young men to overlook the point that diet is a part of environment as both were honor students, held Phi Beta Kappa keys, had been awarded all available scholastic honors, were considered brilliant by their professors and fellow classmates, and were recognized everywhere as the finest types our educational system has produced.

"If neither heredity nor environment plays a part in developing intelligence, then what we've been taught is false," said the first student.

"But what we've been taught is true because it's based on facts," said the second student.

"True," said the first student. "So what Hooper says must be false."

"If what Hooper says is false then he hasn't become the world's most brilliant baby by living on a diet of crib slats and turnips, and he can't possibly be a Ph.D. at the age of two, delivering a lecture to an audience of college students from his baby buggy."

"That's true if what he says is false."

"And what he says is definitely false. We've already decided that."

"Right."

"Then Hooper isn't there. It's contrary to the rules of logic for him to be, to exist in the future, or to have ever been; hence, he just isn't," said the first student, with conviction.

No sooner had he uttered these words than Hooper disappeared. His body became opaque, then transparent. Then there was a puff of smoke, and he was gone, the fact of his existence wiped out by the logical thinking of the two students.

Ten years later the two students whose logic had been responsible for Hooper's disappearance were sitting in a train on their way to Washington, D. C. Both were now eminent scientists whose contributions to humanity had fulfilled in every respect the great expectations of their university.

One had worked on the Manhattan Project devoting his time and energies to the development of the atom bomb. The other was the discoverer of a deadly new strain of bacteria with which it will be possible to wipe out the entire population of the earth in ten seconds flat.

Both had received the Congressional Medal of Honor seventeen times, all existing army awards, a twenty-gun salute from the U. S. Navy, an honorary membership in the National Association of Manufacturers, over a dozen Presidential citations, and recognition everywhere as great humanitarians.

"You know what?" said the first humanitarian.

"No," said the second humanitarian. "What?"

"We made a mistake about young Hooper."

"How come?"

"He said he had become the world's most brilliant baby by living on a diet of crib slats and turnips."

"That's right."

"Diet is a part of environment."

"I see what you mean. What he said didn't conflict with what we were taught after all."

"So what he said was true."

"And if what he said was true, then he must still be alive."

"Right."

"That's logic."

"Hooper is alive then. It's contrary to the rules of logic for him not to be, not to have been, or not to be in the future; hence, he just is," said the two humanitarian scientists, with conviction.

No sooner had they uttered these words than Hooper materialized out of thin air. There was a huff and a puff, and a flash of lightning, and there he was, sitting in his baby buggy in the aisle of the train, as substantial as he ever had been.

"Gentlemen," he said, shaking his teething ring in their faces, "hereafter, don't leap to hasty conclusions."

But he knew they would.

An Egg a Month from All Over

Idris Seabright

When the collector from Consolidated Eggs found the mnxx bird egg on the edge of the cliff, he picked it up unsuspiciously. A molded mnxx bird egg looks almost exactly like the chu lizard eggs the collector was hunting, and this egg bore no visible sign of the treatment it had received at the hands of Jreel just before Krink's hatchet men caught up with him. The collector was paid by the egg; everything that came along was grist to his mill. He put the molded mnxx bird egg in his bag.

George Lidders lived alone in a cabin in the desert outside Phoenix. The cabin had only one room, but at least a third of the available space was taken up by an enormous incubator. George was a charter member of the Egg-of-the-Month Club, and he never refused one of their selections. He loved hatching eggs.

George had come to Phoenix originally with his mother for her health. He had taken care of her faithfully until her death, and now that she was gone, he missed her terribly. He had never spoken three consecutive words to any woman except her in his life. His fantasies, when he was base enough to have any, were pretty unpleasant. He was forty-six.

On Thursday morning he walked into Phoenix for his mail. As he scuffled over the sand toward the post office substation, he was hoping there would be a package for him from the Egg-of-the-Month Club. He was feeling tired, tired and depressed. He had been sleeping badly, with lots of nightmares. A nice egg package would cheer him up.

The South American mail rocket, cleaving the sky overhead, distracted him momentarily. If he had enough money, would he travel? Mars, Venus, star-side? No, he didn't think so. Travel wasn't really interesting. Eggs. . . . Eggs (but the thought was a little frightening), eggs were the only thing he had to go on living for.

The postmistress greeted him unsmilingly. "Package for you, Mr. Lidders. From the egg club. You got to brush for it." She handed him a slip.

George brushed, his hand shaking with excitement. This must be his lucky morning. It might even be a double selection; the package seemed unusually big. His lips began to lift at the corners. With a nod in place of thanks, he took the parcel from the postmistress, and went out, clutching it.

The woman looked after him disapprovingly. "I want you to stay away from that gesell, Fanny," she said to her eleven-year-old daughter, who was reading a postcard in the back of the cubicle. "There's something funny about him and his eggs."

"Oksey-snoksey, mums, if you say so. But lots of people hatch eggs."

The postmistress sniffed. "Not the way he hatches eggs," she said prophetically.

On the way home George tore the wrapper from the box. He couldn't wait any longer. He pulled back the flaps eagerly.

Inside the careful packing there was a large, an unusually large, pale blue-green egg. Its surface stood up in tiny bosses, instead of being smooth as eggs usually were, and the shell gave the impression of being more than ordinarily thick. According to the instructions with the parcel, it was a chu lizard egg from the planet Morx, a little-known satellite of Amorgos. It was to be incubated at a temperature of 76.3 C. with high humidity. It would hatch in about eight days.

George felt the surface of the egg lovingly. If only Mother were here to see it! She had always been interested in his egg hatching; it was the only thing he had ever wanted to do that she had really approved of. And this was an unusually interesting egg.

When he got home he went straight to the incubator. Tenderly he laid the *soi-disant* chu lizard egg in one of the compartments; carefully he adjusted the temperature control. Then he sat down on the black and red afghan on his cot (his mother had crocheted the coverlet for him just before she passed away), and once more read the brochure that had come with the egg.

When he had finished it, he sighed. It was too bad there weren't any other eggs in the incubator now, eggs that were on the verge of hatching. Eight days was a long time to wait. But this egg looked wonderfully promising; he didn't know when the club had sent out an egg that attracted him so. And from one point of view it was a good thing he hadn't any hatchings on hand. Hatching, for all its excitement, was a sort of ordeal. It always left him feeling nervously exhausted and weak.

He had lunch, and after lunch, lying under the red and black afghan, he had a little nap. When he woke it was late afternoon. He went over to the incubator and looked in. The egg hadn't changed. He hadn't expected it would.

His nap hadn't cheered or refreshed him. He was almost more tired than he had been when he lay down to sleep. Sighing, he went around to the other side of the incubator and stared at the cage where he kept the things he had hatched out. After a moment he took his eyes away. They weren't interesting, really—lizards and birds and an attractive small snake or two. He wasn't interested in the things that were in eggs after they had hatched out.

In the evening he read a couple of chapters in the *Popular Guide to Egg Hatchery*.

He woke early the next morning, his heart hammering. He'd had another of those nightmares. But—his mind wincingly explored the texture of the dream—but it hadn't been all nightmare. There'd been a definitely pleasurable element in it, and the pleasure had been somehow connected with the egg that had come yesterday. Funny. (Jreel, who had molded the mnxx bird egg from its original cuboid into the present normal ovoid shape, wouldn't have found it funny at all.) It was funny about dreams.

He got grapes from the cupboard and made *café à la crème* on the hotplate. He breakfasted. After breakfast he looked at his new egg.

The temperature and humidity were well up. It was about time for him to give the egg a quarter of a turn, as the hatching instruction booklet suggested. He reached in the compartment, and was surprised to find it full of a dry, brisk, agreeable warmth. It seemed to be coming from the egg.

How odd! He stood rubbing the sprouting whiskers on his upper lip. After a moment he tapped the two gauges. No, the needles weren't stuck; they wobbled normally. He went around to the side of the incubator and checked the connections. Everything was sound and tight, nothing unusual. He must have imagined the dry warmth. Rather apprehensively, he put his hand back in the compartment—he still hadn't turned the egg—and was relieved to find the air in it properly humid. Yes, he must have imagined it.

After lunch he cleaned the cabin and did little chores. Abruptly, when he was half through drying the lunch dishes, the black depression that had threatened him ever since Mother died swallowed him up. It was like a physical blackness; he put down the dish undried and groped his way over to a chair. For a while he sat almost unmoving, his hands laced over his little stomach, while he sank deeper and deeper into despair. Mother was gone; he was forty-six; he had nothing to live for, not a thing. . . . He escaped from the depression at last, with a final enormous guilty effort, into one of his more unpleasant fantasies. The imago within the molded mnxx bird egg, still plastic within its limey shell, felt the strain and responded to it with an inaudible grunt.

On the third day of the hatching, the egg began to enlarge. George hung over the incubator, fascinated. He had seen eggs change during incubation before, of course. Sometimes the shells got dry and chalky; sometimes they were hygroscopic and picked up moisture from the air. But he had never seen an egg act like this one. It seemed to be swelling up like an inflating balloon.

He reached in the compartment and touched the egg light-

ly. The shell, that had been so limey and thick when he first
got it, was now warm and yielding and gelatinous. There was
something uncanny about it. Involuntarily, George rubbed
his fingers on his trouser leg.

He went back to the incubator at half-hour intervals.
Every time it seemed to him that the egg was a little bigger
than it had been. It was wonderfully interesting; he had never
seen such a fascinating egg.

He got out the hatching instructions booklet and studied
it. No, there was nothing said about changes in shell surface
during incubation, and nothing about the egg's incredible in-
crease in size. And the booklets were usually careful about
mentioning such things. The directors of the Egg-of-the-
Month Club didn't want their subscribers to overlook anything interesting that would happen during the incubation
days. They wanted you to get your money's worth.

There must be some mistake. George, booklet in hand,
stared at the incubator doubtfully. Perhaps the egg had been
sent him by mistake; perhaps he hadn't been meant to have
it. (He was right in both these suppositions: Jreel had meant
the egg for Krink, as a little gift.) Perhaps he ought to get
rid of the egg. An unauthorized egg might be dangerous.

Hesitantly he raised the incubator lid. It would be a shame,
but—yes, he'd throw the egg out. Anything, anything at all
might be inside an egg. There was no sense in taking chances.
He approached his hand. The imago, dimly aware that it was
at a crucial point in its affairs, exerted itself.

George's hand halted a few inches from the egg. He had
broken into a copious sweat, and his forearm was one large
cramp. Why, he must have been crazy. He didn't want—he
couldn't possibly want to—get rid of the egg. What had been
the matter with him? He perceived very clearly now what he
thought he must have sensed dimly all along: that there was
a wonderful promise in the egg.

A promise of what? Of—he couldn't be sure—but of
warmth, of sleep, of rest. A promise of something he'd been
wanting all his life. He couldn't be any more specific than
that. But if what he thought might be in the egg was actually
there, it wouldn't matter any more that Mother was dead and

that he was forty-six and lonely. He'd—he gulped and sighed deeply—he'd be happy. Satisfied.

The egg kept on enlarging, though more slowly, until late that evening. Then it stopped.

George was in a froth of nervous excitement. In the course of watching the egg's slow growth, he had chewed his finger-nails until three of them were down to the quick and ready to bleed. Still keeping his eyes fixed on the egg, he went to the dresser, got a nail file, and began to file his nails. The operation soothed him. By midnight, when it became clear that nothing more was going to happen immediately, he was calm enough to go to bed. He had no dreams.

The fourth and fifth days passed without incident. On the sixth day George perceived that though the egg was of the same size, its shell had hardened and become once more opaque. And on the eighth day—to this extent the molded mnxx bird egg was true to the schedule laid down in the booklet for the chu lizard—the egg began to crack.

George felt a rapturous excitement. He hovered over the incubator breathlessly, his hands clutching the air and water conduits for support. As the tiny fissure enlarged, he kept gasping and licking his lips. He was too agitated to be capable of coherent thought, but it occurred to him that what he really expected to come out of the egg was a bird of some sort, some wonderful, wonderful bird.

The faint pecking from within the egg grew louder. The dark fissure on the pale blue-green background widened and spread. The halves of the shell fell back suddenly, like the halves of a door. The egg was open. There was nothing inside.

Nothing. Nothing. For a moment George felt that he had gone mad. He rubbed his eyes and trembled. Disappointment and incredulity were sickening him. He picked up the empty shell.

It was light and chalky and faintly warm to the touch. He felt inside it unbelievingly. There was nothing there.

His frustration was stifling. For a moment he thought of crumpling up newspapers and setting the cabin on fire. Then he put the halves of the shell down on the dresser and went wobblingly toward the door. He'd—go for a walk.

The mnxx bird imago, left alone within the cabin, flitted about busily.

The moon had risen when George got back. In the course of his miserable wanderings, he had stopped on a slight rise and shed a few salty tears. Now he was feeling, if not better, somewhat more resigned. His earlier hopes, his later disappointment, had been succeeded by a settled hopelessness.

The mnxx bird was waiting behind the door of the cabin for him.

In its flittings in the cabin during his absence, it had managed to assemble for itself a passable body. It had used newspapers, grapes, and black wool from the afghan as materials. What it had made was short and squat and excessively female, not at all alluring, but it thought George would like it. It held the nail file from the dresser in its one completed hand.

George shut the cabin door behind him. His arm moved toward the light switch. He halted, transfixed by the greatest of the surprises of the day. He saw before him, glimmering wanly in the moonlight from the window, the woman of his—let's be charitable—dreams.

She was great-breasted, thighed like an idol. Her face was only a blur; there the mnxx bird had not felt it necessary to be specific. But she moved toward George with a heavy sensual swaying; she was what George had always wanted and been ashamed of wanting. She was here. He had no questions. She was his. Desire was making him drunk. He put out his hands.

The newspaper surface, so different from what he had been expecting, startled him. He uttered a surprised cry. The mnxx bird saw no reason for waiting any longer. George was caressing one grape-tipped breast uncertainly. The mnxx raised its right arm, the one that was complete, and drove the nail file into his throat.

The mnxx bird was amazed at the amount of blood in its victim. Jreel, when he had been molding the imago with his death wishes for Krink, had said nothing about this. The inhabitants of the planet Morx do not have much blood.

After a momentary disconcertment, the mnxx went on with its business. It had, after all, done what it had been molded to do. Now there awaited it a more personal task.

It let the woman's body it had shaped collapse behind it carelessly. The newspapers made a whuffing sound. In a kind of rapture it threw itself on George. His eyes would be admirable for mnxx bird eyes, it could use his skin, his hair, his teeth. Admirable material! Trembling invisibly with the joy of creation, the mnxx bird set to work.

When it had finished, George lay on the sodden carpet flaccidly. His eyes were gone, and a lot of his vital organs. Things were over for him. He had had, if not all he wanted, all he was ever going to get. He was quiet. He was dead. He was satisfied.

The mnxx bird, on the fine strong wings it had plaited for itself out of George's head hair, floated out into the night.

The Perfect Woman

Robert Sheckley

Mr. Morcheck awoke with a sour taste in his mouth and a laugh ringing in his ears. It was George Owen-Clark's laugh, the last thing he remembered from the Triad-Morgan party. And what a party it had been! All Earth had been celebrating the turn of the century. The year Three Thousand! Peace and prosperity to all, and happy life. . . .

"How happy is your life?" Owen-Clark had asked, grinning slyly, more than a little drunk. "I mean, how is life with your sweet wife?"

That had been unpleasant. Everyone knew that Owen-Clark was a Primitivist, but what right had he to rub people's noses in it? Just because he had married a Primitive Woman. . . .

"I love my wife," Morcheck had said stoutly. "And she's a hell of a lot nicer and more responsive than that bundle of neuroses you call *your* wife."

But of course, you can't get under the thick hide of a Primitivist. Primitivists love the faults in their women as much as their virtues—more, perhaps. Owen-Clark had grinned ever more slyly, and said, "You know, Morcheck old man, I think your wife needs a checkup. Have you noticed her reflexes lately?"

Insufferable idiot! Mr. Morcheck eased himself out of bed, blinking at the bright morning sun which hid behind his curtains. Myra's reflexes—the hell of it was, there was a germ of truth in what Owen-Clark had said. Of late, Myra had seemed rather—out of sorts.

"Myra!" Morcheck called. "Is my coffee ready?" There was a pause. Then her voice floated brightly upstairs. "In a minute!"

Morcheck slid into a pair of slacks, still blinking sleepily. Thank Stat the next three days were celebration-points. He'd need all of them just to get over last night's party.

Downstairs, Myra was bustling around, pouring coffee, folding napkins, pulling out his chair for him. He sat down, and she kissed him on his bald spot. He liked being kissed on his bald spot.

"How's my little wife this morning?" he asked.

"Wonderful, darling," she said after a little pause. "I made Seffiners for you this morning. You like Seffiners."

Morcheck bit into one, done to a turn, and sipped his coffee.

"How do you feel this morning?" he asked her.

Myra buttered a piece of toast for him, then said, "Wonderful, darling. You know, it was a perfectly wonderful party last night. I loved every moment of it."

"I got a little bit veery," Morcheck said with a wry grin.

"I love you when you're veery," Myra said. "You talk like an angel—like a very clever angel, I mean. I could listen to you forever." She buttered another piece of toast for him.

Mr. Morcheck beamed on her like a benignant sun, then frowned. He put down his Seffiner and scratched his cheek. "You know," he said, "I had a little ruck-in with Owen-Clark. He was talking about Primitive Women."

Myra buttered a fifth piece of toast for him without answering, adding it to the growing pile. She started to reach for a sixth, but he touched her hand lightly. She bent forward and kissed him on the nose.

"Primitive Women!" she scoffed. "Those neurotic creatures! Aren't you happier with me, dear? I may be Modern—but no Primitive Woman could love you the way I do—and I adore you!"

What she said was true. Man had never, in all recorded

history, been able to live happily with unreconstructed Primitive Woman. The egoistic, spoiled creatures demanded a lifetime of care and attention. It was notorious that Owen-Clark's wife made him dry the dishes. And the fool put up with it! Primitive Women were forever asking for money with which to buy clothes and trinkets, demanding breakfast in bed, dashing off to bridge games, talking for hours on the telephone, and Stat knows what else. They tried to take over men's jobs. Ultimately, they proved their equality.

Some idiots like Owen-Clark insisted on their excellence.

Under his wife's enveloping love, Mr. Morcheck felt his hangover seep slowly away. Myra wasn't eating. He knew that she had eaten earlier, so that she could give her full attention to feeding him. It was little things like that that made all the difference.

"He said your reaction time had slowed down."

"He did?" Myra asked, after a pause. "Those Primitives think they know everything."

It was the right answer, but it had taken too long. Mr. Morcheck asked his wife a few more questions, observing her reaction time by the second hand on the kitchen clock. She *was* slowing up!

"Did the mail come?" he asked her quickly. "Did anyone call? Will I be late for work?"

After three seconds she opened her mouth, then closed it again. Something was terribly wrong.

"I love you," she said simply.

Mr. Morcheck felt his heart pound against his ribs. He loved her! Madly, passionately! But that disgusting Owen-Clark had been right. She needed a checkup. Myra seemed to sense his thought. She rallied perceptibly, and said, "All I want is your happiness, dear. I think I'm sick. . . . Will you have me cured? Will you take me back after I'm cured—and not let them change me—I wouldn't want to be changed!" Her bright head sank on her arms. She cried—noiselessly, so as not to disturb him.

"It'll just be a checkup, darling," Morcheck said, trying to hold back his own tears. But he knew—as well as she knew—that she was really sick.

It was so unfair, he thought. Primitive Woman, with her

coarse mental fiber, was almost immune to such ailments. But delicate Modern Woman, with her finely balanced sensibilities, was all too prone. So monstrously unfair! Because Modern Woman contained all the finest, dearest qualities of femininity.

Except stamina.

Myra rallied again. She raised herself to her feet with an effort. She was very beautiful. Her sickness had put a high color in her cheeks, and the morning sun highlighted her hair.

"My darling," she said. "Won't you let me stay a little longer? I may recover by myself." But her eyes were fast becoming unfocused.

"Darling . . ." She caught herself quickly, holding on to an edge of the table. "When you have a new wife—try to remember how much I loved you." She sat down, her face blank.

"I'll get the car," Morcheck murmured, and hurried away. Any longer and he would have broken down himself.

Walking to the garage he felt numb, tired, broken. Myra—gone! And modern science, for all its great achievements, unable to help.

He reached the garage and said, "All right, back out." Smoothly his car backed out and stopped beside him.

"Anything wrong, boss?" his car asked. "You look worried. Still got a hangover?"

"No—it's Myra. She's sick."

The car was silent for a moment. Then it said softly, "I'm very sorry, Mr. Morcheck. I wish there were something I could do."

"Thank you," Morcheck said, glad to have a friend at this hour. "I'm afraid there's nothing anyone can do."

The car backed to the door and Morcheck helped Myra inside. Gently the car started.

It maintained a delicate silence on the way back to the factory.

The Hunters

Walt Sheldon

The spaceship lay in the valley, just as reported. Lon and Jeni could see it from the ridge.

Lon finally said, "We'll keep going. We'll go further into the hills. Chara Canyon—there's a stream there."

"And when they reach Chara?"

Lon turned slowly. Her eyes were unblown tinder, smoking, not yet aflame. They wouldn't flame. That was her way, the woman's way, quiet and patient and always there behind him, following where he led. She was his wife. She had followed from the shining city when the bombs from space began to fall and the great black columns of smoke were monuments in the sky. She had skinned her hands helping with the cabin logs, washing clothes in the stream; she had bloodied them butchering game.

They were not alone. There were others who had fled to the great mountains, the spine of the continent, but they were scattered among the slopes and canyons, and stayed close to their cabins and mudhuts and caves.

"When they reach Chara—" Lon shrugged.

"I know, I know. I shouldn't have said that. It's too big to think about."

He thought: When it's this big the mind doesn't accept. You keep on doing whatever you were doing.

A twinkle of light down the slope caught his eye. It was

242

only a few hundred yards below. His eyes darted in that direction, and he squinted and saw the figures moving up toward them. The light had been a reflection—the sun catching one of their strange weapons.

"Come on, Jeni!"

"To the cabin?"

"No, no. We'll have to leave the cabin—they'll discover it in a day or so. Chara Canyon—"

They started north. He glanced back once more at the thing in the valley, there on the dry plain. It was longer than a city block, projectile shaped, mirror bright. It was about what he had expected: the radio reports in the past month had been full of descriptions of the others. One by one the radio reports had stopped, as the cities had fallen.

They kept to the ridge, but stayed within the tree shadows. It was cooler in the shadows. They did not run, but walked with long strides.

By looking left Lon could catch shuttered glimpses of the sky and the big round valley that stretched away to the west. He could still see the hunters once in a while, coming diagonally up the slope, as if to cut them off. Faintly, at times, he could hear their throaty voices.

At the north end of the ridge Lon and Jeni headed downslope. The mouth of Chara Canyon, a break in the mountains to their right, was only a mile or so ahead. They heard the report of a weapon, releasing echoes that tumbled all through the hills. The report came from the ridge top behind them, and they knew the hunters were following.

At the bottom of the slope they came to a dry stream bed. Lon jumped across, then held out his hand for Jeni. She missed. She fell, twisting her ankle.

"Oh, Lon!"

"You've got to keep going, darling—you've got to keep going!"

"Yes. I know."

He helped her along, with his hand around her waist. He saw how she kept the pain from showing. She quirked her lips in a funny way each time her injured foot touched ground, and kept her face rigid otherwise.

244 FIFTY SHORT SCIENCE FICTION TALES

He stared at that face with his usual quiet wonder. Her features were still small and delicate; still fine porcelain. There was that same compassion about her, after everything that had happened. He remembered what she had said nearly a year ago when the invading things first came out of the sky. Aircraft had lanced upward to meet them, firing . . . several of the things had been destroyed. Lon and Jeni had seen one explode over the city. It made a great orange ball in the air, and the ball grew and turned over and over, and smoke curled around it like shriveled skin. Jeni said: "Those poor things, those poor creatures in there. . . ."

And then they had fled. They were luckier than most. Lon had worked for an aircraft plant and owned a small plane. They flew west, flying at night so the shining projectiles wouldn't find them; they begged and stole fuel and sometimes, Lon swore, they conjured it up. They crashed upon landing in the mountains, and had used parts of the plane to start their cabin.

Another shot sounded, and this time it was terribly near. He dared to turn his head. The hunters were halfway down the shoulder of the ridge. They gestured and called to each other.

"In here!" He led Jeni into a grove of white-barked trees. Jeni's lips were tight, but a whimper forced its way through.

He held her more tightly, lifting. His heart stuttered violently. His legs ached. Jeni—fragile Jeni—was heavy.

He stumbled, and she fell with him. They lay there, at the roots of a white-barked tree, in each other's arms, and they looked into each other's eyes and knew they couldn't go on.

They heard the shouting voices.

She said, "I don't feel anything. Funny. I'm not angry or afraid or anything."

They clung to each other suddenly. He ran his lips along her cheeks and hair and he wiped the tears from her cheek with his own and he murmured things without really hearing them.

"I'm glad we're together," said Jeni.

They heard the breaking of the underbrush.

Abruptly, he stood. He faced the approaching sounds and

made fists at his sides. His eyes were wild. "Damn you! Damn you! Damn you!" he cried.

"It's their way," said Jeni. "They're hunters. It's their way." There was no anger in her voice.

A creature emerged from the white-barked trees. He stood there and stared at Lon, and stared at Jeni upon the ground. He seemed a little frightened himself. He lifted his weapon.

Lon stared back, taking in every strange detail. It was his first close look at one of these invaders from the planet called Earth, which was third from the Sun and had one Moon.

He waited for the noise of the weapon, wondering if he would hear it.

The Martian and the Magician

Evelyn E. Smith

Ever since childhood I had grown accustomed to being followed by Things wherever I went. I was never lonely. There was always a reptilian *zok* from Mars, who changed progressively into a more and more fearsome variety of monster as I grew familiar with the initial horror. I was never harmed, since the *zokk* had to throw so much energy into projecting themselves from Mars (or *Zokk*, as the natives called it) that they had none left with which to execute any malevolent projects.

Naturally the *zokk* do not follow just anyone about. Twenty years before, my father, a small-time sorcerer, had gone on one of the rare expeditions to Mars—rare because the *zokk* consider human beings a table delicacy, which makes Earthmen take rather a dim view of the journey. Dad was so miffed when the *zZik* or emperor of the *zokk* ate Dad's best friend that he retaliated by eating the *zZik's* infant son.

How he managed to do this and yet get back I never found out. Actually, Dad never was more than a second-rate wizard at best. But the publicity he got for his feat enabled him to make quite a good thing of a small shop dealing in jokes, spells, and love potions that he subsequently opened in the Times Square neighborhood—where business is brisk in that line of goods.

Sorcery, the history books say, used to be called science up until the latter part of the Twentieth Century. Then the FBI discovered an atomic scientist muttering over his work in what they took to be Russian. He was immediately brought before an investigating committee, soon broke down and confessed that he hadn't been speaking Russian at all but chanting a spell to make his atom bomb work.

It turned out that all the scientists had been doing the same thing, making a lot of hoopla about inventing stuff—atom bombs, jet planes, television—when actually they did it all with witchcraft. Seems all the magicians had gone underground since the Age of Enlightenment and had been passing off their feats as science—except for a few unreconstructed gypsies.

The first reaction of the populace was, as usual, to burn the wizards. However, a smart politician, and one of the best sorcerers we ever had, pointed out that without witchcraft modern technology would disappear. "Where would your movies, your refrigerators, your hot and cold running water be?" he asked—because, of course, all those things are done by magic.

In the next election, running on the Third or Sorcerers' Party ticket, he made mincemeat out of the Republicans and Democrats and was elected president. Enemies whispered that he had bewitched the voting machines, but that wasn't true; he'd won fair and square through mass hypnosis.

Things proceeded apace after sorcerers could come out into the open. We reached the inhabitants of other planets and some of them unfortunately reached us . . . but that's another story. The only ones Earthmen couldn't handle in the long run, though, were the *zokk*. They could look at you and just say, without any charms or signs or anything, "Drop dead" and you'd drop dead, no matter how many protective spells you were under. They couldn't project their powers effectively through space—a lucky thing for Dad and me because, although ordinarily they didn't put themselves out for mere Earthmen, they sure had it in for us Bennetts.

This brings us to my twenty-first birthday. I was having the usual argument with Dad. "Son," he said, "I want to make you a full partner in the shop. You know I'm not a well man—my heart isn't good—and I want to be sure that when I'm gone you'll be provided for."

"Hell, Dad," I told him, "I don't want to go in for small-time stuff. I want to leave the Solar System, project myself out into the Galaxy."

He shook his gray head. "Wiser men than you have tried, Bob, and failed. And they used ships powered by hundreds and hundreds of poltergeists. You couldn't even begin to afford a dozen."

"Poltergeist power!" I sneered. "I want to get there by thought projection, like the *zokk*." The *zokk* could reach outer space easily enough but, being awful snobs, they rarely bothered.

"No, no, Bob, you mustn't try that!" Dad pulled his beard in agitation. "Earthmen can't manage thought projection and most of those who've tried have gone mad. It does something to our brain cells. Promise me you'll give up your experiments."

"Nonsense, Dad. Look, I can thought-project a little even now." I sent his *Kabala* zooming across the room. I was pretty proud of myself, because up to then I hadn't been able to levitate anything bigger than a pocket edition.

He got all excited—jealous, I thought. "You muttered a spell under your breath!"

"I did not either," I said, hurt.

"Sorry, son." He calmed down. "It must have been your subconscious muttering the spell. What you ought to do is see a good psychiatrist. People say Dr. McCrindle is one of the best witch doctors."

That's always the way when you discover something new; everybody thinks you're crazy. Still, no use arguing with Dad—if my theories bore fruit I would be doing him and thousands like him out of their livelihood.

I got up. "Well, I can't sit around talking any longer. Got a date with the prettiest girl on Broadway." And, smoothing down my hair with a few drops of our highest-priced love potion, I was off to meet Linda.

I whistled for my Thing as I left the shop—that always annoyed them—but no *zok* appeared. Come to think of it, I hadn't seen one around for some time; but I knew that every now and then the one currently assigned to me would go off on a bender. Poor things, they didn't ordinarily get much chance to travel. The zZik didn't like to let his subjects pick up any democratic foolishness from visiting foreign parts.

I was just as happy, because when I was with Linda three was definitely a crowd—even if the third was a scaly man-eating lizard. She was waiting for me inside the little bistro we always patronized, and she was looking as beautiful as ever.

"Hello, Bob," she greeted me, "you don't seem very happy. Anything wrong?"

"Not really." We sat down at our usual table. "Dad wants me to become a full partner in the shop, but I feel I'm not the type to spend the rest of my life behind a counter."

"You're right, Bob. You're meant for something better."

I told her my plans to thought-project a ship beyond the Solar System. I even showed her. "Look!" and I lifted the cruet stand six feet above the table. Only one vinegar bottle fell off.

The proprietor came over. "Listen, magic man, any more funny business and out you go on your ear."

I got home a little after midnight, went through the darkened shop to our little apartment in the back. Dad wasn't in the living room. Tom, our black cat, sat in Dad's easy chair. "Where's Dad, Tom?" I asked.

Of course Tom couldn't answer; he could only meow. He wouldn't be able to speak until his sentence was up, which would be another eight years. The authorities had turned him into a cat for sorcery with intention to defraud.

But he led the way into the bedroom and there was Dad lying on the bed, gasping. His face was a funny color.

"I'll get a doctor!" I yelled.

He shook his head weakly. "No use, Bob. I know I'm dying. But, before I go, there's something I must tell you, something you must know. . . ."

"Yes, Dad?"

"Bob, you're . . . you're not . . ." With a horrible gurgle, he fell back against the pillows. He'd died without finishing whatever it was he was trying to say.

Well, there I was, stuck with the shop. I could sell it to finance my experiments, but I knew well enough that's just what Dad wouldn't have wanted me to do. I couldn't make up my mind what the next step should be.

I was sitting in the shop one afternoon a couple of days after the funeral, waiting for Linda to bring some sandwich fixings for a picnic lunch, when a steely-eyed character breezed in, flashing a badge.

"Bob Bennett?" I admitted my identity. "I'm from the FBI, investigating *zokk* activity. I understand you're being followed by Things."

"Haven't seen 'em for weeks," I told him. "Besides, I'm used to them; they don't bother me." I wished he would go away. I was getting hungry.

"Perhaps you'll be interested to know," he said, "that they've developed full-power projection."

This put another face on things. As long as the *zokk* just hovered about trying to scare me, that was okay, but if they now had the power to injure me . . . "What precautions would you suggest I take?" I asked.

"Put yourself under our protection. We'll form a cordon around you at all times. Even a *zok* would hesitate to attack fifty or sixty of us, charmed to the teeth."

"Supposing it takes another shape," I pointed out. "Then how'll you know what it is? It might even pretend to be one of your men."

"That's easy. Because we've developed a *zokk*-finder." He showed me a small boxlike gadget. "See this? Whenever I come within a hundred yards of a suspected *zok*, I press this button. If it is a *zok*, the dial flashes purple."

He pressed the button to show me. Just then Linda walked in the door, carrying a large paper bag. The dial flashed purple.

I laughed myself sick. "And this is government efficiency!" I howled. "That's one hell of a *zokk*-finder!"

The FBI man's face was pale. "It works all right, Bennett. This is a *zok*."

"Nonsense!" I told him angrily. "This is my girl and she isn't a *zok*."

"Very well," he retorted, just as mad as I was, "I'll prove to you that she's a *zok!* I'll recite a spell for turning things into their proper forms."

He took out a piece of chalk and made appropriate symbols on the floor, muttering to himself meanwhile. I watched attentively. Government spells were generally classified top secret and I certainly would be able to use this one in my business if it worked.

It worked all right. Tom—and I must say he was a lot better-looking as a cat—streaked past us in human shape yelling, "Me for the straight and narrow, fellows," as he charged out the door.

Then I looked at Linda. Her face was covered with green scales; she now had four arms instead of two and double the number of red claws. Her three eyes flashed purple. Yet, to me she looked more beautiful than ever.

But the FBI man wasn't paying any attention to her. He was staring at me in horror. I looked down. My pin-stripe had slid down to disclose a set of green scales. I had two sets of arms. I could see in four dimensions. In short, I was a *zok*, too.

I looked at Linda, enlightenment dawning. "Then I'm . . . ?"

"Yes, your highness. The sorcerer who kidnaped you changed you into human form instead of eating you. *Zokk* are poisonous to the human system, as even a *yuj* would know. With typical cheap human sentimentality, Bennett raised you as his own son. You are, of course, Prince *zZuk*, heir apparent to the throne of *Zokk*. We've been trying to get you back for years, but only recently have we developed our thought-projection far enough to get sufficient power to take you. We were afraid you might not return voluntarily."

I . . . a *zok* . . . a Martian . . . a prince. The Galaxy lay open before me. "I'll go back voluntarily," I murmured, taking her four little hands in mine, "on one condition—that you'll be my wife and rule *Zokk* with me . . . when *zZik* passes on, of course," I added quickly. "Which won't be too long," I thought.

Three pairs of eyelashes swept her exquisitely scabrous emerald cheeks. "I am yours, *zZuk*," she whispered.

"But what'll we do with this fellow from the FBI?" I

wanted to know. "Can't release him until we get away."

"Dearest," she said apologetically, "in my anxiety to be with you I brought bread but forgot to get anything to put inside the sandwiches."

"Can you cook?" I asked her.

She drew herself up haughtily. "Of course you do not know, your highness, that the prime criterion of true femininity in *Zokk* is the ability to cook."

"Well, sweetheart," I said, "what are we waiting for?"

Barney

Will Stanton

August 30th. We are alone on the island now, Barney and I.
It was something of a jolt to have to sack Tayloe after all
these years, but I had no alternative. The petty vandalisms
I could have forgiven, but when he tried to poison Barney
out of simple malice, he was standing in the way of scientific
progress. That I cannot condone.

I can only believe the attempt was made while under the
influence of alcohol, it was so clumsy. The poison container
was overturned and a trail of powder led to Barney's dish.
Tayloe's defense was of the flimsiest. He denied it. Who else
then?

September 2nd. I am taking a calmer view of the Tayloe
affair. The monastic life here must have become too much for
him. That, and the abandonment of his precious guinea pigs.
He insisted to the last that they were better suited than
Barney to my experiments. They were more his speed, I'm
afraid. He was an earnest and willing worker, but something
of a clod, poor fellow.

At last I have complete freedom to carry on my work
without the mute reproaches of Tayloe. I can only ascribe
his violent antagonism toward Barney to jealousy. And now
that he has gone, how much happier Barney appears to be!
I have given him complete run of the place, and what sport

it is to observe how his newly awakened intellectual curiosity carries him about. After only two weeks of glutamic acid treatments, he has become interested in my library, dragging the books from the shelves, and going over them page by page. I am certain he knows there is some knowledge to be gained from them had he but the key.

September 8th. For the past two days I have had to keep Barney confined and how he hates it. I am afraid that when my experiments are completed I shall have to do away with Barney. Ridiculous as it may sound there is still the possibility that he might be able to communicate his intelligence to others of his kind. However small the chance may be, the risk is too great to ignore. Fortunately there is, in the basement, a vault built with the idea of keeping vermin out and it will serve equally well to keep Barney in.

September 9th. Apparently I have spoken too soon. This morning I let him out to frisk around a bit before commencing a new series of tests. After a quick survey of the room he returned to his cage, sprang up on the door handle, removed the key with his teeth, and before I could stop him, he was out the window. By the time I reached the yard I spied him on the coping of the well, and I arrived on the spot only in time to hear the key splash into the water below.

I own I am somewhat embarrassed. It is the only key. The door is locked. Some valuable papers are in separate compartments inside the vault. Fortunately, although the well is over forty feet deep, there are only a few feet of water in the bottom, so the retrieving of the key does not present an insurmountable obstacle. But I must admit Barney has won the first round.

September 10th. I have had a rather shaking experience, and once more in a minor clash with Barney I have come off second best. In this instance I will admit he played the hero's role and may even have saved my life.

In order to facilitate my descent into the well I knotted a length of three-quarter-inch rope at one-foot intervals to make a rude ladder. I reached the bottom easily enough, but

after only a few minutes of groping for the key, my flashlight gave out and I returned to the surface. A few feet from
the top I heard excited squeaks from Barney, and upon obtaining ground level I observed that the rope was almost completely severed. Apparently it had chafed against the edge of
the masonry and the little fellow perceiving my plight had
been doing his utmost to warn me.

I have now replaced that section of rope and arranged
some old sacking beneath it to prevent a recurrence of the
accident. I have replenished the batteries in my flashlight and
am now prepared for the final descent. These few moments
I have taken off to give myself a breathing spell and to bring
my journal up to date. Perhaps I should fix myself a sandwich as I may be down there longer than seems likely at the
moment.

September 11th. Poor Barney is dead an soon I shell be
the same. He was a wonderful ratt and life without him is
knot worth livving. If anybody reeds this please do not disturb anything on the island but leeve it like it is as a shryn to
Barney, espechilly the old well. Do not look for my body as
I will caste myself into the see. You mite bring a couple of
young ratts an leeve them as a living memorial to Barney.
Females—no males. I sprayned my wrist is why this is written
so bad. This is my laste will. Do what I say an don't come
back or disturb anything after you bring the young ratts like
I said. Just females.

Goodby

Talent

Theodore Sturgeon

Mrs. Brent and Precious were sitting on the farmhouse porch when little Jokey sidled out from behind the barn and came catfooting up to them. Precious, who had ringlets and was seven years old and very clean, stopped swinging on the glider and watched him. Mrs. Brent was reading a magazine. Jokey stopped at the foot of the steps.

"MOM!" he rasped.

Mrs. Brent started violently, rocked too far back, bumped her knobby hairdo against the clapboards, and said, "Good heavens, you little br—darling, you frightened me!"

Jokey smiled.

Precious said, "Snaggletooth."

"If you want your mother," said Mrs. Brent reasonably, "why don't you go inside and speak to her?"

Disgustedly, Jokey vetoed the suggestion with "Ah-h-h. . . ." He faced the house. "MOM!" he shrieked, in a tone that spoke of death and disaster.

There was a crash from the kitchen, and light footsteps. Jokey's mother, whose name was Mrs. Purney, came out, pushing back a wisp of hair from frightened eyes.

"Oh, the sweet," she cooed. She flew out and fell on her knees beside Jokey. "Did it hurt its little, then? Aw, did it was . . ."

Jokey said, "Gimme a nickel!"

"Please," suggested Precious.

"Of course, darling," fluttered Mrs. Purney. "My word, yes. Just as soon as ever we go into town, you shall have a nickel. Two, if you're good."

"Gimme a nickel," said Jokey ominously.

"But, darling, what for? What will you do with a nickel out here?"

Jokey thrust out his hand. "I'll hold my breath."

Mrs. Purney rose, panicked. "Oh, dear, don't. Oh, please don't. Where's my reticule?"

"On top of the bookcase, out of my reach," said Precious, without rancor.

"Oh, yes, so it is. Now, Jokey, you wait right here and I'll just . . ." and her twittering faded into the house.

Mrs. Brent cast her eyes upward and said nothing.

"You're a little stinker," said Precious.

Jokey looked at her with dignity. "Mom," he called imperiously.

Mrs. Purney came to heel on the instant, bearing a nickel.

Jokey, pointing with the same movement with which he acquired the coin, reported, "She called me a little stinker."

"Really!" breathed Mrs. Purney, bridling. "I think, Mrs. Brent, that your child could have better manners."

"She has, Mrs. Purney, and uses them when they seem called for."

Mrs. Purney looked at her curiously, decided, apparently, that Mrs. Brent meant nothing by the statement (in which she was wrong) and turned to her son, who was walking briskly back to the barn.

"Don't hurt yourself, Puddles," she called.

She elicited no response whatever and, smiling vaguely at Mrs. Brent and daughter, went back to her kitchen.

"Puddles," said Precious ruminatively. "I bet I know why she calls him that. Remember Gladys' puppy that—"

"Precious," said Mrs. Brent, "you shouldn't have called Joachim a word like that."

"I s'pose not," Precious agreed thoughtfully. "He's really a—"

Mrs. Brent, watching the carven pink lips, said warningly,

"Precious!" She shook her head. "I've asked you not to say that."

"Daddy—"

"Daddy caught his thumb in the hinge of the car trunk. That was different."

"Oh, no," corrected Precious. "You're thinking of the time he opened on'y the bottom half of the Dutch door in the dark. When he pinched his thumb, he said—"

"Would you like to see my magazine?"

Precious rose and stretched delicately. "No, thank you, Mummy. I'm going out to the barn to see what Jokey's going to do with that nickel."

"Precious . . ."

"Yes, Mummy,"

"Oh—nothing. I suppose it's all right. Don't quarrel with Jokey, now."

"Not 'less he quarrels with me," she replied, smiling charmingly.

Precious had new patent-leather shoes with hard heels and broad ankle straps. They looked neat and very shiny against her yellow socks. She walked carefully in the path, avoiding the moist grasses that nodded over the edges, stepping sedately over a small muddy patch.

Jokey was not in the barn. Precious walked through, smelling with pleasure the mixed, warm smells of chaff dust, dry hay, and manure. Just outside, by the wagon-door, was the pigpen. Jokey was standing by the rail fence. At his feet was a small pile of green apples. He picked one up and hurled it with all his might at the brown sow. It went *putt!* on her withers, and she went *ergh!*

"Hey!" said Precious.

Putt-ergh! Then he looked up at Precious, snarled silently, and picked up another apple. *Putt-ergh!*

"What are you doing that for?"

Putt-ergh!

"Hear that? My mom done just like that when I hit her in the stummick."

"She did?"

"Now this," said Jokey, holding up an apple, "is a stone. Listen." He hurled it. *Thunk-e-e-e-ergh!*

Precious was impressed. Her eyes widened, and she stepped back a pace.

"Hey, look out where you're goin', stoopid!"

He ran to her and grasped her left biceps roughly, throwing her up against the railings. She yelped and stood rubbing her arm—rubbing off grime, and far deeper in indignation than she was in fright.

Jokey paid her no attention. "You an' your shiny feet," he growled. He was down on one knee, feeling for two twigs stuck in the ground about eight inches apart. "Y'might've squashed 'em!"

Precious, her attention brought to her new shoes, stood turning one of them, glancing light from the toecaps, from the burnished sides, while complacency flowed back into her.

"What?"

With the sticks, Jokey scratched aside the loose earth and, one by one, uncovered the five tiny, naked, blind creatures which lay buried there. They were only about three-quarters of an inch long, with little withered limbs and twitching noses. They writhed. There were ants, too. Very busy ants.

"What are they?"

"Mice, stoopid," said Jokey. "Baby mice. I found 'em in the barn."

"How did they get there?"

"I put 'em there."

"How long have they been there?"

" 'Bout four days," said Jokey, covering them up again. "They last a long time."

"Does your mother know those mice are out here?"

"No, and you better not say nothin', ya hear?"

"Would your mother whip you?"

"*Her?*" The syllable came out as an incredulous jeer.

"What about your father?"

"Aw, I guess he'd like to lick me. But he ain't got a chance. Mom'd have a fit."

"You mean she'd get mad at him?"

"No, stoopid. A fit. You know, scrabbles at the air and

get suds on her mouth, and all. Falls down and twitches."
He chuckled.

"But—why?"

"Well, it's about the on'y way she can handle Pop, I guess.
He's always wanting to do something about me. She won't let
'um, so I c'n do anything I want."

"What do you do?"

"I'm talunted. Mom says so."

"Well, what do you do?"

"You're sorta nosy."

"I don't believe you can do anything, stinky."

"Oh, I can't?" Jokey's face was reddening.

"No, you can't! You talk a lot, but you can't really do anything."

Jokey walked up close to her and breathed in her face the
way the man with the grizzly beard does to the clean-cut
cowboy who is tied up to the dynamite kegs in the movies on
Saturday.

"I can't, huh?"

She stood her ground. "All right, if you're so smart, let's
see what you were going to do with that nickel!"

Surprisingly, he looked abashed. "You'd laugh," he said.

"No, I wouldn't," she said guilelessly. She stepped forward,
opened her eyes very wide, shook her head so that her gold
ringlets swayed, and said very gently, "Truly I wouldn't, Jokey. . . ."

"Well—" he said, and turned to the pigpen. The brindled
sow was rubbing her shoulder against the railing, grunting
softly to herself. She vouchsafed them one small red-rimmed
glance and returned to her thoughts.

Jokey and Precious stood up on the lower rail and looked
down on the pig's broad back.

"You're not goin' to tell anybody?" he asked.

"'Course not."

"Well, awright. Now lookit. You ever see a china piggy
bank?"

"Sure I have," said Precious.

"How big?"

"Well, I got one about this big."

"Aw, that's nothin'."

"And my girl-friend Gladys has one *this* big."

"Phooey."

"Well," said Precious, "in town, in a big drugstore, I saw one THIS big," and she put out her hands about thirty inches apart.

"That's pretty big," admitted Jokey. "Now I'll show you *something*." To the brindled sow, he said sternly, "You are a piggy bank."

The sow stopped rubbing herself against the rails. She stood quite still. Her bristles merged into her hide. She was hard and shiny—as shiny as the little girl's hard shoes. In the middle of the broad back, a slot appeared—or had been there all along, as far as Precious could tell. Jokey produced a warm sweaty nickel and dropped it into the slot.

There was a distant, vitreous, hollow bouncing click from inside the sow.

Mrs. Purney came out on the porch and creaked into a wicker chair with a tired sigh.

"They are a handful, aren't they?" said Mrs. Brent.

"You just don't know," moaned Mrs. Purney.

Mrs. Brent's eyebrows went up. "Precious is a model. Her teacher says so. That wasn't too easy to do."

"Yes, she's a very good little girl. But my Joachim is—uh, talented, you know. That makes it very hard."

"How is he talented? What can he do?"

"He can do anything," said Mrs. Purney after a slight hesitation.

Mrs. Brent glanced at her, saw that her tired eyes were closed, and shrugged. It made her feel better. Why must mothers always insist that their children are better than all others?

"Now, my Precious," she said, "—and mind you, I'm not saying this because she's my child—my Precious plays the piano very well for a child her age. Why, she's already in her third book and she's not eight yet."

Mrs. Purney said, without opening her eyes, "Jokey doesn't play. I'm sure he could if he wanted to."

Mrs. Brent saw what an inclusive boast this might be, and wisely refrained from further itemization. She took another tack. "Don't you find, Mrs. Purney, that it is easy to make a child obedient and polite by being firm?"

Mrs. Purney opened her eyes at last, and looked troubledly at Mrs. Brent. "A child should love its parents."

"Oh, of course!" smiled Mrs. Brent. "But these modern ideas of surrounding a child with love and freedom to an extent where it becomes a little tyrant—well! I just can't see that! Of course I don't mean Joachim," she added quickly, sweetly. "He's a *dear* child, really. . . ."

"He's got to be given everything he wants," murmured Mrs. Purney in a strange tone. It was fierce and it was by rote. "He's *got* to be kept happy."

"You must love him very much," snapped Mrs. Brent viciously, suddenly determined to get some reaction out of this weak, indulgent creature. She got it.

"I hate him," said Mrs. Purney.

Her eyes were closed again, and now she almost smiled, as if the release of those words had been a yearned-for thing. Then she sat abruptly erect, her pale eyes round, and she grasped her lower lip and pulled it absurdly down and to the side.

"I didn't mean that," she gasped. She flung herself down before Mrs. Brent, and gabbled, "I didn't mean it! Don't tell him! He'll do things to us. He'll loosen the house beams when we're sleeping. He'll turn the breakfast to snakes and frogs, and make that big toothy mouth again out of the oven door. Don't tell him! Don't tell him!"

Mrs. Brent, profoundly shocked, and not comprehending a word of this, instinctively put out her arms and gathered the other woman close.

"I can do lots of things," Jokey said. "I can do anything."

"Gee," breathed Precious, looking at the china pig. "What are you going to do with it now?"

"I dunno. I'll let it be a pig again, I guess."

"Can you change it back into a pig?"

"I don't hafta, stoopid. It'll be a pig by itself. Soon's I forget about it."

"Does that always happen?"

"No. If I busted that ol' china pig, it'd take longer, an' the pig would be all busted up when it changed back. All guts and blood," he added, sniggering. "I done that with a calf once."

"Gee," said Precious, still wide-eyed. "When you grow up, you'll be able to do anything you want."

"Yeah." Jokey looked pleased. "But I can do anything I want now." He frowned. "I just sometimes don't know what to do next."

"You'll know when you grow up," she said confidently.

"Oh, sure. I'll live in a big house in town, and look out of the windows, and bust up people and change 'em to ducks and snakes and things. I'll make flies as big as chicken hawks, or maybe as big as horses, and put 'em in the schools. I'll knock down the big buildings an' squash people."

He picked up a green apple and hurled it accurately at the brown sow.

"Gosh, and you won't have to practice piano, or listen to any old teachers," said Precious, warming to the possibilities. "Why, you won't even have to—*oh!*"

"What'sa matter?"

"That beetle. I hate them."

"Thass just a stag beetle," said Jokey with superiority. "Lookit here. I'll show you something."

He took out a book of matches and struck one. He held the beetle down with a dirty forefinger, and put the flame to its head. Precious watched attentively until the creature stopped scrabbling.

"Those things scare me," she said when he stood up.

"You're a sissy."

"I am not."

"Yes you are. *All* girls are sissies."

"You're dirty and you're a stinker," said Precious.

He promptly went to the pigpen and, from beside the trough, scooped up a heavy handful of filth. From his crouch, Jokey hurled it at her with a wide overhand sweep, so that it splattered her from the shoulder down, across the front of her dress, with a great wet gob for the toe of her left shiny shoe.

"Now who's dirty? Now who stinks?" he sang.

Precious lifted her skirt and looked at it in horror and loathing. Her eyes filled with angry tears. Sobbing, she rushed at him. She slapped him with little-girl clumsiness, hand-over-shoulder fashion. She slapped him again.

"Hey! Who are you hitting?" he cried in amazement. He backed off and suddenly grinned. "I'll fix you," he said, and disappeared without another word.

Whimpering with fury and revulsion, Precious pulled a handful of grass and began wiping her shoe.

Something moved into her field of vision. She glanced at it, squealed, and moved back. It was an enormous stag beetle, three times life-size, and it was scuttling toward her.

Another beetle—or the same one—met her at the corner.

With her hard black shiny shoes, she stepped on this one, so hard that the calf of her leg ached and tingled for the next half-hour.

The men were back when she returned to the house. Mr. Brent had been surveying Mr. Purney's fence-lines. Jokey was not missed before they left. Mrs. Purney looked drawn and frightened, and seemed glad that Mrs. Brent was leaving before Jokey came in for his supper.

Precious said nothing when asked about the dirt on her dress, and, under the circumstances, Mrs. Brent thought better of questioning her too closely.

In the car, Mrs. Brent told her husband that she thought Jokey was driving Mrs. Purney crazy.

It was her turn to be driven very nearly mad, the next morning, when Jokey turned up. Most of him.

Surprising, really, how much beetle had stuck to the hard black shoe, and, when it was time, turned into what they found under their daughter's bed.

Project Hush

William Tenn

I guess I'm just a stickler, a perfectionist, but if you do a thing, I always say, you might as well do it right. Everything satisfied me about the security measures on our assignment except one—the official Army designation.

Project Hush.

I don't know who thought it up, and I certainly would never ask, but whoever it was, he should have known better. Damn it, when you want a project kept secret, you *don't* give it a designation like that! You give it something neutral, some name like the Manhattan and Overlord they used in World War II, which won't excite anybody's curiosity.

But we were stuck with Project Hush and we had to take extra measures to ensure secrecy. A couple of times a week, everyone on the project had to report to Psycho for DD & HA—dream detailing and hypnoanalysis—instead of the usual monthly visit. Naturally, the commanding general of the heavily fortified research post to which we were attached could not ask what we were doing, under penalty of court-martial, but he had to be given further instructions to shut off his imagination like a faucet every time he heard an explosion. Some idiot in Washington was actually going to list Project Hush in the military budget by name! It took fast action, I can tell you, to have it entered under Miscellaneous "X" Research.

Well, we'd covered the unforgivable blunder, though not easily, and now we could get down to the real business of the project. You know, of course, about the A-bomb, H-bomb, and C-bomb because information that they existed had been declassified. You don't know about the other weapons being devised—and neither did we, reasonably enough, since they weren't our business—but we had been given properly guarded notification that they were in the works. Project Hush was set up to counter the new weapons.

Our goal was not just to reach the Moon. We had done that on June 24, 1967 with an unmanned ship that carried instruments to report back data on soil, temperature, cosmic rays and so on. Unfortunately, it was put out of commission by a rock slide.

An unmanned rocket would be useless against the new weapons. We had to get to the Moon before any other country did and set up a permanent station—an armed one—and do it without anybody else knowing about it.

I guess you see now why we on (*damn* the name!) Project Hush were so concerned about security. But we felt pretty sure, before we took off, that we had plugged every possible leak.

We had, all right. Nobody even knew we had raised ship.

We landed at the northern tip of Mare Nubium, just off Regiomontanus, and, after planting a flag with appropriate throat-catching ceremony, had swung into the realities of the tasks we had practiced on so many dry runs back on Earth.

Major Monroe Gridley prepared the big rocket, with its tiny cubicle of living space, for the return journey to Earth which he alone would make.

Lieutenant-colonel Thomas Hawthorne painstakingly examined our provisions and portable quarters for any damage that might have been incurred in landing.

And I, Colonel Benjamin Rice, first commanding officer of Army Base No. 1 on the Moon, dragged crate after enormous crate out of the ship on my aching academic back and piled them in the spot two hundred feet away where the plastic dome would be built.

We all finished at just about the same time, as per schedule, and went into Phase Two.

Monroe and I started work on building the dome. It was a simple prefab affair, but big enough to require an awful lot of assembling. Then, after it was built, we faced the real problem—getting all the complex internal machinery in place and in operating order.

Meanwhile, Tom Hawthorne took his plump self off in the single-seater rocket which, up to then, had doubled as a life-boat.

The schedule called for him to make a rough three-hour scouting survey in an ever-widening spiral from our dome. This had been regarded as a probable waste of time, rocket fuel, and manpower—but a necessary precaution. He was supposed to watch for such things as bug-eyed monsters out for a stroll on the Lunar landscape. Basically, however, Tom's survey was intended to supply extra geological and astronomical meat for the report which Monroe was to carry back to Army Headquarters on Earth.

Tom was back in forty minutes. His round face, inside its transparent bubble helmet, was fish-belly white. And so were ours, once he told us what he'd seen.

He had seen another dome.

"The other side of Mare Nubium—in the Riphaen Mountains," he babbled excitely. "It's a little bigger than ours, and it's a little flatter on top. And it's not translucent, either, with splotches of different colors here and there—it's a dull, dark, heavy gray. But that's all there is to see."

"No markings on the dome?" I asked worriedly. "No signs of anyone—or anything—around it?"

"Neither, Colonel." I noticed he was calling me by my rank for the first time since the trip started, which meant he was saying in effect, "Man, have *you* got a decision to make!"

"Hey, Tom," Monroe put in. "Couldn't be just a regularly shaped bump in the ground, could it?"

"I'm a geologist, Monroe. I can distinguish artificial from natural topography. Besides—" he looked up—"I just remembered something I left out. There's a brand-new tiny crater near the dome—the kind usually left by a rocket exhaust."

"Rocket exhaust?" I seized on that. "*Rockets,* eh?"

Tom grinned a little sympathetically. "Spaceship exhaust, I should have said. You can't tell from the crater what kind of propulsive device these characters are using. It's not the same kind of crater our rear-jets leave, if that helps any."

Of course it didn't. So we went into our ship and had a council of war. And I do mean war. Both Tom and Monroe were calling me Colonel in every other sentence. I used their first names every chance I got.

Still, no one but me could reach a decision. About what to do, I mean.

"Look," I said at last, "here are the possibilities. They know we are here—either from watching us land a couple of hours ago or from observing Tom's scoutship—or they do not know we are here. They are either humans from Earth—in which case they are in all probability enemy nationals—or they are alien creatures from another planet—in which case they may be friends, enemies or what-have-you. I think common sense and standard military procedure demand that we consider them hostile until we have evidence to the contrary. Meanwhile, we proceed with extreme caution, so as not to precipitate an interplanetary war with potentially friendly Martians, or whatever they are.

"All right. It's vitally important that Army Headquarters be informed of this immediately. But since Moon-to-Earth radio is still on the drawing boards, the only way we can get through is to send Monroe back with the ship. If we do, we run the risk of having our garrison force, Tom and me, captured while he's making the return trip. In that case, their side winds up in possession of important information concerning our personnel and equipment, while our side has only the bare knowledge that somebody or something else has a base on the Moon. So our primary need is more information.

"Therefore, I suggest that I sit in the dome on one end of a telephone hookup with Tom, who will sit in the ship, his hand over the firing button, ready to blast off for Earth the moment he gets the order from me. Monroe will take the single-seater down to the Riphaen Mountains, landing as close to the other dome as he thinks safe. He will then proceed the rest of the way on foot, doing the best scouting job he can in a spacesuit.

"He will not use his radio, except for agreed-upon non-sense syllables to designate landing the single-seater, coming upon the dome by foot, and warning me to tell Tom to take off. If he's captured, remembering that the first purpose of a scout is acquiring and transmitting knowledge of the enemy, he will snap his suit radio on full volume and pass on as much data as time and the enemy's reflexes permit. How does that sound to you?"

They both nodded. As far as they were concerned, the command decision had been made. But I was sitting under two inches of sweat.

"One question," Tom said. "Why did you pick Monroe for the scout?"

"I was afraid you'd ask that," I told him. "We're three extremely unathletic Ph.D's who have been in the Army since we finished our schooling. There isn't too much choice. But I remembered that Monroe is half Indian—Arapahoe, isn't it, Monroe?—and I'm hoping blood will tell."

"Only trouble, Colonel," Monroe said slowly as he rose, "is that I'm one-*fourth* Indian and even that . . . Didn't I ever tell you that my great-grandfather was the only Arapahoe scout who was with Custer at the Little Big Horn? He'd been positive Sitting Bull was miles away. However, I'll do my best. And if I heroically don't come back, would you please persuade the Security Officer of our section to clear my name for use in the history books? Under the circumstances, I think it's the least he could do."

I promised to do my best, of course.

After he took off, I sat in the dome over the telephone connection to Tom and hated myself for picking Monroe to do the job. But I'd have hated myself just as much for picking Tom. And if anything happened and I had to tell Tom to blast off, I'd probably be sitting here in the dome all by myself after that, waiting . . .

"*Broz neggle!*" came over the radio in Monroe's resonant voice. He had landed the single-seater.

I didn't dare use the telephone to chat with Tom in the

ship, for fear I might miss an important word or phrase from our scout. So I sat and sat and strained my ears. After a while, I heard *"Mishgashu!"* which told me that Monroe was in the neighborhood of the other dome and was creeping toward it under cover of whatever boulders were around.

And then, abruptly, I heard Monroe yell my name and there was a terrific clattering in my headphones. Radio interference! He'd been caught, and whoever had caught him had simultaneously jammed his suit transmitter with a larger transmitter from the alien dome.

Then there was silence.

After a while, I told Tom what had happened. He just said, "Poor Monroe." I had a good idea of what his expression was like.

"Look, Tom," I said, "if you take off now, you still won't have anything important to tell. After capturing Monroe, whatever's in that other dome will come looking for us, I think. I'll let them get close enough for us to learn something of their appearance—at least if they're human or nonhuman. Any bit of information about them is important. I'll shout it up to you and you'll still be able to take off in plenty of time. All right?"

"You're the boss, Colonel," he said in a mournful voice. "Lots of luck."

And then there was nothing to do but wait. There was no oxygen system in the dome yet, so I had to squeeze up a sandwich from the food compartment in my suit. I sat there, thinking about the expedition. Nine years, and all that careful secrecy, all that expenditure of money and mind-cracking research—and it had come to this. Waiting to be wiped out, in a blast from some unimaginable weapon. I understood Monroe's last request. We often felt we were so secret that our immediate superiors didn't even want *us* to know what we were working on. Scientists are people—they wish for recognition, too. I was hoping the whole expedition would be written up in the history books, but it looked unpromising.

Two hours later, the scout ship landed near the dome. The lock opened and, from where I stood in the open door of our dome, I saw Monroe come out and walk toward me.

I alerted Tom and told him to listen carefully. "It may be a trick—he might be drugged. . . ."

He didn't act drugged, though—not exactly. He pushed his way past me and sat down on a box to one side of the dome. He put his booted feet up on another, smaller box.

"How are you, Ben?" he asked. "How's every little thing?"

I grunted. "*Well?*" I know my voice skittered a bit.

He pretended puzzlement. "Well *what?* Oh, I see what you mean. The other dome—you want to know who's in it. You have a right to be curious, Ben. Certainly. The leader of a top-secret expedition like this—Project Hush they call us, huh, Ben—finds another dome on the Moon. He thinks he's been the first to land on it, so naturally he wants to—"

"Major Monroe Gridley!" I rapped out. "You will come to attention and deliver your report. Now!" Honestly, I felt my neck swelling up inside my helmet.

Monroe just leaned back against the side of the dome. "That's the *Army* way of doing things," he commented admiringly. "Like the recruits say, there's a right way, a wrong way and an Army way. Only there are other ways, too." He chuckled. "Lots of other ways."

"He's off," I heard Tom whisper over the telephone. "Ben, Monroe has gone and blown his stack."

"They aren't extraterrestrials in the other dome, Ben," Monroe volunteered in a sudden burst of sanity. "No, they're human, all right, and from Earth. Guess *where.*"

"I'll kill you," I warned him. "I swear I'll kill you, Monroe. Where are they from—Russia, China, Argentina?"

He grimaced. "What's so secret about those places? Go on!—guess again."

I stared at him long and hard. "The only place else—"

"Sure," he said. "You got it, Colonel. The other dome is owned and operated by the Navy. The goddam United States Navy!"

The Great Judge

A. E. Van Vogt

"Judgment," said the rad, "in the case of Douglas Aird, tried for treason on August 2nd, last—"

With a trembling movement of his fingers, Aird turned the volume control higher. The next words blared at him:

"—That Douglas Aird do surrender himself one week from this day, that is, on September 17, 2460 A.D. to his neighborhood patrol station, that he then be taken to the nearest converter, there to be put to death—"

Click!

He had no conscious memory of shutting off the rad. One instant the sound roared through his apartment, the next there was dead silence. Aird sank back in his chair and stared with sick eyes through the transparent walls out upon the shining roofs of The Judge's City. All these weeks he had known there was no chance. The scientific achievements that, he had tried to tell himself, would weigh the balance in his favor—even as he assessed their value to the race, he had realized that the Great Judge would not consider them from the same viewpoint as himself.

He had made the fatal error of suggesting in the presence of "friends" that a mere man like Douglas Aird could govern as well as the immortal Great Judge, and that in fact it might be a good idea if someone less remote from the needs of the mass of the people have a chance to promulgate de-

272

crees. A little less restriction, he had urged, and a little more individuality. With such abandon he had spoken on the day that he succeeded in transferring the nervous impulses of a chicken into the nervous system of a dog.

He had attempted to introduce the discovery as evidence that he was in an excited and abnormal state of mind. But the magistrate pronounced the reason irrelevant, immaterial and facetious. He refused to hear what the discovery was, ruling coldly:

"The official science investigator of the Great Judge will call on you in due course, and you will then turn your invention over to him complete with adequate documentation."

Aird presumed gloomily that the investigator would call in a day or so. He toyed with the possibility of destroying his papers and instruments. Shudderingly, he rejected that form of defiance. The Great Judge's control of life was so complete that he permitted his enemies to remain at large until the day of their execution. It was a point made much of by the Great Judge's propaganda department. Civilization, it was said, had never before attained so high a level of freedom. But it wouldn't do to try the patience of the Great Judge by destroying an invention. Aird had a sharp conviction that less civilized methods might be used on him if he failed to carry through the farce.

Sitting there in his apartment, surrounded by every modern convenience, Aird sighed. He would spend his last week alive in any luxury he might choose. It was the final refinement of mental torture, to be free, to have the feeling that if only he could think of something he might succeed in escaping. Yet he knew escape was impossible. If he climbed into his hopjet, he'd have to swoop in at the nearest patrol station, and have his electronic registration "plates" stamped with a signal. Thereafter, his machine would continuously give off vibrations automatically advising patrol vessels of the time and space limitations of his permit.

Similar restrictions controlled his person. The electronic instrument "printed" on his upper right arm could be activated by any central, which would start a burning sensation of gradually increasing intensity.

There was absolutely no escape from the law of the Great Judge.

Aird climbed to his feet wearily. Might as well get his material ready for the science investigator. It was too bad he wouldn't have an opportunity to experiment with higher life forms but—

Aird stopped short in the doorway of his laboratory. His body throbbed with the tremendousness of the idea that had slammed into his mind. He began to quiver. He leaned weakly against the door jamb, then slowly straightened.

"*That's it!*" He spoke the words aloud, his voice low and intense, simultaneously utterly incredulous and hopeful to the point of madness. It was the mounting hope that brought a return of terrible weakness. He collapsed on the rug just inside the laboratory, and lay there muttering to himself, the special insanities of an electronician:

". . . have to get a larger grid, and more liquid and—"

Special Science Investigator George Mollins returned to the Great Judge's Court and immediately asked for a private interview with the Great Judge.

"Tell him," he told the High Bailiff of the Court, "that I have come across a very important scientific discovery. He will know what is meant if you simply say 'Category AA.' "

While he waited to be received, the Science Investigator arranged his instruments for readier transport, and then he stood idly looking around him at the dome-vaulted anteroom. Through a transparent wall, he could see the gardens below. In the profusion of greenery, he caught the glint of a white skirt, which reminded him that the Great Judge was reputed to have at least seven reigning beauties in his harem at all times.

"This way, sir. The Great Judge will receive you."

The man who sat behind the desk looked about thirty-five years old. Only his eyes and his mouth seemed older. From bleak blue eyes and with thin-lipped silence, the immortal, ever-young Great Judge studied his visitor.

The latter wasted no time. The moment the door shut behind him, he pressed the button that released a fine spray of gas straight at the Great Judge. The man behind the desk simply sagged in his chair.

The visitor was calm but quick. He dragged the limp body around to his instrument case, and removed the clothes of the upper body. Swiftly, he swabbed the body with the liquid he had brought, and began to attach his nodes. Half a dozen on one side and a dozen on the other. The next step was to attach the wires to his own body, lie down and press the activator.

The question that puzzled Douglas Aird on the day that he succeeded in transferring the nervous impulses of a chicken into the nervous system of a dog was: How complete was the transference?

Personality, he argued with himself, was a complex structure. It grew out of many quadrillions of minute experiences and, as he had discovered, finally gave to each body its own special neural vibration.

Would it be possible by artificially forcing that exact vibration upon another body to establish a nerve energy flow between the two bodies? A flow so natural and easy that every cell would be impregnated with the thoughts and memories of the other body? A flow so complete, that, when properly channeled, the personality of one body would flow into the other?

The fact that a dog acted like a chicken was not complete proof. Normally, he would have experimented very carefully before trying it on a human being. But a man doomed to die didn't have to think of risks. When the Science Investigator called on him two days before the date of the execution, he gassed the man, and made the experiment then and there.

The transference was not absolutely complete. Blurred memories remained behind, enough to make the routine of going to the Great Judge's Court familiar and easy. He had worried about that. It was important that he follow the right etiquette in approaching a man who normally permitted no one near him but people he had learned to trust.

As it turned out, he did everything right. The moment he felt the blurring sensation which marked the beginning of the transfer of his personality from the body of the Science Investigator to the body of the Great Judge, Aird acted. He released a gas toward the Great Judge that would revive the man in about five minutes. Simultaneously, he sprayed his present body with instantaneous anesthetic gas. Even as he sank into unconsciousness, he could feel the sharp, hard personality of the Great Judge slipping into the Investigator's body.

Five minutes later Douglas Aird, now in the body of the Great Judge, opened his eyes, and looked around him alertly. Carefully, he disconnected the wires, packed the instruments—and then called a bailiff. As he had expected, no one questioned the actions of the Great Judge. It was the work of an hour to drive to the apartment of Douglas Aird, transfer the Great Judge's personality to the body of Douglas Aird— and at the same time return the personality of the Science Investigator into its proper body. As a precaution, he had the Science Investigator taken to a hospital.

"Keep him there for three days under observation," he commanded.

Back at the Great Judge's Court, he spent the next few days cautiously fitting himself into the pleasant routine of a life of absolute power. He had a thousand plans for altering a police state into a free state, but as a scientist he was sharply aware of the need for orderly transition.

It was at the end of a week that he inquired casually about a traitor named Douglas Aird. The story was interesting. The man had, it seemed, attempted to escape. He had flown some five hundred miles in an unregistered hopjet before being grounded by a local patrol. Immediately, he fled into the mountains. When he failed to report on the morning of the day set for his execution, the printed instrument on his right arm was activated. Shortly before dusk, a tired, distracted, staggering scarecrow of a man, screaming that he was the Great Judge, appeared in a mountain patrol station. The execution was then carried out with no further delay. The report concluded:

"Seldom in the experience of the attending patrol officers has a condemned man approached the converter with so much reluctance."

The Great Judge, sitting at his desk in the luxurious court, could well believe it.

Emergency Landing

Ralph Williams

The funny part about this is that Burke was perfectly sober. Not that he is in the habit of coming on watch drunk, but then it just isn't the sort of thing that happens to a sober person. I had the evening watch that day, and when he relieved me at midnight he was absolutely normal.

When I left he was settling down in the chief's chair with a detective story magazine. The CAA frowns on that—the magazine, I mean, not the chief's chair—but most of us do read on duty, especially on the midnight watch, because ordinarily there is nothing to do at an intermediate landing field between midnight and eight but report the weather once an hour, and reading is about the only way to keep from getting sleepy. But once in a while things do happen, which is why they keep a twenty-four-hour watch at these places.

It must have been around one-twenty that things began to happen on this night. About that time Burke glanced up at the clock and decided it was time to start taking his weather—a job that wasn't likely to prove very interesting, since conditions had been "ceiling and visibility unlimited" all evening, and the forecasts stubbornly maintained that they would continue so—so he put aside his magazine and stepped outside to read the thermometers. It was while he was spinning the psychrometer crank and gazing around the sky for signs of cloudiness that he saw this plane coming in.

When he first saw it, he says, it was just a dot of light sliding slowly down the sky toward the field. The first thing that struck him as queer about this ship was that he couldn't hear the engines, even though it couldn't have been over half a mile from the west boundary. It seemed to be gliding in; this was a very silly thing to do with nothing but the boundary lights and beacon as a guide. Another thing, it was strange that any plane at all would be landing here after dark, in good weather, since there was none based at our field, and it was only about once in a blue moon that we had a visitor. Burke wondered about that, but then he remembered that he had to get his weather in the sequence, so he ran inside and put it on the wire.

By the time he could get to the window for another look, the stranger was just landing. He could see it more plainly now in the flashes from the beacon, and if it was a plane, it was like none he'd ever seen or even heard of. It looked more like an airship—only not like an airship either. This may sound silly, but Burke says if you can imagine a flying submarine, that is just what it looked like, and he should know, being ex-Navy. He says it reminded him of the old gag the recruit instructors like to pull: If you were on guard and saw a battleship steaming across the parade ground, what would you do? It even had *U.S. Navy 1156* painted on its side in big black letters.

There was still no sound from the engines, but there was a faint blue exhaust from somewhere around its tail, and it was plain that the ship was under control—that is, if it really was there, and not just Burke's sins beginning to catch up with him. When it was about thirty yards from the watchhouse, this exhaust stopped, and it settled gently to the ground on two broad skis that ran the length of the ship. It drifted down like a feather, but when the weight came on those skis they sank a good three inches into the unsurfaced runway. Burke began to wonder about secret Navy inventions, stratosphere planes, and stuff like that. Also he wondered whether he ought to call the chief, and decided not to since the chief is apt to be cranky when someone wakes him up in the middle of the night and makes him drive the six miles from his home to the field. Burke compromised by making an entry in the

log that *Navy 1156* had landed at 0141. Then he walked out
to the ship and waited for someone to get out. When he got
close enough, just to satisfy his own curiosity, he gave one of
the ski struts a good hearty kick. It was solid enough, all
right. He almost broke his toe.

There was a glassed-in compartment in the upper part of
the nose that looked like the control room, and through the
glass Burke could see someone in a blue coverall and flight
cap fussing with some instruments. He was so busy watching
this fellow that he didn't notice the door open behind him
until a voice spoke almost over his shoulder.

"Hey," the voice said, "what's the name of this place?"

Burke spun around and looked up at an open door in the
side of the ship and another man in the same blue coverall
and flight cap. This one wore a web pistol belt, though, and a
funny, bulky-looking pistol in the holster. He had a lieutenant's stripes on his shoulder and Burke automatically high-
balled him.

"Parker, sir," he answered, "Parker, North Dakota."

The lieutenant turned and relayed this information to
someone back in the ship. Then he and Burke stared at each
other. Burke was on the point of mustering up courage to ask
what the score was when another man came into view. This
was the one who had been in the control room, and Burke
saw that he was a commander. He, too, stared curiously at
Burke.

"Can we get some water here?" he asked.

"Sure." Burke indicated the pump, visible in the light from
the open watchhouse door. "Right over there."

The lieutenant eyed the pump doubtfully. "We might get
it out of there in about a week," he said.

The commander jumped. "A week! My God, man, we have
a mission to perform. We can't stay around here for a week.
We have to be out by morning."

"Yes, sir, I know, but we're going to need a lot of water.
Those Jennies will suck it up like a thousand-horse centrifugal
when we hit that warp, or whatever it is."

"About how much?"

The lieutenant pulled a cigarette out of his pocket and lit
it thoughtfully. "Well, we're almost dry now, and we'll need

every drop we can carry. At least twenty-five-thousand gallons."

The commander turned back to Burke. "How about it?" he demanded. "Can we get that much water around here?"

Burke mentally pictured a five-hundred-gallon tank, multiplied by fifty. That was a lot of water. He found himself agreeing with the lieutenant that it would be hardly feasible to get it out of the watchhouse well, if a person was in a hurry.

"There's the river," he said, "but it'd be kind of hard to find in the dark."

"Never mind that. We'll pick it up in the visors. Which way?"

"South," Burke told him. "About five miles."

"Thanks."

For an instant longer they stared sharply at him, as if fascinated by his appearance, and he in turn began to realize that there was something obscurely alien about these people—nothing definite, just a hint of difference in the way they handled their words, a certain smooth precision in their movements. It made him vaguely uneasy, and he felt a distinct sense of relief when the commander turned and spoke to the lieutenant.

"Come on," he said. "Let's get her up."

The two officers disappeared into the ship. A seaman stepped into view and threw a switch and the door began silently to close. Burke suddenly remembered there were questions he wanted to ask.

"Hey," he shouted. "Wait a minute."

The door slid open a foot and the seaman's head popped out. "Stand clear," he warned. "If you're caught in the field when we start to go up, you'll go with us."

Before Burke could open his mouth to speak the face disappeared and the door closed again. Burke prudently retired to the watchhouse porch.

Presently the ship lifted into the air, the exhaust flared out softly, and she spun on her tail and headed southward. Burke watched until the blue glow had faded out into the starry sky, then went inside and looked thoughtfully at the log. There are no regulations covering the landing of submarines at intermediate fields, and the CAA does not approve of unorthodox use of its facilities.

Finally he came to a decision and sat down to the typewriter.

"0152," he wrote. "*Navy 1156* took off."

Obviously Suicide

S. Fowler Wright

"In about two seconds the Earth would dissolve in a blaze of fire," the research worker at the N. U. Laboratories told his wife. "There would be a burst of light and—one planet less in the universe. The amazing aspect is its very simplicity. It could be made in a back-yard shed. All one needs is a combination of three substances, all easy to obtain, and then nothing more than a loop of heated wire."

"Wouldn't it be common prudence to get rid of these substances entirely?" she asked.

"Unfortunately, they are so widely distributed, and in such general use, that their complete destruction would be quite impossible."

"You mean that if this should become known, any lunatic—or any criminal without hope of escape or pardon—could destroy the human race in a form of universal suicide?"

"It is impossible not to be apprehensive." The research worker calmly lit his pipe. "It is known to our Grade-A men—that is, to about thirty, now. We are sworn to secrecy as to its ingredients, which I should not think to disclose, even to you. But if there should be one among us who now, or in the future—"

"How has it become known to so many?"

"The possibility was first raised at the weekly conference

which is attended by all of the first grade. Several of us worked separately upon it, by experiment to a point and, beyond that, by mathematical calculations. All reached the same conclusion. It is hardly a matter which could be put to experimental test, but the conclusion is beyond reasonable doubt."

"Then it should surely be wiped out and forgotten as completely as possible from the minds of all of you who share such perilous knowledge."

"We have discussed that already, and shall do so again at a special meeting tomorrow. It may be decided in that way. But differences of opinion are natural among so many. At our last meeting, there were three who objected at once. No scientific fact, they argued, should be treated in such a way. . . . The trouble is that, though the calculations may be destroyed, the process and ingredients are too simple to be put out of mind—especially out of such minds as ours."

"Yet it seems the only sensible thing to do. . . . And if any object, I should say the best thing to do would be to put them in a lethal chamber before they would have time to do a mischief which none could limit."

Grafton agreed to that. There was no more said, and his wife slept.

But he found that he could not sleep. During the past week he had been imagining what it would be like to live in a world in which it was common knowledge that anyone could destroy it at an instant's caprice. Even the threat, which might soon be on every unscrupulous tongue—"Give me what I demand, or we shall all be gone in the next hour"—would be one which the bravest might find it hard to ignore.

Apart from that, how long would it be likely that the Earth *would* exist, if this knowledge were once at large? Each month there were thousands of suicides of men of different races, of every disposition. Would there be none who would elect an exit of so dramatic a kind? Cast this knowledge abroad, and it would become improbable that Earth could endure for a further week. Yet what could now be done?

But his wife, being refreshed by a night of dreamless sleep, proposed what to him had a startling sound.

Women are more practical and more ruthless than men.

She had looked at the bed where a young child slept, and she thought of his sister, a year older, in the next room. Then she said: "If it were possible for the thirty to be destroyed before they could give their knowledge to other men, it would be the best thing that could happen now."

He said: "Oh, but my dear, think who they are! There's Professor Gribstein and Dr. Thornton and—"

"I never did like Dr. Thornton," she replied, as a woman would.

He did not give two thoughts to this criminal suggestion at the time, and it might never have re-entered his mind had there not been a discussion in the Council which became heated when it was clear that a substantial minority were indisposed to put the knowledge aside. One even suggested that they should make a public announcement of their discovery, so that they might become a Council of Thirty who would control a world that would crouch around them in abject fear. . . . And then the idea came to his mind of how simply it could be done. . . . At their next meeting, when they would all be assembled together, and he could be absent! He could have a bad cold! A *real* cold! It would be easy to contrive that. . . . The scentless deadly gas which was for use in the next war—a herd of two hundred cattle had been destroyed in seventeen seconds by a smaller quantity than was in the little cylinder on the high shelf of the room where they always met! Kept for special security there. And most effectually sealed. But a corrosive acid could be timed to eat through the cylinder wall. (They would not know how they died, nor more important, would anyone else.) It was certainly an attractive idea. And even Maude, a kind-hearted, sentimental woman, said it was the right thing to do. When he came to consider the matter, *he* didn't like Dr. Thornton either. . . . And it would certainly leave him in an unrivaled position!

So, when the Council met again, it was done.

And no one suspected him in the least.

His one mistake was that he told Maude, thinking that she would approve, as indeed she did.

He said that the power was now in his hands alone, and he must consider the wisest course.

Maude thought of many things. Among these was the doubt

of what, if or when he were dying, he might be tempted to do. She looked again at a sleeping child, and then did the practical thing.

It was a purlieu in which poisons were not hard to procure. She gave it to him in his morning coffee.

It was a clear case of suicide, for she was able to say that he had told her of the twenty-nine deaths which had preceded his own, that they were due to some carelessness of omission on his part, and his remorse had been painful to see.

It was very necessary to avoid suspicion falling upon herself. She had two children for whom to live. And she was aware of the gravity with which the law might regard the death of one man—though it seemed to take lightly the killing of millions.

Six Haiku

Karen Anderson

1

The white vapor trail
   Scrawls slowly on the sky
      Without any squeak.

2

Gilt and painted clouds
   Float back through the shining air,
      What, are there stars, too?

3

In the heavy world's
   Shadow, I watch the sputnik
      Coasting in sunlight.

4

Those crisp cucumbers
   Not yet planted in Syrtis—
      How I desire one!

5

In the fantastic
   Seas of Venus, who would dare
      To imagine gulls?

6

When Proxima sets
   What constellation do they
      Dream around our sun?